P9-CWE-630

"Quake! Everybody outside!"

Jak was first to reach the door, hesitating with his fingers gripping the handle.

J.B. held Mildred's hand as they weaved across the heaving floor, looking like a couple of drunks trying to make a decorous exit from a frontier gaudy.

"Door's jammed," the teenager yelled. There was a ferocious shudder, and the kerosene lamp crashed onto the floor, rolling under one of the beds and plunging the room into momentary darkness.

But that lasted for only a few seconds. A flicker of orange flame snaked out of the blackness as the dust-dry blankets caught fire, followed by the crackling of the floorboards igniting in the fierce heat.

"Windows are all shuttered and locked from the outside," the Armorer shouted.

Already it was hard to breathe.

**Other titles in the
Deathlands saga:**

JAMES AXLER

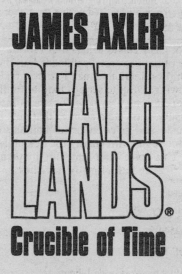

DEATH LANDS®

Crucible of Time

A GOLD EAGLE BOOK FROM
WORLDWIDE®

TORONTO • NEW YORK • LONDON
AMSTERDAM • PARIS • SYDNEY • HAMBURG
STOCKHOLM • ATHENS • TOKYO • MILAN
MADRID • WARSAW • BUDAPEST • AUCKLAND

If you purchased this book without a cover you should be aware
that this book is stolen property. It was reported as "unsold and
destroyed" to the publisher, and neither the author nor the
publisher has received any payment for this "stripped book."

This is for Chef David Mitchell of Florida. Apart from
being one of the greatest Deathlands fans, he is also just
about the most remarkable man I've ever had the privilege
of knowing. Despite serious long-term illness and
countless operations, David demonstrates incredible grace
under pressure, showing a courage that puts Ryan Cawdor
in the shade, and gives enormous amounts of precious
time to his own charity for sick children.
This book is for him with my thanks
and all of my best wishes.

First edition January 1999

ISBN 0-373-62544-8

CRUCIBLE OF TIME

Copyright © 1999 by Worldwide Library.

All rights reserved. Except for use in any review, the
reproduction or utilization of this work in whole or in part
in any form by any electronic, mechanical or other means,
now known or hereafter invented, including xerography,
photocopying and recording, or in any information storage
or retrieval system, is forbidden without the written permission
of the publisher, Worldwide Library, 225 Duncan Mill Road,
Don Mills, Ontario, Canada M3B 3K9.

All characters in this book have no existence outside the
imagination of the author and have no relation whatsoever to
anyone bearing the same name or names. They are not even
distantly inspired by any individual known or unknown to the
author, and all incidents are pure invention.

® and TM are trademarks of the publisher. Trademarks indicated
with ® are registered in the United States Patent and Trademark
Office, the Canadian Trade Marks Office and in other countries.

Printed in U.S.A.

"Belief is exercised through shared thoughts and words of wisdom.
Blind belief can only be exercised along the barrel of a rifle."

—From: *Happiness Is the Good Book and a Warm Gun*
by Blessed Bob "Bobcat" Bobson,
Apocalypse Press, Waco, Texas

THE DEATHLANDS SAGA

This world is their legacy, a world born in the violent nuclear spasm of 2001 that was the bitter outcome of a struggle for global dominance.

There is no real escape from this shockscape where life always hangs in the balance, vulnerable to newly demonic nature, barbarism, lawlessness.

But they are the warrior survivalists, and they endure—in the way of the lion, the hawk and the tiger, true to nature's heart despite its ruination.

Ryan Cawdor: The privileged son of an East Coast baron. Acquainted with betrayal from a tender age, he is a master of the hard realities.

Krysty Wroth: Harmony ville's own Titian-haired beauty, a woman with the strength of tempered steel. Her premonitions and Gaia powers have been fostered by her Mother Sonja.

J. B. Dix, the Armorer: Weapons master and Ryan's close ally, he, too, honed his skills traversing the Deathlands with the legendary Trader.

Doctor Theophilus Tanner: Torn from his family and a gentler life in 1896, Doc has been thrown into a future he couldn't have imagined.

Dr. Mildred Wyeth: Her father was killed by the Ku Klux Klan, but her fate is not much lighter. Restored from predark cryogenic suspension, she brings twentieth-century healing skills to a nightmare.

Jak Lauren: A true child of the wastelands, reared on adversity, loss and danger, the albino teenager is a fierce fighter and loyal friend.

Dean Cawdor: Ryan's young son by Sharona accepts the only world he knows, and yet he is the seedling bearing the promise of tomorrow.

In a world where all was lost, they are humanity's last hope....

Chapter One

Ryan Cawdor moaned and blinked open his eye.

His head felt like someone had been using it to grind flour. He cautiously parted his lips and swallowed, tasting the bitterness of bile. It seemed as if a gang of muties had been using his mouth for an outhouse.

"Fireblast!" he whispered, his voice sounding high, thin and cracked.

The flash of dazzling light that had drilled through the optic nerve into the forepart of his brain had made him close his good right eye immediately. He took several long, slow breaths, trying to gain a measure of control over mind and body.

All he knew was that the mat-trans jump had been a bad one. The leap from one gateway to another was never a pleasant experience, but some jumps were worse than others.

"Bad one," he muttered to himself.

There was only the briefest memory of starting the jump. All of them had sat down on the floor with its pattern on steel disks, matched by the ones in the ceiling. His back settled against the cold armaglass, with Krysty Wroth at his right and Dean, his son, on his left. Doc Tanner, Mildred Wyeth,

J.B. Dix and Jak Lauren had ranged themselves around the hexagonal chamber.

The door had been slammed, triggering the mechanism that would whisk them from that location to someplace else in the blighted remnants of the United States, now known as Deathlands. They had no control over their destination.

Ryan sat still, swallowing hard to avoid throwing up. He eased open his eye again, squinting to see how his companions had survived the jump.

The first thing he noticed was the color of the armaglass walls of the chamber. They had been blue; now they were a deep maroon, like venous blood.

As far as Ryan could tell, everyone else was still alive and breathing. Krysty's head was on her shoulder, mouth open, her fiery scarlet hair coiled tight at her nape. Her long fingers were clenched tightly into the palms of her hands, and he could make out a worm of bright blood inching across the pale skin. Her emerald eyes were clamped shut, and a thread of saliva dangled from a corner of her lips.

"Bad one," Ryan repeated.

"Yeah, compadre, it was." The almost inaudible voice came from the far side of the mat-trans unit, from J. B. Dix, the Armorer, as he'd been known during the years when the two men had ridden together on the war wags of the legendary Trader.

He struggled to sit upright, feeling in one of the deep pockets of his coat for his spectacles. He wiped the lenses on his sleeve and perched them back on his narrow nose, then picked his beloved fedora hat from his lap and jammed it on his head. "Yeah, bad one, bro," he said.

"Doc looks in a sorry way."

J.B. nodded. "And the kid doesn't look like he's ready for action."

"Not 'kid,' old man." Jak's lids peeled back, revealing the ruby eyes of the true albino. His skin, as white as new-fallen snow, was smudged with dirt across the high cheekbones.

Jak Lauren, from West Lowellton in Louisiana, was still only sixteen years of age, as skinny as a lath, with the wiry strength of a self-trained acrobat. His mane of white hair hung across his shoulders, onto his leather-and-canvas camouflage jacket. Like the other companions, he carried a blaster at his hip—a satin-finish Colt Python, with the long, six-inch barrel. But his favorite weapons were the half-dozen leaf-shaped throwing knives that he wore concealed about his person. Jak was able to take the eye out of the jack of diamonds at twenty paces.

Or kill a man at three times that distance.

"Damn it all to hell, Dad. That was a bad one. Worst jump I can ever remember." Dean Cawdor, at age eleven, was a mirror image of his father. He was the fruit of a brief liaison Ryan had with Sharona Carson, wife of the baron of Towse. Though Dean hadn't been long in Ryan's life, the one-eyed man loved him fiercely.

"One of the worst, son, that's for bastard sure."

Ryan was aware that Krysty was recovering consciousness. She coughed, then retched, putting her head in her hands.

"Gaia! That was…"

"A bad one," chorused Ryan, Jak, Dean and J.B.

Krysty managed a wan smile. "Yeah. Had a foul dream, if that's the right word for what passes dribbling through your skull during a jump."

Ryan nodded. "I was strapped to a table of polished chrome, and men with white robes and masks were working on me with long tubes and needles. Probing at my arteries, sucking my blood through into a whirling machine."

"I was crawling through tunnels that were filling with warm mud," J.B. said.

Jak shook his head. The snowy mane whirling like a torrent of meltwater spray. "Can't remember. Just know was frightening. Old women in it, holding small knives. Pecked like beaks of birds. Blood on snow like petals of roses."

"What was your dream, Krysty?" Ryan asked, holding her hand in his.

"Only recall bits, lover. I was held captive by a man who stood always in the shadows. I could save myself if I could complete a puzzle. Just one last piece was needed, but I couldn't find it. Didn't know what shape and size it was. So it was totally impossible, but I had to keep on searching." She shuddered and squeezed Ryan's hand so hard he almost cried out. "Nightmare alley, lover. That's what it was. One of those black nightmares when you think you've actually lost your mind somewhere during the jump. Your brain's been swirled apart."

Mildred Wyeth had recovered consciousness while Krysty was talking.

"Know what you mean," she said, coughing, pressing her hands against her brown eyes to regain control. "My dream was about traveling back in the days of Amtrak, when I was a little girl. Before skydark, I was wandering from platform to platform in a huge station, trying to find the right train. Then I was in a train car but nobody knew where it was going. Just endless and pointless. It was like running and staying still."

She smiled at J.B. and patted him on the arm, using his help to get upright, staggering a little.

Ryan admired her toughness, knowing that he would almost certainly puke if he didn't stay sitting a while longer. But he already knew what a tough person Mildred was.

She had been born way back, on December 17, 1964. Mildred was black, and a doctor, and came from Lincoln, Nebraska. Her father, a Baptist minister, had been burned alive less than a year after her birth by firebombing racists who hid their cowardice beneath white hoods.

Her beaded plaits rattled and whispered as she shook her head to try to clear it. Two weeks after her thirty-sixth birthday, she had gone into the hospital for minor abdominal surgery that had gone badly wrong. Ironically, since cryonics was her medical specialty, she had been frozen to save her life. Very shortly after that the world blew apart. But she slept dreamlessly on, her body monitored by a small, timeless nuke reactor, until she was finally woken by Ryan and the others.

She pulled J.B. to his feet, adjusting her Czech ZKR 551, a 6-shot target revolver, in its holster. Before being frozen, Mildred had been a silver-medal winner in the free pistol shooting at the 1996 Olympics. And she was the best shot with a handgun that Ryan Cawdor had ever seen.

Mildred rubbed her forehead. "I know everyone says the same, but that was a mother of a bad one." She looked down at the motionless figure of Doc Tanner, who lay at her feet. "Old-timer looks a lot less than well," she said.

The old man lay flat on his back, gnarled hands down at his sides. His grizzled hair was matted with sweat, and his breathing was harsh and irregular. Ryan crawled across the chamber, seeing that Doc had been bleeding from both ears, as well as from nose and mouth. His pale blue eyes were tight shut. It looked like he might have had some sort of convulsion, as his massive Le Mat pistol had been jolted loose from the holster on his hip.

"Doc. Doc?"

There was no response. Mildred moved to join Ryan. She lifted an eyelid, peering down at Doc. "Seems to be in shock," she said. "Know how delicate the old bastard's mind is at the best of times? Well, this isn't the best of times. Especially after what happened in Puerto Rico."

"'It was the worst of times and it was the best of times.'" The voice was weak, the eyes still closed. Doc swallowed hard. "*A Whale with Two*

Kitties, or some title. 'A far better rest I come from than was ever known.' Quoting and misquoting. Hither and thither. Not to mention yon.''

"Sounds in bad shape," Krysty said quietly.

The old man struggled to a sitting position, aided by Mildred. He wagged a forefinger at her. "Anoint thee, witch. Thou rump-fed runyon! There's nothing wrong with my mind that a truly bad jump won't cure." He hesitated, looking puzzled. "That is not quite what I meant to say, I think. I mean that it was a poor jump and it has sadly addled my pate for a few moments. Sadly addled. Badly sadly addled."

"Did you have any dreams while you were in the jump, Doc?" Ryan asked.

"I think that I did."

There was a long pause. Jak had got to his feet and was leaning against the armaglass wall, eyes closed, sucking in deep breaths. He ran his fingers through his long hair, bringing a semblance of order to it, then leaned down to help Dean to his feet.

"Well?" Mildred snapped.

Doc put his head on one side and peered up at her, like an inquisitive buzzard. "Well what, madam?"

"You said you had a dream during the jump, Doc. What was the dream about?"

"Ah, yes. Indeed. The dream. By the Three Kennedys, but it was passing strange! I was visiting an elderly aunt in Boston. It seems that I was betrothed to Emily, but not yet married. Aunt Alberta lived in a huge, rambling mansion, on Beacon Hill, looking down toward the Common. A somewhat gloomy building, with stained glass at every door and window.''

"Is this going to take long, Doc?'' Mildred asked. "I have a life to get on with.''

Doc ignored her. "She had a number of cats. Dozens. Those very furry ones. Persians, I think they are called. They moved silently through the corridors, like a great gray wave, rippling up and down the stairs. And their eyes were green gold in hue, and they always seemed to be watching me. No matter where I went or what I did.''

Ryan coughed. "Mebbe you could finish this story later, Doc, when we settle for the night. Sounds like it's going to go on for a while.''

Doc shook his head. Mopping at his smeared vest with the blue swallow's-eye kerchief that he always carried with him. "No, my dear Ryan. I am nearly done.''

"Really?'' J.B. said, disbelievingly.

"Oh, indeed yes. The dream was that I found myself on the upper landing, which was where the maids' quarters had once been. It was thick with dust, and slates were gone from the roof, showing the leaden sky. Birds had nested up there, and the floor was covered in feathers and the brittle bones of dead pigeons. I stood at the end wall, turned and saw that my way back to the stairs was blocked by this silent army of cats, gazing at me with an infinite menace.''

He closed his eyes and sat quiet. After a few moments of stillness, Krysty nudged him with the silvered toe of her boot. "And?" she prompted. "What happened then?"

"I woke up, dear lady. That was what was so strange about the dream. It just stopped dead like a brougham breaking an axle and losing its rear wheels. I may never recover from Jamaisvous's damnable manipulations, and I believe I was fortunate to avoid the depths of an all-consuming nightmare."

"That's it, Doc?" Dean asked. "It just stops? That's not much of a dream."

"I can tell you it prickled the short hairs at my nape, dear boy."

Ryan moved to stand by the door. "Now we've finished with dream telling, I reckon we might do well to get going. See what sort of a redoubt we've ended up in."

Everyone got ready for moving to condition red, without Ryan even having to remind them. Blasters were drawn and checked quickly, cocked and held firm.

The one-eyed man put his left hand onto the cold metal of the handle of the armaglass door, looking around at his companions. "Here we go," he said quietly.

"Do it, lover," Krysty said with a smile.

"Got any kind of feeling?"

She hesitated a moment, using her inherited mutie powers, trying to locate any imminent danger to them. "No. Nothing close by here."

Ryan opened the door of the mat-trans chamber.

Chapter Two

At first the air seemed to have the familiar stale, flat taste to it.

The redoubts were generally vast military complexes, built during the intense second cold war that dominated life in the period immediately before the horrors of skydark and the following long winters. Many were hastily erected in wilderness areas, often using swathes of national parks, causing great bitterness from liberals and conservationists. A number of bloody confrontations had erupted between the National Guard and outraged citizens.

The total number of redoubts was unknown. Some were scattered throughout the world, and a few in the old United States were on a much more modest scale, concealed in isolated houses.

As Ryan led the way out of the gateway, he wondered what kind of place they'd find. The fact that everything was still functioning meant that the master reactor control was still working: keeping the place secure; checking the lights and air quality; operating a tight and sometimes lethal security system; working as it had been designed to do around a hundred years earlier.

But some of the redoubts had been infiltrated, and moving into a strange complex was always fraught

with danger. There were usually on condition red
for much of the time.

He found himself in a small, square room, about
a dozen feet across. Most of the redoubts that he'd
visited had been abandoned and stripped bare, but
some had obviously been deserted in the prenuke
panic the last few hours before the missiles darkened the skies and the United States became Deathlands. In the past they'd found arms, food and beds.

Sometimes people.

Muties.

"Seems safe, lover," Krysty said, following close
on his heels.

J.B. sniffed the air. "Not too bad. Smelled a lot
worse."

The room was painted in a light cream color, with
a matte finish. It was totally empty, except for a
small rectangular plastic-topped table against the
side wall, with four tubular steel legs. There was a
single narrow shelf on the opposite flank, but that,
too, was empty.

Occasionally they had come across prenuke graffiti, but these walls were flawless and clean.

There was another vanadium-steel sec door on the
opposite side of the room.

"Ready?" Ryan asked, finger light on the trigger
of his 9 mm SIG-Sauer P-226 pistol. He reached out
with his left hand to depress the cold metal handle
and inch the door open.

"Air tastes better here than in chamber," Jak
said. "Fresher."

Ryan hesitated, taking in a deep breath, as did everyone else.

"Kind of a pine scent." Mildred sniffed again. "Feel the rush through the sinuses."

"Yeah," Ryan agreed nodding, still holding the handle. "Must mean we're close to a forest of some kind."

"Let's go look," J.B. suggested. "Forest means there's game."

The heavy door swung slowly open, revealing what they'd all expected to see—a large room containing the main control section of the mat-trans unit. Digital displays on more than forty screens were in constant flux, altering every nanosecond, endlessly changing numbers, codes and formulas, monitoring every aspect of what had once been called Project Cerberus, which was a tiny cog in the infinitely complex system known to the selected few as the Totality Concept.

The far side of the rows of control consoles was dominated by a huge sec steel door. It was in the closed position, sealing off that section of the redoubt against anything short of a full nuke-missile attack.

"Down to orange," Ryan said, holstering his pistol. If by any amazing chance the sec door started to open, it would give them a good half-minute warning.

The rest of the group of friends put away their blasters and wandered around the rows of desks, seeing if anything had been left behind that might give them a clue as to where they were and what had happened.

"The waste bins are devoid of any contents," Doc declared.

"No notes or anything like that," Mildred said, perching herself comfortably in a dark gray orthopedic swivel chair, revolving slowly, head back, looking up at the rounded ceiling. "Sec cameras are still functioning. Wonder if anyone's watching us. Probably not, I guess." She lifted a hand in a casual wave to the nearest of the security devices that had a tiny ruby light glowing at its top.

"Nothing," J.B. said, taking off his glasses and wiping them carefully on his sleeve. "Place swept as clean as this is, likely means no food or weapons in the rest of the redoubt. Might as well move on, Ryan."

"Sure. Back onto red."

As was usual, Dean hurried forward to operate the mechanism that opened and closed the sec doors. He moved to the side of the entrance, sticking his blaster in his belt, laying both hands on the green steel lever, ready at his father's word to shift it to the upward position that would start the ponderous door moving slowly, opening the way to the rest of the complex.

It was a moment of considerable danger.

Ryan gestured for the others to back away, taking cover behind the control consoles. He moved to the opposite side of the door from Dean, crouching as close to the concrete floor as he could get, his blaster drawn again, ready to squint through the narrow gap that would appear beneath the sec door.

"Go, Dean. Ready to stop instantly on my word."

The boy threw his weight against the green lever, heaving it up. There was the familiar faint rumbling sound of buried gears engaging, deep within the walls. Ryan felt the trembling of movement through his knees, seeing the almost imperceptible beginning of action.

Somewhere, from the far side of the vast door, he could just catch the faint sound of a warning siren. If there was anyone living in the redoubt, it would give them ample warning of the arrival of intruders.

A narrow gap appeared between the bottom of the door and the floor, and Ryan flattened himself to peer beneath it. He saw the corridor outside, brightly lit, and the wall. There was no sign of any kind of life.

"Hold it."

The gap was about seven inches.

"Krysty, you feel anything?"

There was a pause while the flame-headed woman closed her eyes and pushed her mind to go questing into the redoubt. "No, lover. Can't feel anything."

"All the way, Dad?"

"Sure."

The lever moved from the horizontal and the great weight of sec steel began to slide slowly upward again. Ryan crouched on hands and knees, watching as more of the passage outside was revealed. He saw concrete, sloping to an arched roof that was illuminated by strip lighting, and he could also see the first of an expected number of sec cameras, fixed high up where the roof and walls ran into one another.

The door was now almost completely open, leaving a gap of better than six feet. "Stop it right there, Dean. I'll take a look outside in the corridor."

The barrel of the powerful blaster probed the air in front of him as he glanced around the corner of the opening, checking both ways. Both were empty.

"Clear," he said, easing down the hammer on the SIG-Sauer.

The scent of pines was noticeably stronger out in the passage, and he could feel a light draft coming from the right.

"Everyone ready?"

Most of the redoubts that they'd visited had the same sort of layout. The gateway chamber and control room were almost always in the deepest part, often far below ground level. Ryan turned to the left, walking only a few paces along the curving passage before coming up against a wall of raw, impenetrable rock, dark granite streaked with bands of silvery quartz. Again, this feature was common to most redoubts.

"Back the other way," Ryan said.

He walked past the rest of them, taking the lead. Krysty fell in behind him, followed by Jak, Dean and Doc. Mildred came sixth with J.B. bringing up the rear.

Now the wide sweep of the passage opened up

before him, with sec cameras dotted in the angle between wall and ceiling, about every thirty paces. The tiny ruby lights flickered on and off, under the random control of comp central.

Ryan paused, looking up at them, wondering whether there was anyone watching the master screens that he knew would be hidden deep in the heart of the redoubt.

Anyone?

Or anything?

They continued for about two hundred yards, always curving to the right, the concrete floor of the wide corridor sloping slightly upward.

"Like being inside the Guggenheim in old New York," Mildred commented.

"What's a Guggenheim?" Dean asked.

"An art gallery, Dean. One of the best. The design is sort of based on the shell of a snail, so it winds round and round. Only difference with this place is that you start at the top in the Guggenheim and work your way to the bottom."

They hadn't passed any side entrances, which wasn't all that unusual. Quite often the section of the redoubt that housed the mat-trans unit was buried in the part of the complex farthest from the center and the entrance.

"There," Jak said, pointing ahead.

The round-roofed passage widened, becoming a clear, steep ramp that stopped abruptly at the single sec-steel door of a large freight elevator.

"Anything?" Ryan asked, turning toward Krysty. She hesitated a moment, closing her eyes. Ryan noticed that her sentient red hair was coiled loosely at her nape. It was generally safe to assume that if the hair had been bunched tight then there might have been danger in the air.

"Nothing." She paused. "Well, there's the faint scent of piñon, floating around from some place outside." She flashed him a brilliant smile, teeth gleaming in the flat overhead lighting. "Wouldn't mind a little time resting among fresh mountain pines, lover."

"No hostiles? That's good," J.B. said, taking off his fedora and fanning his face with the brim. "Kind of warm. Feels like the air-con's not working properly."

Jak moved ahead, peering at the controls of the elevator. He turned back to face the others, his snowy hair floating around his narrow face. "Control code's at side," he called, voice dull in the stillness of the concrete vault.

"Makes life easier." Mildred and the others had all bunched up, close by the elevator.

"Four and two and six and six and seven," Jak said, peering at the neatly printed card. "Go for it, Ryan?"

"Seems a most discreditful breach of security to leave the code placed there for everyone to see." Doc made a moue of disapproval, shaking his head and tutting between his perfect teeth. "Heads should roll."

J.B. replaced his hat, tweaking it into place. "Probably had to do it during the last evac before skydark. Chaos must have reigned, and they had to put the code up to save time. Time must've been real tight with the nukes already up and flying.''

Ryan nodded. ''Makes sense. Let's go onto red again, friends. All right, Jak? Press it in.''

The teenager's tongue slipped out to lick his pale lips as he concentrated on entering the correct code, making sure that each button was properly depressed.

''Moving,'' he announced.

They could all hear the faint hum of distant machinery, a sonorous, deep sound, seeming to vibrate through the marrow of their bones. There was a light above the door showing the progress of the elevator.

The Armorer had his head on one side, listening to the noise. ''Like it's kind of high,'' he said.

Ryan had been thinking the same. It was taking such a long time, the exit from the shaft had to be a good way off. But that again wasn't unusual.

''Don't like it.'' Krysty had a taken a couple of steps away from the others, glancing back over her shoulder.

The indicator light showed that the cage was three-quarters of the way down.

''Bad feeling?'' Ryan asked, his voice ragged in the sudden tension. ''Someone coming?'' He looked away down the brightly lit tunnel.

Krysty's feelings were so often right that they could never, ever be ignored.

''Can't tell you. Not like muties or...''

''Nearly here,'' Jak called. ''What we do, Ryan?''

Apart from Krysty, they were all gathered in a tight knot in front of the sec door.

There was a faint electronic sound, like a tiny bell, warning of the arrival of the elevator.

"Danger...close," Krysty stammered.

The elevator door hissed open, and there was the deafening boom of a blaster.

Chapter Three

Ryan felt the hot breath of the lead shot as it sliced by, just over his head.

Krysty's warning had come just in time. He had shouted out for everyone to get down on the floor a fraction of a second before the dull metal door opened. He took a moment to see that there was nobody in the rectangular cage and, in the same moment, he saw the gaping mouths of a pair of sawed-down scatterguns, jerry-rigged with what looked like fishing line and a crude arrangement of two-by-fours. The whole thing was set to shoot when the door opened.

"Crude but effective," Ryan said as he stood, brushing cement dust off his pants.

"Twelve-gauges." The Armorer crouched carefully outside the elevator, holding the door open with his left hand, peering at the smoking barrels of the booby trap.

Mildred was rubbing her left elbow where she'd gone down awkwardly. "Bitching bastards! Why they want to do that to fellow Americans?"

"Because, my dear Dr. Wyeth, the long dead assassins imagined that if anyone attempted to come this way, they would probably be of the Russian persuasion."

The woman nodded. "Guess that you might be right...for once, Doc."

He made her a low bow, the ferrule of his ebony swordstick scraping on the stone floor.

"Good job you felt the danger, lover," Ryan said.

Krysty gave him a tremulous half smile, waving away the fumes from the quadruple shotgun. "Yeah. Just about have taken us off at the shoulders."

"Reckon that it's safe to use the elevator?" J.B. asked, staring into the empty cage, holding the Uzi at the ready in his right hand.

Ryan sniffed, rubbing the side of his nose with his index finger. "Fireblast! I don't know."

"After my experience at the hands of that madman in Puerto Rico, I am somewhat averse to making another jump quite so soon." Doc ran a hand through his grizzled locks. "Mayhap we could take the ride to the top and then exercise especial care once we arrive up there."

"Why not?" Ryan said.

He led the way into the elevator, bouncing up and down a couple of times to test the springiness of the main support cables, half expecting them to suddenly give way and plunge the cage the rest of the way to the bottom of the shaft.

But everything felt right.

He beckoned to the others, waiting until they were all inside before releasing the door mechanism. "When we reach the top, everyone get down on the floor before the doors slide open. Press the control, Jak.''

The door hissed shut, and the albino teenager pressed the recessed button that carried the illuminated symbol of an arrow pointing upward.

Ryan flexed his knees to absorb the movement, watching the lighted panel above the door that showed their progress up the deep shaft. His index finger was tight on the trigger of the powerful SIG-Sauer. Everyone was on full condition red, blasters cocked and ready for instant use.

The humming of the predark machinery sounded smooth and fluid, taking them steadily toward the top part of the old redoubt. Nobody spoke.

''Right,'' Ryan said finally, as the orange light gleamed close to the top.

There was a slight jolting as the cage came to a halt. A moment's pause, then the steel sec door slid open, revealing a brightly lit corridor.

Ryan relaxed. No shooting. No mines. No trap waiting for them.

''Let's go take a look,'' he said, standing and stepping warily out of the cage, glancing both ways and seeing that there was no sign of anyone or anything.

''There's a notice.'' Krysty walked across the far side of the passage, to where a large multicolored plan of the redoubt was fixed to the wall. A hand-lettered piece of faded, pale blue paper was tacked next to it.

''What say?'' asked Jak, last out of the elevator, allowing the door to slide shut behind him.

"Gaia! Give me a chance."

They gathered around the tall flame-haired woman as she read the notice, following the clumsy writing with her long index finger.

It was short and to the point.

"To anyone it concerns. This redoubt is now fully emptied on orders of Washington. Emergency quarters available only on limited basis in Section JA 33."

Beneath it, in a different hand, someone had scrawled in pencil: "And put your head between your legs and kiss your ass goodbye."

J.B. shook his head. "Means there won't likely be any armament anywhere. Shame."

"But it might mean some food and beds." Ryan looked up at the map. "Section JA 33. Where the...? The green box up close to the main entrance is marked JA."

"There it is," Mildred said. "Right by the entrance. Same level as we're on here."

"Wouldn't mind a good night's sleep in a decent bed before we tackle the outside world." Krysty glanced at Ryan. "What do you think, lover?"

"Sounds good to me. Let's go find this section. Best stay on orange."

FOLLOWING THE COLOR-CODED wall markings, it was easy to find their way through the maze of deserted corridors to Section JA 33. The whole complex was completely cleansed, with the majority of the side doors locked tight. Those few that responded to Jak's eager hands were echoing vaults of empty darkness.

"Here we are," J.B. said, pointing with the muzzle of the Uzi at the letters and numbers, painted in green. "Must be through that door."

"Watch out for boobies," Ryan warned. "Open it real careful."

But there was no wired gren or cocked scattergun behind the sec door, just the same kind of setup that they'd seen on earlier occasions. Four white-walled rooms each contained a dozen metal-framed beds, each with a rolled, plastic-covered mattress and neatly folded gray blankets. An olive green metal locker stood alongside each bed.

There was a pair of identical bathrooms. When Mildred turned on the chromed faucets, nothing happened for several long seconds, then there was a distant gurgling sound, rushing closer. The water that gushed out was initially rust colored and cold, but it quickly cleared and began to warm up, eventually pouring out, steaming.

Jak had immediately headed straight for the dining and kitchen section.

"Ace on line!" he called. "Plenty food."

"CURRIED KING-CRAB gumbo," Doc said, allowing the words to roll off his tongue. "*Succulent* is the word that springs to my mind."

The white dish bore an Army stamp. It sat on the table in front of Doc, brimming with a variegated sludge, his spoon settled on one side.

"You mean it actually tastes like something?" Mildred asked. "The label on the cans I'm eating claimed that it was tender chunks of pan-fried boneless chicken, tenderized for my dining pleasure, in a flavorsome sauce with handpicked herbs and spices. With smoked beans on the side."

"And?"

She smiled at Doc. "And it tastes like different sorts of shit."

"My can said it was a lobster bisque with assorted spring vegetables." Krysty took another hesitant mouthful, blowing to try to cool it, running it around her mouth, shaking her head. "I can taste plenty of chemical additives. Salt. Lot of sugar. Not much lobster."

"I'll finish what you don't want," offered Dean, who had polished off his bowl of food and was sitting back, watching the others.

"Go open another can for yourself," J.B. said. "My beef stew's better than a lot of things I've eaten. Things like dead rat and road-killed toad."

"I confess that my soup is passingly adequate." Doc slurped another mouthful, a thread of the orange liquid running over his stubbled chin.

"How about you, lover?" Krysty asked, glancing sideways at Ryan. "What wonderful blue-ribbon delicacy did you pick off the shelves?"

Ryan stirred the bowl with his spoon, peering down at the speckled liquid, picking up a lump of something green and staring at it. "I think this is a pea. The strands of yellow are probably cheese."

"Cheesy peas," Doc said, smiling toothily. "Or

is it peasy cheese? Greasy and freezy. Easy on the palate with a hint of teasy.''

''Yeah, we get the idea, Doc,'' Mildred told him, dabbing at her lips with one of the paper napkins she'd discovered in a drawer in the kitchen.

''My apologies. That tendentious old habit of mine of thoughtlessly engaging my mouth before I have allowed my poor, tired brain to operate.''

They carried on eating in silence, broken only by Jak's slurping and the rattle of spoons on dishes. The albino teenager went out into the kitchen and after several minutes reappeared with a fresh bowl of food.

''Gaia! What is that?''

''Chicken rice ginger lemon-grass. Want some? Big can. Plenty left.''

She shook her head. ''Thanks a lot, Jak, but no thanks. Think what I've eaten should charge up the battery for a day or so.'' Krysty yawned, laying down her spoon. ''Right now I think I might head for bed.''

Everyone seemed to feel the same, and in a minute Jak was left alone at the Formica-topped table, busily finishing off his Thai chicken.

RYAN AND KRYSTY TOOK one of the rooms, pushing a pair of beds together and overlaying some of the blankets. The dormitory, like the rest of the redoubt, was kept at a constant seventy degrees, the air dry and slightly dusty. The faint scent of pines seemed to have disappeared.

J.B. and Mildred took the second of the rooms,

leaving Doc, Dean and Jak to share a third. The old man was complaining loudly that his stomach felt a little disturbed, blaming it on the curried king-crab gumbo. "Best fasten up your seat belt, dear boy," he said to Dean. "I fear that we are all in for a somewhat bumpy evening."

IT WAS RELATIVELY RARE for them to be able to spend a night feeling completely safe and relaxed. The outer doors of the redoubt were undeniably closed and sec locked, and Ryan had personally slipped the double bolts that sealed off the JA 33 section of the complex.

Ryan and Krysty went to bed naked, which was unusual. Her Smith & Wesson Model 640 double-action blaster, with the snub-nose barrel, was tucked under the pillow. Ryan had laid his long blaster— the 7.62 mm SSG-70 Steyr bolt-action rifle—on the floor on his side of the makeshift double bed. The SIG-Sauer P-226 pistol was beside it.

He worked the dimmer switch, reducing the room to near darkness before padding across to climb in next to Krysty, feeling the warmth of her body.

"Hi, lover," she whispered, reaching out to him, allowing her fingers to trail down across the scarred chest, over the flat, muscular wall of his stomach, lower, finding him instantly hard, ready for her. They teased and touched each other with the tender, sure knowledge of longtime lovers.

"Quickie to start?" he asked quietly, his fingers caressing the soft flesh between her slightly parted thighs.

"Mmm... Quicker the better, lover."

Ryan rolled on top of her, guiding himself with his right hand, starting the steady, rhythmic pressure. He supported some of his weight on his elbows, kissing her mouth, sliding a little way up the bed to make the contact deeper.

He could feel her amazing control, her body seeming to shrink about him, squeezing him tight, waves of pressure gripping him and sucking him deeper. Her body rose to meet him on every thrust, her mouth open, eyes closed.

"Not yet..." she whispered.

He held back, trying to set his mind onto something else, slowing himself to meet her readiness, aware of her muscles butterflying around him, sensing her breath coming faster.

Krysty moaned, her fingers digging into his back. "Yes, lover, yes."

Ryan closed his eye, biting his lip so hard with the intensity of his orgasm that he was vaguely aware of a thread of hot blood trickling down his chin. Krysty's back arched under him and she was motionless for a frozen moment, then she bucked and heaved, crying out in her passion.

For several long, soft moments, they clung to each other, letting their breath return to normal, feeling each other's heartbeat.

"Another?" Ryan asked.

"Why not?"

JAK HAD FALLEN instantly into a deep sleep, on his back, snoring quietly. He had stripped off to a

T-shirt and pants, using only a single blanket to cover his skinny body. The taped hilt of one of his throwing knives protruded from beneath the Army-issue pillow.

Dean, as well, had fallen asleep quickly, his blaster on top of the neat pile of clothing beside his cot.

Doc had peeled off his cracked knee boots and the ancient frock coat and breeches, then stretched out on a bed. His swordstick and the ponderous Le Mat blaster were on the floor at his side.

Though he felt very tired, partly due to his recent experiences in Puerto Rico, sleep refused to come gently to him from out of the good night. He found himself slipping into that uneasy land that dwelled part in light and part in dark, where gibbering specters came unbidden and restful slumber was an eternity away, where madness waited in the shadows.

Doc lay on his back, staring sightlessly up at the white ceiling, trying to steady his breathing, but he was all too conscious of the blood pounding in his ears.

He carried a silver half-hunter watch in one of the pockets of his frock coat and he finally sat up, leaned down and fumbled for it. Angling it toward the dim light, he tried to catch the reflection off the slender hands. "Five and twenty minutes past two," he muttered.

A nagging headache pounded behind his temple, and his stomach was still churning from the predark soup, a churning that was becoming more insistent.

"It would be wise to go to the toilet," Doc said,

standing, knees creaking and cracking. He stooped to pull on his pants, then padded barefoot toward the door.

Jak stirred at the movement, blinking open a ruby eye, his hair spilling across the pillow like frozen spray. "Where goin', Doc?" he mumbled, still half-asleep.

"I must worship at the shrine of Thomas Crapper," Doc replied. "Back in a jiffy, or less."

As he left the room, his head was spinning, and he began to fear that he was about to lose control of his lower bodily functions. He moved fast along the short stretch of corridor, past several other doors, until he reached the white-tiled washroom.

Doc sighed with relief as he sat on the flush. "Welcome to the cloacal throne, Theophilus," he said quietly. "For which relief, much, much thanks."

HE WAS RUNNING after a steaming locomotive, along a deserted platform. The train seemed to be empty, apart from the last car, where the window was down and an attractive young woman was peeking out, her arms around the shoulders of two little children. A boy and a girl.

"Run faster, my dear one," she called. "And we can be safe together."

"I am trying, sweet Emily. Before God, I am trying my very best!"

But the train was pulling away, smoke billowing from the stack, floating along the platform, covering the last car, hiding the dream vision of Doc's wife and children.

"No," he said so loudly that he woke himself up, finding he was still sitting in the bathroom, trousers crumpled around his ankles.

Doc sighed, then cleaned himself and pulled up his pants. He washed his hands, then left the bathroom section, emerging again into the passage. He was still half-asleep and he turned right instead of left, so tired he was barely able to keep his eyes open, stumbling along toward the dormitory.

He reached what he thought was the correct door, turned the chromed handle and pushed it open. Part of his waking mind was aware that the room was unexpectedly cold. The opening of the door triggered stark overhead lighting, showing him three metal tables, with a sluice drain at the foot of each, and eight rows of labeled steel cabinets. One of them stood partly open, showing Doc that it was big enough to conceal a fully grown man.

It was bitterly cold, his breath pluming out around him like fog.

"By the Three Kennedys!" he exclaimed. "But this is not our sleeping quarters."

Behind him, the entrance door had been hissing silently closed, shutting with a solid click. Doc spun and found that some kind of internal lock had operated, and he couldn't open the door from the inside.

At the same moment, he saw the notice above the entrance and the single word Morgue.

Doc began to bang on the door, yelling for help at the top of his voice, feeling the first feather touch of panic.

Chapter Four

Ryan slid the SIG-Sauer into the greased holster, stooping to lace up his steel-toed combat boots. "You're sure about the sec lock out of this section?"

Jak nodded. "Soon as saw Doc gone, Dean and me went looking. Still locked and bolted from inside. No sign Doc anywhere. Sure would've heard if attacked."

"We've got to find him, Dad. There's no telling what could happen in here!"

Ryan straightened. J.B., Mildred and Krysty were all fully dressed, sitting on beds in the dormitory. By his wrist chron it was nearly five in the morning.

"Don't worry, son. We'll find him. He couldn't get far." The one-eyed man turned to Krysty.

"You feel him, lover?" he asked.

She shook her head. "Not really. You know I can't properly distinguish one person from another. Not when there's several of us around."

"You check the bathroom, Jak?" J.B. asked. "Didn't have a stroke or heart attack on the john, did he?"

"First place looked. Clean as knife blade in there. Shouted for him. No answer."

"Are there some locked rooms?" Mildred bit her lip worriedly. "Old fart's got to be someplace."

Ryan stood a moment, locked in thought, nibbling at a ragged edge of a torn nail. "Best we stay together," he decided. "If he hasn't gotten outside of the section, then there aren't many places he can be."

"MORTUARY," MILDRED SAID, trying the handle. "And the lock's engaged."

The friends stood in a silent half circle. They'd checked the outside sec bolts to Section JA 33, confirming what Jak had said. And they'd gone all through the whole section, calling out for Doc, waiting together in the oppressive stillness to try to catch the sound of a possible reply, filtering through the thick concrete walls.

But there was nothing.

Now there was only this one locked door.

Ryan rapped on it with the butt of his blaster, pausing to listen for any noise from behind the gray sec door. He knocked again, shouting out, "Doc! You in there, Doc?"

"Silent as a grave," Mildred muttered. "Likely to be cold in there, if the power system's still working. Yeah, likely to be real cold."

"Best shoot out the lock." Ryan gestured for the others to move back out of the way. "Shouldn't be triple vanadium steel, just for a mortuary."

"Doc used to sing that song," J.B. said. "Why build a wall around a graveyard, 'cause nobody wants to get in? Why build a wall round a grave-yard, 'cause nobody wants to get out?''

Ryan nodded. ''Yeah.''

He positioned the four-and-a-half-inch barrel within a couple of inches of the lock, turned his head away and squeezed the trigger three times.

There was an eruption of orange sparks, and the high-powered rounds shattered the fastening on the morgue's door, the shock of the triple explosion jolting clear up his arm to the shoulder. Ryan holstered the blaster and reached out, turning the handle, pushing the door open.

Cold air rushed into the passage, like white spray, all of them feeling the biting chill.

''Doc!'' Mildred called, her voice ragged with the first edge of panic, pushing past Ryan, running into the disinfected, freezing room.

''Here.'' The voice in reply came whispering from the deep shadows at the very rear of the mortuary, near the rows of deep cabinets.

Doc was sitting, arms huddled around himself, ice frosted in his hair, his face as white as polished ivory. Only his pale blue eyes showed any sign of life.

Mildred knelt at his side, finger going to the angle of neck and shoulder, feeling for a pulse. ''Very slow,'' she said urgently. ''Got to move him and warm him up.''

Ryan and J.B. bent down, locking their hands beneath the old man's thighs, steadying him as they lifted. Doc's head lolled to the right, his eyes closing.

"What about the hot water in the showers?" Krysty suggested. "Raise his temperature."

"Yeah. Make a bed ready for him with plenty of blankets. Get him stripped off."

Now that the first shock of finding Doc so close to his unexpected date with the Grim Reaper had passed, Mildred had assumed her calm, professional demeanor.

DOC'S BODY FELT FROZEN, the skin like parchment. The flesh was white, blotted with patches of blue and a deeper purple. Veins stood out on the back of his hands like dark whipcord. The frost melted away once they got him out of the freezing mortuary into the rest of the complex.

"Strip him off," Mildred ordered. "One of you should…maybe both of you should get in the shower with him to support him. Jak, you and Dean and Krysty get the bed ready for him." Ryan and J.B. carefully laid the motionless body on the tiled floor, peeling quickly out of their clothes, modestly keeping on their underwear, while Mildred had turned the chrome faucets, releasing a steady stream of warm water.

"Don't have it too hot for starters," Ryan said. "Shock could kill him."

"Why don't you go teach your grandma to suck eggs," Mildred snapped.

Ryan didn't respond to the gibe, taking one arm and lifting, while the Armorer took the other side. They eased Doc into a sitting position under the shower, kneeling alongside to hold him steady.

"He could mebbe take it just a little hotter," J.B. suggested.

Mildred adjusted the thermostat control. "How about that, John?"

"Better."

The water was now hot enough to steam, condensation streaming down the white tiles. All three men were soaked, huddled close together.

"How's he doing?" Mildred asked, peering through the fog. "How's the pulse?"

Ryan checked it at Doc's right wrist, closing his good eye to keep out the torrent of hot water. "Still a tad slow. But not far off normal."

"Maybe we should get him straight into a bed," Mildred said thoughtfully.

Doc's eyes blinked open and he gazed around, his expression blankly puzzled as he took in Ryan and J.B. on either side of him on the floor of the shower. Then he became aware of his own nakedness. Finally he turned his head and saw Mildred staring down at him.

"By the..." he began, coughing as water gushed into his open mouth.

"Shut it, Doc," Mildred hissed. "Not the time for your humor."

"Where...? I was freezing in a desperately cold place. What...?" His fine set of perfect teeth were chattering like someone with an ague.

"Get him up and out of there, guys." Mildred had found an armful of large white towels, made from a thick, fluffy material, in a closet.

The water was turned off, the last drops streaming

down the sluice, vanishing through the chromed drain cover. Ryan and J.B. helped Doc out, almost carrying him between them along the short stretch of corridor to the dormitory.

"Here," Mildred said, giving J.B. and Ryan a towel each, giving a third one to Krysty, keeping the fourth towel for herself.

Both women started to rub the old man dry, scrubbing at his pallid skin until it glowed with the friction. Doc moaned, opening his eyes for a moment.

"Where is your sense of dignity, ladies?" he asked softly. "I am shamed."

"You'd have been dead, Doc, if we hadn't got to you in time. That morgue was Arctic cold."

He swallowed hard and nodded at Mildred. "For once I cannot find the means to argue with you, madam. Except—" his hands dropped to cover his groin "—I think that I can dry myself in the private parts."

"Sure, help yourself, Doc." Mildred handed him the towel. "Scrub well, then we'll get you under the blankets for an hour or so. You'll be fine."

MILDRED'S JUDGMENT WAS dead-on. Just the single hour had drifted by when the long shape under the heaped blankets began to stir. Coughing, the tangled head appearing into the stark lights of the dormitory.

"By the Three Kennedys! That place was cold as death itself. But now I am myself."

"Thought we might eat some more of them stored cans, Doc," Ryan said.

"'Those' stored cans, lover," Krysty corrected. "Sounds like a good idea. Then we can mebbe get outside and see where we've ended up."

"Smelled that pine scent again," Dean said, sitting cross-legged on the bed next to Doc.

"Me, too," Ryan agreed. "One of the nicest smells I've ever smelled."

Doc's teeth had stopped chattering, and some color had returned to his seamed cheeks. He ran his long fingers through his mane of silvery hair. "I would not be averse to spending some time in the pines, in the pines, where the sun never shines." He laughed. "And I'll shiver the whole night through."

AFTER THEY'D FINISHED EATING and disposed of the dirty dishes and cans in the clattering garbage dispenser, Ryan called them all together. "Make sure you got all of your clothes and weapons," he said.

Everyone went through the motions of checking their blasters, though Ryan knew it was hardly likely that any of them, even absentminded Doc, would walk out into Deathlands unarmed.

He then led the way out of the living quarters, with J.B. carefully closing the sec door behind them.

The main entrance was only about three hundred yards away, past a number of locked side doors. One of them was labeled on the central map as being the armory, and J.B. spent a little time there trying to work it open. But it blankly resisted all of his efforts.

"Wish we'd gotten some plas-ex," he muttered, finally giving up. "Though from what we've seen, they'd likely have stripped it bare before the final vac.''

"USUAL CODE, DAD?" Dean asked, pausing by the control pad at the side of the enormous double sec doors.

"Try it."

"How about the risk of a booby?" Krysty queried. "Though I don't feel anything."

"Doubt they'd put one on the outer doors." Ryan shook his head. "No. Their only worry was obviously of someone coming in the back door, through the mat-trans. Try the 3-5-2 code, son. See what it brings us."

It brought success, and the familiar sound of gears, muffled and distant, as the hidden machinery began to open the double doors, shifting hundreds of tons of vanadium steel strong enough to withstand anything except a direct nuke hit.

Ryan had positioned himself at the center of the gates, the SIG-Sauer drawn and cocked. He squinted through the widening gap, watching for any sign of danger, ready to warn Dean to instantly reverse the number code and close the sec doors at the first hint of a threat.

But he kept silent, watching as the doors slid wider and wider, revealing forty or fifty feet of the ground outside. There was bright sun, throwing stark shadows, and the smell of pines flooded into the redoubt.

"Oh, that is wonderful," Krysty said, sighing,

throwing back her head and drawing in a great lungful of the scented air. "Just smell the green."

Dean moved away as the doors hissed and shuddered to their full width.

There was a wide plateau of bare rock just outside, then the fringes of what looked like a solid wall of green pines towering skyward.

Ryan stepped into the opening, glancing toward the blue sky, noting the streaks of white clouds, with some swelling thunderheads away to the north. A bird of prey, looking like a bald eagle, was riding a thermal a thousand feet above him, scanning the forest below for signs of potential food.

The blaster slid back into its holster as Ryan stood, feet apart, taking in a deep breath of the fresh, bright air. "Fireblast! But that's good."

He turned toward the Armorer, who'd taken the tiny comp sextant out of one of his capacious pockets. "Where do you put us?" he asked.

"Just a minute."

Jak had been scanning the ground outside the sec doors for any signs of life, animal, human or mutie. "See nothing. Looks like nobody found place."

Ryan nodded. "That forest seems solid as a wall. Must've grown fast and sealed off any road there might have been way back around the long winters."

"What's that?" Mildred had shaded her eyes against the brightness of the sun, peering out toward the west, over the tops of the trees.

"What?" Ryan and the others looked to where

she was pointing—all except J.B., who was still fiddling with the controls of the minisextant.

"Silvery," she said. "Big lake. Or...or maybe even a sea of some kind."

"Cific Ocean," J.B. said, putting the instrument back in one of his pockets. "Near as I can make it, we're in the middle of California."

"Really!" Ryan looked across at his old friend. "Bit more specific?"

J.B. had an amazing memory for the topography of the old, long-gone United States of America.

"I'd say that the closest of the old villes to where we are now would be Fresno."

"I took part in a free-pistol competition there, back in '99." Mildred smiled at the memory. "Beat everyone in the Pan-American Games. Scored 996 if I remember right. Four more than a skinny little guy from Brooklyn."

"Fresno would've been around fifty miles west of us, over yonder." J.B. pointed to where there was the glint of distant water, the sun flickering off the lenses of his spectacles. "That's the Cific, all right."

"But it only looks to be a scant forty or so leagues away," Doc said. "Surely the coast should be closer to 150 good miles off?"

Ryan squinted down, running the gray dust through his fingers. "You're forgetting skydark, Doc. Word from the old ones who lived through it was that most all of western California simply slipped into the sea. Hundred percent death toll. The San Andreas Fault went at hour one, and the whole maze of seismic lines opened up like wet string. Dumped the land into the sea, bringing the coast way up into the foothills of the Sierras.''

"I forgot that!" Doc exclaimed. "What a fuzzy-minded old fool I am, to be sure, to be sure. So, we could be close to that part of California where the tall trees used to be."

J.B. nodded. "National parks in this region, and we know that redoubts often got themselves built in such places. Sequoia and King's Canyon.'' He shaded his eyes with the brim of his fedora. "The tall trees, Doc.''

Ryan had walked across the plateau, looking down at the clearly man-made surface of impacted gravel, still showing the century-old marks of deeply ridged tires. As he closed on the fringe of sky-scraping pines, he noticed that there were the remains of some stubby stone bollards circling the edge of the roadway. At one point there were the traces of a two-lane blacktop running toward the northwest. But the greening had enveloped the road, and it vanished under the shadowy branches.

"We stuck here, lover?" Krysty said at his side, her hand resting lightly in the crook of his right elbow. "Be a shame if we can't do some exploring. It seems such a beautiful place."

"It does." He put his arm around her shoulders, feeling the sun-warmed material of her white shirt. "You don't feel any stickies in the neighborhood, do you?"

"No. Nothing, except for some sort of background wildlife sensations. Can't say I'm aware of any sense of danger.''

"I'm sure we can use that old highway as a sort of lodestar to get us away from here. Trees aren't impenetrable. Should be able to move through them.''

"We goin', Ryan?" Jak asked.

"Why not? Everyone ready to do some back-country hiking? Then let's go.''

He began to pick his way between the striated trunks of the pines, heading downhill, using the barely visible remnants of the blacktop to guide him.

The others were strung out behind him.

Chapter Five

A rust-colored squirrel darted up the tree that stood close to the pathway, chattering angrily at the invasion of its territory. A jay perched on a high, feathery branch, swaying backward and forward in the rising wind, dark, beady eyes watching the seven humans far below it.

Ryan had been a little optimistic about the ease of following the old, lost road through the woods. For some of the time, it was almost as though there had never been a road through the woods. Time and the weather had washed parts of it away, and the fast-growing pines had broken through the tarmac in many places. But it was at least some sort of guide, carrying them gradually downhill from the abandoned redoubt.

It was around noon when the friends finally found themselves nearing the bottom of the slope, and the end of the winding, hidden highway.

The sun had been a constant presence, breaking through the pools of dappled shadow. The scent of the pines was so strong and omnipresent that they'd almost stopped noticing it. Away toward the far north, the sky was darkening with banks of snowy thunderheads.

The tall, slender pines that had masked the main

entrance to the redoubt had gradually been absorbed into a region of mixed forest. They strolled through a magnificent mixture of ancient oaks, shivering aspens, white firs, dogwoods, sugar pines and cottonwoods, with a smattering of massive sequoias.

The flowers and shrubs were just as impressive: vivid orange and startling white lilies, chiquapin, lupine and bracken ferns. There was a wealth of bird life, including ravens, owls and bright chickadees, which prompted Doc into an impersonation that he claimed was someone called W. C. Fields. He became annoyed when only Mildred had ever heard of the comedian.

Once they paused near a crystal-fresh spring, resting for a few minutes and heard the howling of coyotes, several miles away to the east, in the higher country.

"Used to be bear and bobcats around here," Mildred commented. "I wouldn't be surprised if they made a good recovery without man to hunt them out."

DOC HAD a nasty coughing fit, doubled over, and hawked up threads of green phlegm into the bed of pine needles under his feet. "I feared there that I was about to vomit copiously," he spluttered.

Mildred approached and laid a hand on his sweat-dewed forehead. "Kind of hot," she commented. "Could be that you're in for a touch of flu, Doc."

"I confess to feeling a few inches below par, Dr. Wyeth. Slight headache and soreness in the throat. Perhaps it is only a touch of the sun. Or a mild attack of altitude sickness. Or it might all be in the fevered imagination of a foolish old man. Let us proceed, shall we?''

THEY HAD EMERGED from the forest onto the buckled remnants of an old highway and followed it as it meandered north and eastward, sometimes between the high walls of a sheer gorge with a river running along its bottom.

''There's a sign,'' Dean said, running ahead of the others to a bullet-pocked, rusting road sign. ''One ninety-eight,'' he called back to them.

J.B. took off his fedora and scratched his forehead. ''Sounds right. Have a feeling it's a highway that runs through Visalia, all the way toward the coast. Linked up with what used to be Highway 101. Way we're heading, I reckon we should finish up in the heart of the national park. See taller trees than you ever imagined.''

''Is there one that you can drive a wag clear through?'' Krysty asked.

''Believe there used to be, but I think it fell some years before skydark.'' Mildred shook her head, her beaded, plaited hair rattling. ''I expect the trees in the park should be something. If the quakes didn't bring them all crashing down.''

The foaming river tumbled over vast rounded boulders, in a flurry of ceaseless, busy foam. The rumbling noise seemed to fill the canyon.

''Running water always make me want to take a leak,'' Mildred said.

''Nobody stopping you, my dear lady,'' Doc

stated. "You have a thousand miles of backcountry to choose from."

"I'll wait awhile. Good training for the muscles. May be a rest area just around the corner."

THEY CAME ACROSS a rest area, less than a quarter mile around the next bend. It was off to the right, set back into a wide recess under the cliffs, across the highway from the river.

A central area housed the rest rooms, as well as a number of shaded tables and benches. The rusting remains of barbecue units were visible here and there among the coarse grasses.

Ryan glanced sideways at Krysty, the silent question visible in his eye. She paused a moment, then shook her head. "Nothing human or mutie, though I get the feeling there are animals close by here."

"Likely coyotes?"

"Could be."

Ryan swallowed hard. "Feel thirsty, lover. Going to take a drink from the river."

Krysty watched him cross the deserted highway, the steepling sun throwing his shadow around his ankles. She glanced down at her own booted feet, seeing one of the Deathlands daisies, white and yellow, growing from the dusty soil. She stepped carefully around it, joining the others by the concrete block at the center of the rest area.

They were looking at a notice board. It was around seven feet high, double sided, with a brown metal frame that was covered in break-resistant, transparent plastic, scratched and weathered over the years.

"Tourist information," Doc said, peering at the faded writing.

One notice warned about the dangers of wild animals such as bears, snakes and panthers, stressing that they weren't tamed and feeding them was totally forbidden under park regulations.

Next to it was a warning about backcountry hiking, making the point that hikers should always register any planned hike and sign on and off with rangers at approved places, marked on the small map on the board.

But what interested Krysty and the others were the crudely hand-lettered, unattributed notices that had been stuck beneath the plastic covers, obscuring some of the original, official messages.

Ryan had rejoined the others, wiping his mouth from his drink, and he read them over Krysty's shoulders.

"War is here. This region is under martial control. Leave now and return to your homes. No photography or videos. Trespassers are likely to be shot on sight."

"Must've gone up in the last hours before the state slipped into the Cific," J.B. said.

"Look on the wall of the john," Mildred said. "Paint's almost gone, but you can read the message. Short and sweet. 'Go home or get shot.' Within a day virtually everyone in the whole country was dead or dying.''

They stood in silence, each of them locked into his or her private thoughts, trying to imagine what those last moments before the skies were filled with missiles had to have been like, the chilling awareness of impending doom.

Ryan whistled softly. ''Spooky to see a reminder like this. Hardly ever see anything anywhere that was so close to those final hours.''

Mildred patted J.B. on the arm. ''Got to go use the facilities, John, or I'll burst.''

''Take care.'' He returned her touch. ''Remember you might find spiders or snakes or scorpions in an abandoned building like that. Looks as if the roof's been torn open on the far side there. Watch out.''

''I'll be fine. Back in a minute.''

The outer door had lost all of its paint from a hundred years of weathering, and there were deep scratches down its surface, leaving raw splinters of white wood. The brass handle was covered in a thick coating of green verdigris. Mildred turned it, finding it seized up solid. She put more of her weight behind it, and it creaked stiffly, then jerked inward.

Mildred could see dazzling sunlight spearing through the damaged roof, and a pile of dried leaves scuffed around her boots. She sniffed, wrinkling her nose at the hot, acrid smell of stale urine that filled the place, surprising after such a long time.

The inner door stood slightly ajar, and Mildred had the momentary illusion that something had moved inside the rest room. But she decided that it was only the leaves that carpeted the tiled floor.

She was conscious of the growing pressure on her bladder, and she pushed open the heavy door with the heel of her left hand, her right already reaching down for the silver buckle on her thick leather belt.

Her head passed directly through the lancing sunshine, making her blink, blinded for a moment. The door swung shut behind her, and the bitter, feral smell was much stronger.

Mildred heard a rustling sound, though she was standing quite still, and there wasn't a breath of wind in the claustrophobic building.

And she became suddenly aware that she wasn't on her own. There was the whisper of steady, rhythmic breathing, and a patch of darkness in the black shadows in the far corner.

Her vision was already adjusting to the mix of light and shade, and she froze, hand inching toward the butt of the Czech revolver on her hip.

It was an enormous black panther, crouched on its haunches, the tip of its tail flicking from side to side. She could see the golden eyes, fixed on her, the ears flattened along the angular skull. The beast, at least twelve feet in length, began to make a purring sound and it stretched its front paws, honed, curved claws scratching on the floor.

Its jaws opened, and she caught the taint of its hot, rancid breath, seeing the ivory glint of the teeth.

''Good God,'' Mildred whispered, aware that the short hairs were prickling at her nape. There was a dreadful temptation to scream out for help, knowing that J.B. and the others would be with her in less than five beats of the heart, their blasters ripping the magnificent creature to ragged fur and shards of bloodied bone.

But her razored mind overrode that temptation, knowing that the panther would leap at her and bear her to the ground, powerful hind legs ripping at her belly, spilling her guts all over the floor, teeth clamping on her skull, crunching the fragile bones, squeezing eyes from their sockets. That would take only a brace of beats of her heart.

"Slow and easy," she whispered to herself, keeping her eyes locked to those of the beast.

Her fingers were on the butt of the ZKR 551, resting there, waiting to make the next move.

The panther growled, deep in its chest, and its back twitched with the desire to charge and rend and kill.

Mildred stood very, very still.

OUTSIDE, THE SIX companions had found a patch of shade to sit down in. The conversation had turned, amid that wilderness, to which kind of wood could best be hewed and which burned with the best flame.

"I have hacked away at a log of black walnut," Doc said ruminatively. "There is something slippery about it. However careful you might be in setting the blade of the ax into a straight line, the black walnut always splits in an oddly curved way, with a gentle bent to it."

"That's true, Doc," Ryan agreed. "But nothing burns cleaner and fresher than a cord of apple wood."

"Cherry's mighty sweet," Krysty said. "Uncle Tyas McCann cut down a whole ancient orchard on the edge of Harmony. Whole place, burned it for a winter and a half. Lovely scent."

"Seasoned pine fine winter. Or piñon, most any time. In swamps was hard finding good dry wood."

J.B. looked back over Ryan's shoulder, toward the block of rest rooms. "Mildred's takin' a long time," he stated. "Think she's all right?"

"Would've shouted if she wasn't," Ryan said. "Mebbe a stomach bug got her."

The Armorer stood, stretching. "Think I'll just step over and see whether— Dark night!"

There had been a sudden, shockingly violent trio of noises: a scream, a thunderous roar and a single pistol shot.

Then silence.

Chapter Six

Mildred had managed to get the revolver three-quarters out of its holster. Her index finger caressed the trigger, her eyes still fixed on the panther's face.

The animal was bowstring tense, muscles twitching beneath the coat of fine black fur. Its ears were still flattened against the skull, eyes glowing in the dim light.

Mildred kept the blaster at her side, thumb making contact with the spurred hammer. She was aware of sweat trickling down the small of her back, between her breasts, over her stomach. The salty liquid beaded her forehead, her cheeks.

The huge mutie carnivore was *so* aware of any movement from its intended prey that Mildred didn't dare to move her gun farther, sensing that the panther would react immediately by charging across the rest room at her.

The wind outside stirred some of the dried rubbish, trapped in the splintered ruins of the angled roof, loosing an aspen leaf and sending it spinning down into the warm space, whirling around and around.

Mildred watched it out of the corner of her eyes, also watching the eyes of the panther, seeing that the beast was fascinated by the light brown, spinning leaf.

Somehow, she knew that the falling dead leaf was going to spark the charge, so she readied herself for the fastest draw of her life.

But the panther was quicker, moving from its crouch, powering toward her with a deafening roar of hatred and rage. Mildred screamed and finished drawing the revolver, thumbing and firing in a single fluid action.

The short-fall thumb-cocking hammer fell on the chambered .38 round, and the boom of the powerful handgun filled the rest room.

Mildred was aware of the shudder of the explosion running clear up to her elbow, then the leaping panther hit her, chest high, and knocked her flat on her back.

J.B. WAS QUICKEST, the Uzi gripped in his right hand as he sprinted the few steps toward the rest room, crashing into the door and sending it spinning off broken hinges. Ryan was at his heels, both of them freezing at what they saw inside.

Mildred lay still, sprawled on her back, knees drawn up, one hand gripping the gleaming revolver, pressing the muzzle against the side of the skull of an enormous black panther. It was huddled on top of her, snarling, jaws open, bright crimson blood dribbling over its curved teeth. There was more blood splashed on its chest, toward the right shoulder.

"No," the woman panted, her eyes wide, staring

at the two men, her voice forced through gritted teeth. "Mine."

Ryan was ready to ignore Mildred and chance a shot at the panther, but events moved past him.

The animal was recovering from the first snapped shot. A rumbling deep in its chest threatened another attack. Mildred, shaken by the attack and the fall, squeezed the trigger of the ZKR 551 a second time, the noise of the .38 round muffled by the barrel being jammed against the creature's head.

The bullet smashed through the dense wall of the skull, puddling the brains, exiting on the far side, a chunk of bone and scalp exploding across the room, splattering against the far wall.

The panther screamed, thrashing away from Mildred, legs kicking, clawing at itself. She rolled free, scrambling to the opposite wall of the rest room, holding the revolver ahead of her, gripping the butt in both hands to keep it steady.

"It's done for, Mildred," J.B. said quietly.

Krysty, Doc, Dean and Jak had come inside, past the smashed door, watching the slaughter of the big animal.

"Let me give you a hand, Mildred," Krysty offered.

"Thanks," the woman replied, holstering the warm blaster at a second attempt. She reached to take the proffered hand, pulling herself upright, whistling between her teeth at the nearness of the escape. "Real close call there."

"How did it get in?" Dean asked. He turned his

gaze upward to the hole in the roof. "Oh, yeah. That way."

"Might be a good idea to move on." Ryan holstered his own blaster. "Sound of those two shots might travel a long way through a silent forest."

"WE LOOKING FORWARD to hole up for a day or so?" Ryan asked. "Or keep moving?"

"A rolling stone gathers no bullets, so it is said. Perhaps we might find a decent roof to protect us for the night." Doc stooped and rubbed at his knee. "Upon my soul, but I think that I have wrenched my leg."

Ryan looked around the circle of faces, seeing exhaustion and nervous strain on all of them, but no sign that any of them was frightened.

"Can you walk all right, Doc?"

"Oh, I trust so, my dear fellow. Just a spasm in the tendon behind the right knee. No, nothing to concern yourself about. Personally I would rather like to leave this rest area behind. As you so rightly commented, the noise of the bullets might attract unwelcome company. The sun is already sinking, but the animal inside there will not smell any sweeter. Perhaps a fresh campsite for the night? What think the others?"

Krysty glanced at Ryan, answering first. "Leave this place of death and blood and find a good camp for the night. The smell of the corpse could attract other predators, and there isn't much shelter with the roof and door gone." She shooed a fly away from her face. "Kind of pretty site, but it's tainted, lover."

Mildred nodded. "I agree."

"And me," added Jak Lauren, who'd been quietly honing the blade of one of his taped throwing knives on a convenient stone held in his lap.

"I'm up for moving on, Dad," Dean piped up.

J.B. had been checking over Mildred's blaster, carefully cleaning it and reloading the two spent rounds. "Move on," he said gently.

Ryan grinned. "I'll make it unanimous, friends. Let's go along the blacktop."

THERE WAS ANOTHER road sign, broken in two, three miles down the highway. It looked like it had once given the distance to Sequoia National Park. Someone had painted something across it, but the weather had faded it so far that it had become illegible.

But there was fresher graffiti, neatly done in capital and lowercase letters, painted in gold, with no spelling errors:

Entering the Land of the Children of the Rock. Come in Peace and be Loved. Come with Anger and encounter Eternity.

"Ring any bells?" Ryan asked.

"No," the Armorer replied, while the others shook their heads in silence.

"Quite recent." Ryan rubbed at it with his right

hand, almost expecting it to smear. "Must be some kind of ville or group, I guess."

They saw two more hand-painted signs for the mysterious Children of the Rock: Come with open arms and the Children of the Rock will make you welcome. Come with a closed fist and we will break you.

And: The Children of the Rock will bear witness for the Blessed Savior, but first we will bear arms against followers of Shaitan.

"Bible-punchers," Mildred said. "Used to be a lot of them around, in the tense years before sky-dark. Part religious crazies and part racists and part redneck rifle carriers. Fundamentalist paramilitaries."

J.B. moved his fedora, driving off some persistent insects with bright green bodies and purple, multi-eyed heads. "Read of them. Some of them got triple paranoid and became bitterly antigovernment. Some of them turned to bombers."

"Best keep a good watch," Ryan said. "Mebbe we should walk along in a skirmish line, on condition orange."

"I have the feeling we're being watched," Krysty murmured, looking at Ryan, keeping her eyes fixed on him. "Don't look now, but there's someone up on the ridge to the south of us. Horseman. Take a casual glance."

"Nobody else look," Ryan snapped, rubbing at the back of his neck, spitting in the dirt. He turned slowly with his good eye to look up where Krysty had pointed.

For a moment he saw nothing, just the ridge, lined with the tops of pines. Then he caught the glimmer of movement and focused on the horseman, astride a pinto pony. The distance was too great to be sure, but he thought the man was riding bare back, in shirt and pants of light-colored cotton, with long hair and a bandanna tied across his forehead.

"Native American," he guessed. "Looks like an Apache, but he's sure a long way from home."

Mildred turned and looked at the figure, blurred on the hogback ridge. "You got better seeing with your one eye than most folks with two good eyes, Ryan. I can make out a man on a horse, but he could be the Emperor Napoleon for all I can see."

Doc laughed. "At least you can see the rider, Dr. Wyeth. I can see some tall green trees and that is all. No more."

The sun was beginning to slide down behind the western slopes, giving the sort of light where Jak with his albino eyes came into his own.

"Apache," he said. "Carrying long gun. Sharps .50. Looks to be in twenties. Dressed like Mescalero. Seen us watching him. Riding off."

Sure enough, the horseman had kicked his heels into the flanks of the pinto, moving it off toward the north, away from the friends, and disappeared from sight in a handful of seconds.

"You feel any others, Krysty?" J.B. asked. "Anywhere around?"

"No. Just the one man, going away. Can't hardly feel him at all now."

Ryan turned back to the buckled, weed-strewed

highway, following it with his eye as it twisted and turned before vanishing among the pines.

"Let's go find a place to camp," he said.

IT LOOKED LIKE it might have been another picnic area back before the long winters. But there was no building, or notices; no barbecue pits and just the stumps remaining from what might have been scattered tables and seats, and no messages from the mysterious Children of the Rock.

A narrow river ran along its back, which Ryan and Jak checked for spoor, concluding that no animals, or humans, had been there for several days.

"Looks good to me," Ryan said. "After the run-in with that panther, and our friend on the pony, we'd best keep a careful double watch. Doc, Dean and Jak, do ten through one. Mildred and J.B., watch from one to four. Krysty and me—and I—will keep guard from four until dawn."

"We hunting?" Jak asked.

Ryan shook his head. "Think not. Light's going fast. Remember the size of the panther Mildred chilled. Wouldn't like meeting that on a dark trail. We had plenty to eat back in the redoubt. There's what seems like good, clean water over yonder. We can think about food tomorrow."

RYAN AND KRYSTY LAY under a tall live oak, pulling the lightweight blankets over both of them.

"You feel like some lovemaking, lover?" she whispered.

Ryan hesitated a long, meaningful moment before starting to reply. "Well..."

Krysty laughed and kissed him very gently on the cheek. "Me neither, lover."

"Tomorrow?"

"Mebbe."

Ryan grinned. "And mebbe not. Been a long day. Bit of excitement with Mildred's panther."

Krysty held his hand, running her thumb in a soft circle around the center of his palm. "Not many women could've done that," she said.

Ryan nodded. "True enough. Tomorrow we could think about doing some hunting."

"Don't feel very hungry. Not at the moment, anyway. Thing I feel most like is getting some shut-eye."

Ryan squeezed her hand and rolled over onto his back. Unlike in the redoubt, they were both fully dressed, having just kicked off their boots. Their weapons lay on the ground at their side.

"Sleep well, dearest," he said.

"And you."

THEY WALKED along the steep-sided gorge, gradually moving higher.

The cloudless sky was a deep, rich blue, and a refreshing breeze shifted the tall branches. The night had passed without incident, though Ryan had thought at one point that someone was moving stealthily in the dark woods. But he had looked carefully in among the shadows cast by the hunter's moon and seen absolutely nothing.

He'd checked with Krysty, who hadn't been able to feel any nearby presence.

They were following a narrow game trail that cut up the gradient, away from the rumbling of the water at the bottom of the valley. The higher they climbed, the taller the pines seemed to become.

A little before noon, Krysty laid her hand on Ryan's arm. "Something quite close," she said quietly. "Feels like a number of men."

"Which direction?"

"Ahead of us. Somewhere about where the trail levels out onto a kind of plateau."

The others waited while Ryan crept ahead on hands and knees, the SIG-Sauer drawn, moving as silent as a whisper in a midnight graveyard.

There was some thick brush just where the trail flattened out, and he was able to reach it unobserved. Parting the leaves with his fingers, he peered through.

Krysty's mutie sense had been right.

Chapter Seven

There were five of them, instantly recognizable as Mescalero Apaches, sitting around a small, totally smokeless fire with a pair of skinned rabbits roasting over a pit. They were all short, muscular men, between twenty and twenty-five years old. Their restless ponies were tethered at the far side of the clearing.

Ryan watched them for several long seconds. They were lying down, two of them passing a soapstone pipe backward and forward. It was obvious that they had no idea there was anyone close by, watching them.

The wind shifted a little, bringing the smell of roasting meat to Ryan's nostrils, making him realize that he was feeling kind of hungry. There were two more rabbits, unskinned, tossed on the ground on the far side of the fire.

"Sharing time," he whispered to himself, wriggling back down the slope to rejoin the others.

Jak looked up, his mouth open, ready to call out to the returning figure of Ryan, who lifted a finger to his lips to silence the teenager. He waited until he was among the others to tell them what he'd seen up the hill.

"Five, all warriors, armed with hunting bows and

arrows. Three have rifles of some kind. Couldn't make out the detail. Four of them got pistols stuck in their belts. They weren't especially on the alert.''

J.B. stood up, slinging the Uzi across his shoulder. "And you said they got food?"

"Rabbits. Two cooking, two skinned ready. I don't reckon they'd put up a fight if we took the uncooked pair. Let's go see."

Ryan crawled on hands and knees back up the steep slope, the others spread out on either side of him. The bushes gave them all cover until they were ready to make their move on the fringe of the clearing.

The one-eyed man waited a moment, checking that none of the five Apaches was aware of their presence, less than a dozen yards away. But they all seemed completely relaxed and confident, three of them now sharing the pipe.

He glanced across at the others, all of them waiting for the signal to move forward, all of them with their blasters drawn and cocked.

Ryan nodded. "Now," he said quietly, pushing through the brush, SIG-Sauer leveled at the nearest of the Native Americans.

"Nobody moves and nobody gets hurt," he commanded, gesturing with the muzzle of the handblaster.

For a moment the Apaches sat quite still, shocked at the sudden threatening appearance of the companions, all of them well armed.

"We're kind of short on food, so we'd appreciate

the loan of those two rabbits in the grass there." A pause. "You agree? Well, you don't disagree."

The tallest of the group narrowed his eyes, saying very clearly, "Children of Rock, my brothers."

And he drew the revolver from his belt.

Ryan couldn't believe what he was seeing.

The Mescalero were all covered by cocked weapons, and had absolutely no chance of defending themselves. And all that Ryan had asked for was a couple of rabbits.

It wasn't something men would normally be willing to give up their lives for.

"Don't!" J.B. yelled, as stunned as Ryan, loath to gun down helpless men.

But the event was inexorably set.

The Apaches were going for their blasters, some slower than others, as if they couldn't believe what was happening to them, either.

It was Jak who fired first, squeezing the trigger on his enormous .357 Colt Python.

You couldn't possibly have called it a firefight. Perhaps *massacre* was the only appropriate word for what happened in the next four seconds.

J.B. fired six rounds of 9 mm ammo from the Uzi. Krysty got off two rounds from her double-action Smith & Wesson. Ryan shot down the two nearest Mescalero Apaches with the SIG-Sauer. Mildred only fired once, but the bullet took away the lower jaw of the youngest of the Native Americans, opening up his throat in a welter of gushing blood. Jak had fired once, hitting the leader of the group in the right thigh. Doc leveled the big Le Mat, ready to use the single shotgun round. But he saw that he was already too slow and he held fire. Dean, as well, was unable to get off a shot. It was done.

The Apaches managed a single shot in retaliation. That came from a rusting, rebuilt Colt .45 and exploded into the dirt and leaf mold as the man's trigger finger tightened in his death spasm.

"Hold it," Ryan said unnecessarily.

The warriors were all down, all dead, though a couple still had twitching legs, or scrabbling fingers as the lines of communications went down between limbs and brain.

The air in the clearing was heavy with the smell of cordite, a haze of smoke gradually dissipating. On the spits, over the small fire, the pair of rabbits was cooking nicely.

Ryan holstered the warm blaster, looking across at his oldest friend. "Now, why the fuck did they want to do that?" he asked J.B.

The Armorer shook his head. "Dark night! I couldn't even begin to guess. We had them cold-cocked. Could've blasted them from cover if we'd been minded."

"All for a couple of undersized rabbits," Doc said. "Why? Why on earth did they make us slay them?" His voice was hoarse with emotion.

Krysty looked down at the tangled corpses. "Only kids, some of them," she said quietly. All around them, the forest was still and silent after the burst of gunfire. "You hear him say the name we've seen on graffiti?"

"Children of Rock?" Dean said.

"Yeah. Their chief just said that name, then they all went for their blasters. Must've known that they didn't have a hope of Hades of making it against seven blasters."

She turned to Ryan. "What do you make of it, lover?"

"Children of the Rock? Never heard of them. Not anyone we came across during the time we rode with Trader. All kinds of weird groups.... But not the Children of the Rock. I'm sure I'd have remembered."

J.B. had been quickly checking the corpses, waving away the clouds of green-winged blowflies that were already gathering, drawn by the acrid pools of spilled salt blood. "Mescalero all right," he said. "Long way from their usual hunting grounds, south and east of here."

"We eating rabbits?" Jak asked.

Ryan grinned. Trust the albino teenager to strike at the heart of the business. It hadn't turned out the way they'd wanted, but at least they'd gotten themselves a good meal out of the savage encounter.

"Keep a sharp look and listen out in case they've got companions who might've heard the shots."

THEY TIPPED THE BODIES into the fast-falling river, watching as the foaming water carried them southward toward the distant Cific Ocean.

Then they ate, polishing off the two cooked rabbits, replacing them on the spits with the now skinned animals, moving them as the pink flesh darkened.

They lay back in the filtered sunlight, weapons at their sides, sucking the tender meat off the fragile bones, wiping the grease from their chins. Conversation was held in abeyance until they had all finished eating.

Doc made a halfhearted effort to stifle a belch. "I do most beg your pardon, friends. My rumbling abdominal is simply phenomenal. Run rabbit, run." He belched again, turning it into a sort of part-muffled cough.

"Think it's time we got moving, Ryan." Mildred yawned and stretched. "Help this disgusting old man to get his gastric juices flowing."

As they all stood and readied themselves to get back on the trail, there was a distant rumble of thunder. Through occasional gaps in the swaying high branches, it was possible to see, far north and west, a belt of pewter clouds, scarred and seamed with purple-pink chem lightning.

"Tall pines like this must be vulnerable to lightning strikes," Mildred stated. "We going to try and make it to the old national park and see the really big trees?"

"I'd like that. How about you, lover?"

Ryan grinned. "Sure."

FUELED BY THE RABBIT MEAT, they made good time along the old highway, pressing on through the clear air, gradually climbing higher.

Doc suddenly stopped and sat down, pressing his knuckles to his temples, eyes squeezed tight shut.

"By the Three Kennedys! But I have the most demonic headache."

"Could be altitude sickness," Mildred said, kneeling by Doc. "Any other symptoms?"

"Little tired. Breath short. Nausea. What more can I tell you, madam?"

The woman patted him on the shoulder. "Told me enough, Doc."

"What sort of height are we at?" Krysty asked. "Feel like eight thousand or so."

J.B. checked his pocket comp sextant, which had a reading on height above sea level. "Seven thousand nine hundred. Mebbe we could stop early for the night and take a rest. Give Doc chance to acclimate before we climb higher."

"I am sorry to be such a crashing bore," the old man muttered. "I can hear my pulse beating in my ears. A most unpleasant sensation."

"Rest's best." Mildred glanced over at Ryan. "Could be that he'll be real sick if we don't take a break. Stop for the night now, maybe?"

He looked around. The trail wound temporarily downhill, rippled by the quakes of skydark, lined with scarlet Indian paintbrush, and Sierra poppies, blazing orange against the dark green forest.

"Fine," he said. "Should be water close by. If Doc can make it, we'll take it slow and steady, then camp once we find the river again."

AFTER THEIR ENCOUNTER with the Apaches, Ryan kept them to a strict skirmish line, going on point himself. With only one eye, his peripheral vision was strictly limited, and he walked cautiously, head constantly turning.

Doc seemed to recover a little, stalking along, ferrule of his cane clicking on the blacktop, the wind ruffling his silvery hair. The temperature had dropped, and the sky was once more darkening ahead of them.

From a few steps behind him, Krysty drew Ryan's attention to a figurine fixed to the flank of a stout, lightning-split pine just off the trail to the right.

"Not the Children of the Rock again?"

He stopped and peered at the mannequin. It looked like it had once been a child's toy, but it was stripped naked, with a coil of razored barbed wire wrapped around its sexless loins. Daubs of paint represented blood, as though it had been flogged.

It was crucified, upside down, to the tree, steel pins through the center of each hand and through the crossed ankles. The face was oddly blank, with a water-stained crew cut, indifferent to the myriad tortures the body was suffering.

"Some sickos around here," Mildred said. "Look at the burn marks around the groin."

"It much resembles some sort of religious totem," Doc suggested.

Ryan nodded slowly. "Could be. Seen similar things all over Deathlands."

"Sicko," repeated Mildred, turning away from the tree in disgust.

"Seen animals impaled in swamps," Jak said. "Voodoo medicine."

Doc was breathing hard, his face pale, holding his chest. "Forgive me, but there has been talk of stopping early to take a good rest? I would appreciate that."

"Fine." Ryan looked around. "We'll get a distance away from this place, then camp."

Chapter Eight

It was a peaceful night. They had a tiny fire, glowing bright in the darkness while they sat around it, talking of old days, old stories.

The conversation had turned to the weather. It was obvious there was a storm brewing. J.B. told the tale that Ryan knew from the Trader days, about a sudden tornado in the open plains of old Kansas.

"Sky had gone dark as a beaver hat. Wind rising over the prairie from the north, tasting of winter ice. Flurry of hail pattered down, hard enough to sting if it hit you in the face. The cattle and horses on the farms all spooked, sensing that something bad was coming down on them."

Krysty reached across and tossed a length of broken, dried timber onto the fire, sending a column of golden sparks into the velvet sky.

"There was this guy, had a wife and three little children. They only moved there a few months earlier, from Montclair in Jersey. He thought he knew everything, did Jerzy Pollinger. Fat, with a thin little voice, like a spoiled child. He hadn't listened to the locals who warned him to build well and solid, with a decent storm cellar for shelter against the tornadoes."

"I recall that a cousin of mine was once trapped

in a tornado," Doc began, then looked across at the Armorer. "A thousand apologies, dear friend. I have interrupted you in your story, have I not? Pray proceed."

"Sure, Doc, thanks. One day, with this storm threatening, Jerzy was looking across the windswept plains. Always a wind in Kansas. Drives folks insane. And out in the distance, where the sky meets the land, he saw the beginnings of a twister. Fat and sullen. Wide bellied near the top, sweeping down to a sucking mouth, maybe fifty paces across."

"That all?" Jak asked. "We never got them in swamps."

J.B. looked across the fire at the white-faced youth. "Sure. Mile across at the top. This one was shimmying and advancing toward Jerzy's farm. The air was still all around, but you could hear the storm advancing, rumbling on. Jerzy's wife, Lorena, came out and gave a feeble, despairing sort of cry when she saw death rolling in their direction. By now it was less than a mile off."

Dean lifted a hand to his face and barely managed to smother a yawn. Something large, with white wings, came swooping down from the highest branches, through the clearing, swooping only a few feet above the group of friends, making all of them duck. Then it vanished, twisting and weaving between the trees, before anyone could see it properly.

J.B. carried on with his story. "Jerzy looked around their yard, desperately seeking somewhere to hide from the ravening monster heading their way. He spotted the deep well, bucket hauled up and hooked off at the top. Called out to his wife to look after the children and ran to the well. He hopped over the rim and let himself down, vanishing from sight. Lorena cursed him as she stood there, helpless, knowing that if he'd waited they could have gotten into the well and likely been saved. But as it was, his action had doomed them all to almost certain death.''

"What a bastard," Krysty said. "Should have—"

J.B. took off his glasses and polished them carefully on his sleeve, holding up his other hand to quiet her. "Just wait, Krysty."

"Sorry. Go on."

"Lorena saw nowhere to hide. Just a broken-down concrete culvert that used to be part of the cattle-feeding system, way back before skydark. She caught hold of the little ones and dragged them after her, screaming and crying, and squeezed herself under the old trough, pulling them after her, holding them as tight as tight could be. Keeping her face down, she told them to close their eyes tight shut, say a prayer, and waited for the end.''

Mildred was sitting close to the Armorer and now she reached out and gripped his hand, huddling herself close to him. "Sounds like a story that'll end in tears, John," she commented.

He didn't answer her. "The tornado came down on top of them, sucking and howling like a banshee. Louder than the loudest thunder, she said. It sort of skirted past the house, sucking out the windows, but leaving the roof intact. Then it brushed past them and tugged at Lorena, ripping off most of her clothes, the sand scouring at her skin. She could feel the children crying out. Not hear them. Felt them. Then, just as suddenly as it arrived, the twister was gone again. She blinked open her eyes and looked out and saw it funneling its way across the prairie, off toward the east. And she could make out bits of rubbish and branches and chunks of stuff flying around in it.''

''I heard tell of slivers of straw being driven clean through stout trees,'' Doc said.

J.B. nodded. ''True enough, Doc. Anyway, Lorena got herself up and dusted herself and the children down and went to look for her cowardly husband, fully intending to give him a real piece of her mind.''

''Hear, hear,'' Ryan said, even though he knew the end of the story.

''She reaches the well and peers down into it. Now the clouds have broken up and there's bright sunlight, illuminating right to the bottom of that well. And all the water's gone. Bone-dry. Sucked clear out from the bottom. Bucket and chain gone. Jerzy Pollinger gone. And they never saw hide nor hair of him again, from that day to this. Plain vanished.''

There was a ripple of applause from the others, sitting around the smoldering embers of the fire.

''Excellent tale, John Barrymore,'' Doc said. ''Upon my soul but I have seldom heard a more moral story, so finely narrated. Divine vengeance, indeed.''

"Listen," Jak said suddenly.

Everyone fell instantly silent, straining to hear the noise that had attracted the attention of the teenager, listening for some sound above the gentle murmur of the dying campfire. At first, there was nothing.

"I hear it," Krysty said, brushing back an errant tendril of her fiery hair. "Singing. No, more like chanting. Quite close. Other side of river."

Jak stood, uncoiling with the ease of a serpent. "Yeah."

Now all of them could make it out.

"Reminds me wondrously of the Gregorian chant of monks at their devotions," Doc said.

Krysty stood, looking across at the old man. "Yeah. I can hear what you mean. Sort of spiritual and chilling at the same time."

"Not the kind of church singing that I'm used to," Mildred said. "Too much head in it and not enough heart. Real cold and scary."

"We goin' to take a look?" J.B. asked.

Ryan thought about it. "Could be something to do with that crucified, tortured doll back there. Might be safer to stay where we are and keep quiet."

"I'd like to take me a look, lover."

He sighed. "Guess there can't be any harm if we keep under cover. No noises. Doc?"

"Yes, my dear fellow?"

"That especially means you."

Doc looked hurt. "I can walk just as silent as a vaporous midnight dream picking its tippy-toed way through an endless beach of soft sand, my dear

Ryan. When the occasion merits it, that is, of course.''

"Then do it, Doc. Do it. There's something about that noise I don't much like.''

THEY HEARD THE FIRST SCREAM when they'd only moved about a hundred yards through the woods, a single piercing shriek of gut-wrenching, jagged pain, almost instantly muffled.

"Could be you were right, Ryan,'' Mildred said, eyes gleaming in the dappled moonlight. "Maybe this falls under the category of not our business.''

"Someone out there getting goose cooked.'' Jak's hair blazed like a magnesium torch in the gloom. His eyes glowed like living rubies.

"Can't be too far away from here.'' Ryan paused and listened. It might have been his imagination, but the singers seemed to have missed a beat when the cry came before resuming their dogged, droning chorus.

"I vote for going on.'' Krysty looked around. "How's anyone else feel?''

The decision was unanimous.

AS THEY MOVED SLOWLY through the forest, the sky was clouding over, veiling the moon. It grew suddenly cooler and the wind began to rise from the north, disturbing the topmost branches of the old pines.

Though the scream had seemed to come from not far away, they had been walking for several minutes without a sign or sound of anything.

Ryan held up his hand, bringing the others huddling around him. "Anyone hear anything? Krysty? Can you feel anything out there in the dark?"

"Nothing, lover. Nothing really positive. Just a sort of a vague sense of the dark forces of chaos." She pointed ahead of them, to where the narrow hunting trail wound alongside the river. "There. That way."

The singing had stopped, and there was only the rising breeze, slicing through the woods.

Ryan beckoned them on, picking his way carefully along the overgrown path, knowing that a false step could easily leave one of them with a twisted ankle or worse.

The chanting suddenly resumed, so near in front of them that it made Ryan jump with surprise. He stopped immediately, shading his eye and peering through the blackness, catching a glimpse of glowing fire, less than a hundred yards ahead. As he stared intently at the flickering flames, he could make out several figures moving back and forth against the light.

"Not muties," Krysty whispered.

"What's that cracking noise?" Dean asked curiously.

"Sounds like small-gauge blaster shots. Or firecrackers," J.B. suggested.

"If I might cast my beaver into the ring," Doc said, clearing his throat, "I am of the opinion that the noise is actually the sound of a lash striking sullen human flesh." He shrugged. "Though I may be in error.''

Ryan nodded. ''Could be right, Doc. Whipping.''

THE WIND VEERED, bringing a fountain of crimson-and-golden sparks from the large fire that stood at the center of a clearing, about twenty paces in width. Ryan felt a thin flurry of rain strike his cheeks as he crouched in the shelter of some thorn-bushes.

Smoke was drifting toward them, bitter and acrid, the scent of pine, overlaid with some sort of herbs. Ryan covered his mouth, taken with the desire to cough.

If it came to a firefight, he guessed they would be able to win easily enough, against eighteen naked men and women. But there was no way of knowing whether there was a ville nearby, perhaps with dozens of armed men.

It still wasn't possible to determine the focus of the shuffling snake of people. Each of them held a short-hilted, multilashed whip, which they were using on the back of a person in front of them, giving rise to the wet, sticky sound that Doc had correctly identified. In the flickering light of the big fire, it was easy to see the tendrils of dark blood that were trickling down over the glistening buttocks of each of the participants in the ceremony. But their eyes seemed fixed on something or someone that was out of sight of Ryan and the others. It seemed to be something attached or standing against a broad oak that had its back to Ryan and the watchers.

''We'll move around the edge of the clearing. See

what we can see,'' he whispered, gesturing to the others.

As he led the way, the powerful SIG-Sauer cocked in his right hand, finger on the trigger, Ryan came close to inadvertently opening fire. He was suddenly aware of a creature of some kind, snaking unexpectedly from the leaf mold beneath his boots, a reptile that appeared to have dozens of tiny, stubby legs, carrying it sinuously across the trail, its iridescent orange scales damp with the steadily falling rain.

The singing was growing louder and faster, gathering momentum, the shuffling figures moving more quickly, the blood-clotted lashes rising and falling.

Ryan realized now what the ragged, panted words were. It was the old, old hymn about meeting at the river, the river that flows by the throne of God.

The cold rain was coming with serious intent, slanting down, filtering through the pine needles, dripping onto the forest floor all round them. Ryan could catch the sound of the drops hissing off the burning logs.

Finally he could see the center of attraction fixed to the trunk of the oak tree.

It was uncannily like the little plastic figure that they had seen crucified upside down.

Only this figure wasn't made of plastic.

Chapter Nine

"Jesus Christ!" Mildred was so close to Ryan that he could almost feel her revulsion, sensing her swallowing hard, seeking to avoid throwing up.

"Goodness, gracious me," Doc said, his voice surprisingly mild, considering the horror of the spectacle that the firelight revealed to them.

"Dad, how could they do that to someone?" Dean asked, transfixed by the horrible sight.

It was exactly like the tortured mannequin that they had seen earlier, a naked male, upside down, head dangling toward a pile of dry brushwood beneath the long dark hair. The heads of iron nails glittered at the center of both spread palms. Another, longer spike had been hammered bloodily through the crossed ankles, splintering the bones.

His eyes had been either burned or gouged from their sockets. It was difficult to see, among the dancing shadows, whether the dark caverns were filled with ashes or with clotted blood. The fingers dangled limply, all broken and wrenched out of place. It looked as though the wretch's knees had both been broken with a sledgehammer.

The pallid skin was marked with a number of slicing cuts and purpled bruises, indicating a lengthy period of torture over the previous few hours.

Ryan brushed a few drops of rain from his face. Clearing his vision, he saw that the hideous burning of the plastic man's groin was reproduced here for real. The genitals had been severed, a torn hole filled with congealed blood all that remained of the victim's manhood.

"We could take them all out," J.B. whispered, shoulder pressing against Ryan's arm.

As the rain grew heavier, the cavorting naked figures seemed to be slowing. The singing became even more ragged, their flagellation less frenzied. The water mingled with the streaks of splattered blood, turning it pink, sending it flowing all the way across emaciated bellies and wrinkled thighs and down over the bare feet.

The fire was dying under the torrential downpour, the light sinking in the clearing.

Ryan wondered whether there was any point at all in interfering. The sacrificial prey was doomed. The kindest thing would be to put a 9 mm bullet through his skull and end his suffering.

At one point Ryan had thought the tortured man was dead. Then he drew several racking, shuddering breaths, his whole rib cage heaving with the effort of staying alive. A hank of cloth had been knotted around his mouth to keep him from crying out again. The head turned desperately from side to side, as though he were blindly seeking some sort of salvation.

The leader of the worshipers seemed to be a singularly tall, skinny man. Endowed, Ryan couldn't help noticing, with an extremely large penis that hung almost to his knee, like a length of rejected hose. He had a shaved head, streaming with rain, his eyes wide and staring. His mouth hung open, showing a series of jagged and broken teeth. His whip was bigger than the others, multithonged, which he was using on his own back, lashing his scarred flesh across alternate shoulders.

Now he held up the dripping flail and called out to his followers in a harsh, croaking voice.

"Best we finish before the weather fucks us in our intention," he yelled.

Krysty tugged at Ryan's sleeve. "Are we not going to do something, lover?"

He shook his head. "Man's almost dead."

"Still ease his passing."

Ryan looked sideways at her, seeing the way the storm had flattened her fiery hair against her skull.

"Trader used to say that you didn't clean up shit unless you'd already trodden in it. Not our business, Krysty. Can only lead to trouble."

She tugged harder. "I don't believe what I'm hearing, lover. I don't."

"There's times and there's times. You know that, just as well as I do."

Part of him wanted to put a violent ending to this bloody torture. But the more rational side of his character told him to leave well alone and move on. It wasn't their business. He sighed, rubbing his finger along the side of his nose, huddling his shoulders as the rain beat down even more strongly. The wind was also gathering force, whistling and shrieking through the tall trees, whipping the fire into a steaming inferno.

The dancing had stopped, and the eighteen men and women were gathered around their victim.

"In the name of the gods of sky and land and earth and sun and fire and water and stone and blood... That you might help us to a great harvest, we offer up this worthy sacrifice to you all. He came willing like..." There was a pause, and muffled sniggering from a couple of the women. "Now we offer him to you, through fire and through rain."

He turned to a stout young man. "Light the torch, brother, and then we can go home."

The raging storm made it hard to get the brand lit, but it eventually flared into life, smoking with an orange-red glow, showing that they were using some crudely refined petroleum to help it to burn.

"If you don't, Ryan, then I will," Krysty warned, aiming with her Smith & Wesson blaster. "Sorry, lover. Can't let them do this."

For a fraction of a frozen moment, it crossed his mind to punch her out, knock the blaster from her hands, stop her from disobeying him in front of the others. The crimson rage was blazing, but that microsecond of red-mist rage passed as quickly as it had reared its cobra head.

The teenager, hair dank across his shoulders, was stooping to set light to the pile of brushwood just below the head of the tortured man.

Ryan made his decision. He turned to Mildred, crouched on his left. "Put away their victim. Rest of you, chill as many as you can. Best that none of them escape to carry the word back to their ville.''

Mildred already had her Czech target revolver drawn, in her right hand. She leveled it slowly, blinking away the rain.

Ryan could have spent hours watching Mildred shooting. Her talent with a blaster was truly phenomenal, better than anyone else he'd ever seen in Deathlands. She had once told him that her expertise didn't just extend to holding her breath before gently squeezing the trigger. She was so aware of her own body that she had the ability to judge the single beats of her heart and fire between them.

The rest of them all had their blasters at the ready, peering out through the dripping bushes at the last scenes of the bloody ritual.

''When you're ready,'' Ryan said, leveling his own blaster at the dangling head of the crucified man.

There was a blinding flash of chem lightning, like a purple spear, exploding against the top of one of the pinoo, looo than a hundrod yardo away, igniting the tall tree as it seared its way to the ground. It was followed instantly by a massive rumble of deafening thunder.

The noise drowned out the thin crack of the ZKR 551, though Ryan sensed Mildred shooting and saw the effect of her single shot.

She fired again, at the young man who was concentrating on lighting the fire, bent forward. The .38 round took him through the back of the skull, a little to the left. The round tumbled as soon as it hit the bone, distorting, rolling and slicing through the soft tissues of the brain. It erupted through his open mouth in a welter of gray, pink and scarlet, and white shards of bone, smashing his teeth and shredding his chubby lips. His scream of shock and horror was choked off with a gush of blood and a grue of brain matter.

The rest of the naked coven stopped stock-still. To them it had to have appeared that their companion had been stricken down by a blast from heaven. Like Ryan, they couldn't possibly have heard the sound of the shot above the crash of thunder. And there was the young man rolling on his back, fists clenched, flailing, feet scrabbling in the muddy earth, eyes wide open, the rain splashing on them.

It looked as if some horrific accident had led to him vomiting out his own brains.

The tall leader started to turn toward the undergrowth, the only one of the group to begin to suspect that they were under attack.

Krysty shot him through the upper chest with her first shot, sending him staggering backward, tumbling over his own feet and landing on his back in the remnants of the big fire. He began to yell in a frantic, high-pitched voice.

Then the clearing became a maelstrom of death. It was a far, far worse massacre than that of the Mescalero Apaches—more helpless, defenseless dead.

Most of the dead fell to the chattering spray from the barrel of J.B.'s Uzi, a hail of leaden slaughter that sent them spinning and dancing in a ghastly parody of riotous pleasure. Blood fountained from sliced flesh, turning pink in the torrential downpour.

Because of the shortage of ammo for his Le Mat, Doc was the only one of the seven not to engage in the shooting party, instead watching the butchery, stone-faced.

By a freak of happenstance, one of the women escaped the killing ground. A bullet from Dean's blaster had clipped her right shoulder, but she managed to stagger away, dodging and sliding in the mud, mouth gaping in a silent shriek of horror. Ryan tried a snap shot at her as she slithered on hands and knees behind a clump of aspens, but the bullet stripped off a length of bark and missed her by a good eighteen inches.

"Get her, Jak," he snapped. "Don't want word of this to get out."

The teenager holstered his blaster and was off, a white-haired ghost, vanishing surefooted into the gloom like an avenging angel of savage death.

"J.B., drag that corpse out of the fire," Ryan said, stepping cautiously from cover.

There was little movement in the clearing. One of the older men had been gut shot and was rolling from side to side, clutching the gaping wound in his scrawny belly. Threads of gray-yellow entrails seeped out into the dirt. Ryan holstered the blaster and drew the panga, stooping and cutting open the dying man's jugular, giving him a swift and merciful passing that had been denied to the wretched figure that dangled upside down from the tree. Blood sprayed out, and Ryan stepped neatly to one side to avoid having it splatter over his pants and boots.

The Armorer dragged the tall, skinny corpse from the smoldering remnants of the fire, where it had already begun to blister and scorch, the hair sizzling and stinking in the cool dampness.

They had barely finished checking the bodies when Jak returned to them, wiping the leaf-shaped blade of one of his throwing knives on the sleeve of his jacket, whistling under his breath.

Ryan glanced across at him, eyebrows raised in a question. As more lightning hissed close by and thunder filled the forest, Jak simply nodded.

"Good."

"Think they were those Children of the Rock?" Krysty asked, looking around at the carnage.

"Could be. But we've come across this sort before. Let's get him down off the tree," Ryan said, pointing at the tortured body.

"Seemed more like a crowd of penitents," Mildred suggested, reloading her blaster. "I vacationed a few times in the Southwest and came across them down there. All across New Mexico, and into Colorado. And parts of Arizona. They were real big on crucifixion, I recall."

"And flagellation," Doc added. "Mortifying the body to cleanse the spirit."

They managed to lever out the long iron nails, carefully lowering the raggled body to the wet ground. The center of the storm seemed to have passed them by, and the rain had eased to a steady drizzle.

"We aren't going to bury him, are we, lover?" Krysty asked.

"No. Carry him back down the path and put him in the river. It's in flood, and he'll get carried well away from here. It's all we can do for him."

"How about the rest of them, Dad?" Dean asked.

"Leave them. Soon as we put him in the water, we can move on again. There's far too much blood and too many corpses in this part of Deathlands."

THE CHEM STORM WAS behaving oddly. Having rushed upon them, it had eased away to the south. But within ten minutes the wind had changed and the rain turned back into a torrential downpour, battering at the trees, driven by the howling wind into the faces of Ryan and his companions.

By the time they'd struggled through the darkness down the winding, treacherous path with the heavy body, all of them had taken at least one fall and were covered in slick, dark mud.

"River's around the next bend," J.B. panted. "Need to cross it if we want to get north and west along the highway and get in among the really tall timber."

"Listen to that noise!" exclaimed Doc, who was wrestling with the dead man's legs. "It sounds to me as though that little river has become something of a flood."

Jak was out at point and he suddenly reappeared, shoulders hunched. "Bad news," he yelled, cupping his hands to his mouth.

Ryan rubbed at his good eye. The water had penetrated behind the patch over his missing eye, stinging the socket. "What is it, Jak?"

"River's up."

"Much?"

The teenager grinned wolfishly at the question, holding his long-fingered hands as far apart as they would possibly go. "Plenty," he called.

"We get across?" yelled the Armorer, who was supporting the shoulders of the slippery, naked body, barely managing to keep it up out of the dirt.

"No way. Fucking impossible!"

As soon as Ryan rounded the corner and saw the state of the river, he knew that Jak was correct. There was no way at all that they could cross the foaming inferno that interrupted the trail ahead of them.

Chapter Ten

They heaved the corpse into the river, taking the greatest care that none of them lost their footing and followed it into the tumbling torrent. It dipped and rose, riding the whirlpools and rapids, one arm reaching out of the white frothing bubbles, as though the dead man had revived and was seeking help from the silent watchers on the bank.

"Poor bastard," Mildred said very quietly.

"Least blood price paid. Paid good odds." Jak smiled at the woman.

The lightning and thunder of the chem storm had passed, but the wind had risen to something close to hurricane strength and the rain was so heavy that if you stood with your face upturned there was a risk of drowning. The water was icy cold and tasted of rusty iron on the tongue.

The rippled blacktop vanished beneath the turbulent river and reappeared, tantalizingly close, on the other bank. It was barely twenty yards from side to side. Ryan had no doubt that when the rains ceased, the river would drop within hours and they would be able to continue their journey.

They found a huge sequoia that had fallen, probably a hundred years earlier, during the tremors of skydark, and had barely begun to rot. Its root structure was massively tangled, like a mummified Medusa's hair, forming a cavern a good fifteen feet deep and at least a dozen feet across. Large enough for them all to find shelter.

Within a couple of minutes, J.B. had used one of their precious self-lights to set sparks to some dry leaf mold, some thin, broken twigs and some bigger branches, until there was a bright, roaring fire.

They stripped off their sodden outer garments, keeping on only underclothes, and hung the soaked pants, shirts and vests on the dried roots, turning them now and again as the dark, damp patches gradually became lighter and their white, wrinkled skin resumed its usual color.

The steam from the wet garments hung heavy in the damp air. Ryan glanced out into the teeming rain, conscious of Doc at his elbow.

"You know, dear friend, that this used to be a hell of a beautiful part of the country once upon a while. Now, every place we set our feet, it seems like the shadow of death falls across the land."

Ryan shook his head, running his fingers through his damp, thickly matted hair. "Something's real wrong in these hills. Trees like the gods just finished growing them. Air so fresh you could slice it with a knife. Everything green and pleasant. Yet, like you said, it's as if there's a corpse lying under every bush. Madness. First the Apaches freaking out when there wasn't any need for it. Then those fladgies with their sick games."

He felt Krysty's hand, gentle on his arm, like a

moth's wing, the warmth of her nearly naked body against his.

"Think that it's these Children of the Rock that have tainted things, lover?"

He put his arm around her shoulders. "How do we know? Possible. Either we can keep on and explore a while more, or we turn around and go back and make a jump to someplace else."

"Keep goin'," Jak said from the darkness behind them.

"I'll second that," J.B. called, his words echoing in the cavern.

"And I'll third it," Mildred added. "Soon as we can rest, get ourselves dry and our clothes dry and the rain stops. Then maybe find something to eat."

"Seen game trails," the albino teenager commented, shaking his tumbling mane of snow white hair. "Deer all sorts."

"Won't be much fishing with the river in spate." J.B. took off his glasses, then realized that he had nothing to wipe them on. "We can hole up here. This rain looks like it's here to stay for a while."

Ryan spit out into the rain. "Guess we don't have a lot of choice right now. Just so long as we don't have to massacre anyone else for a while."

IT WAS A LITTLE before dawn. The fire had sunk to a pile of white, glowing embers, and the rain had recently stopped, water still dripping noisily from the pines. A gray mist hung in the trees, about fifty feet up, hiding the soaring tops.

Ryan awakened feeling cold and stiff, yawning

and stretching, feeling the tight muscles creak across his shoulders and the back of his neck.

"Sleep well, lover?" Krysty whispered.

"Getting too old for this sort of thing." He quickly began to dress himself, pulling on his pants and slipping his blaster into the greased holster. "Time I settled down in a snug little log cabin with a warm fire and an old mongrel dog sleeping on the hearth."

"And a snug little wife waiting up the stairs for you to go and join her?"

"Sure. That, too."

Krysty laughed and rolled out of her blanket. In less than half a minute she, too, was dressed and armed.

They made no effort to keep quiet, and within a few moments the others were stirring.

Doc's knee joints cracked like musket shots, and he threw back his head and yawned noisily, showing off his unnaturally splendid set of teeth. "By the Three Kennedys!" he exclaimed. "This may have suited Daniel Boone, but I find it parlously chill. Who let the fire be so sadly neglected?"

"All of us," Dean replied.

"No point in getting it going again." Mildred stood, the beads in her plaited hair tinkling softly. "God, what time is it, John?"

The Armorer checked his wrist chron. "Little after five-thirty."

"I could have used another couple of hours' sleep." She rubbed her eyes. "That's one of the things I hate about Deathlands. You never get to sleep in.''

THEY ALL WENT DOWN to check on the river, finding it was still swollen, racing at five times its previous width, foaming and muddied, carrying all sorts of detritus in its jaws. Even as they watched, a dead animal was swept by, head lolling, its limp body destroyed by the force of the water.

"Wolf?" J.B. asked.

"Could be. Bound to be plenty of them in a forest this size."

Ryan shrugged. "No way of getting over here. Best follow upstream until we can find a place to cross and carry on northward."

ABOUT A HALF MILE upstream they heard the thundering of a cataract, and tasted the coolness of misty spray hanging in the rainbowed air.

The land had changed from open hillside to a steep gorge, with granite rocks gleaming in the dampness of early morning. The sun was peeking over the mountains toward east, casting long shadows across the narrow paths.

Dean had gone a little ahead of the others and he came scampering back, breathless with excitement. "Hot pipe! Fish," he panted. "Lots of fish!"

The ravine was around two hundred yards in length, filled with a thunderous torrent. The water raged over a series of falls, the steepest of them rising fifty feet in a number of minor jumps. And it was there that it was possible to see and appreciate the quantity of fish.

Even in dry times, in midsummer, it would have been an impressive sight. Here, after the heavy downpour, it was unbelievably spectacular.

"Steelheads," J.B. announced, recognizing the silvered, iridescent scales of the trout. They watched as the fishes—thousands of them—swarmed their way upstream, battling the incredible power of the swollen river. Some of them were visibly muties, stretching out well over six feet in length, the sunlight catching their blankly incurious eyes.

"Is that not a truly remarkable sight?" Doc asked. "Nature at her most mysterious."

"Good eating," Krysty said. "Though I don't see how we're going to get close enough to catch any of them."

"Shoot one," Mildred offered. "Size of those bastards, one'll feed us all for a month."

Ryan nodded. "There's a shallow pool under that next falls. If you can put a bullet into one as it's making its leap, it should drop back there and we can grab it easily."

"Good shot in all spray." Jak was grinning widely at the prospect of watching Mildred's ace-on-the-line shooting, as well as anticipating the succulent feast of tender roasted trout that would follow.

"Nobody'll hear the sound of the blaster, even if they're a hundred yards off." J.B. gestured to Mildred. "Go for it," he said, the sun glittering from his glasses.

The polished 6-shot Czech revolver, showing the engraved name of its makers from the Zbrojovka works in Brno, slid from the holster. Mildred thumbed back on the short-fall cocking hammer, the click inaudible against the roaring background of the white-foamed torrent.

She stood with feet slightly apart, perfectly balanced, holding the .38-caliber blaster in both hands, at arm's length in front of her. Mildred looked along the barrel, keeping both eyes open, holding her breath.

Everyone stared at the tumbling water, watching the jostling steelhead as they fought their way toward their ancestral spawning grounds. Ryan was astounded, never having seen such a proliferation of fish anywhere in his life. And some of them were gigantic.

One of them, a good six feet in length, was making its third or fourth effort to negotiate the turbulent, rocky slope, powerful tail flapping with all its power as it seemed to hang suspended in the shining air.

"Now," Ryan whispered.

Mildred squeezed the trigger and the blaster kicked in her hands, the explosion muffled by the roar of the falls.

"Missed," Jak sniggered.

Mildred holstered the blaster and turned to face the teenager, slowly raising the middle finger of her right hand toward him. "Not," she said.

The monstrous trout slid back down among the jagged rocks, landing in the deep pool at the base of the falls. A thread of pale blood leaked into the dark water, circling as the fish flailed in its death throes.

The Armorer warned Jak as the albino started to go into the water to haul out the dying steelhead. "Look out for those jaws. Might only be a trout, but it's a rad-blasted sizable creature to tangle with. Take your hand off at the wrist, easy as winking. Best we all help."

The bullet had struck the mutie fish through the head, blowing a hole the size of a man's fist as it exited. The wound was fatal, but the creature was still thrashing, its tail kicking up a bloody froth.

Despite the wet weather, it wasn't that difficult to scavenge among the tall trees to find enough dry twigs to get a smokeless fire started. The Armorer used his thin-bladed flensing knife to slice the trout into dripping haunches, arranging them carefully on a network of thin branches that suspended them over the bright orange flames.

Krysty and Mildred went hunting with Doc and Dean to try to find something to eat along with the fish, returning with an armful of various roots and herbs that produced a delicious scent as they began to cook.

It took more than an hour before the steelhead was ready to eat. The companions sat around, blowing on their fingertips, peeling off the thick, blackened scales, dropping them hissing into the smoldering ashes.

It was excellent.

Ryan belched, leaning back against the worm-eaten bole of a larch, and yawned. "That was great."

"You feel confident that the flavor of the cooking won't have impinged upon our Native American friends, or upon any more of those religious maniacs?" Doc wiped his mouth on the sleeve of his frock coat.

Ryan sniffed. "Can never be sure, Doc. But a forest as thick as this should swallow up most smells. And the trees are so tall that there's no chance of the smoke being seen. Should be safe enough, I reckon."

"How much farther are we going?" asked Mildred, who'd been watching J.B. meticulously fieldstripping and cleaning her revolver.

"See what one more day brings us," Ryan replied.

Chapter Eleven

Between them the seven companions managed to eat the entire fish at two gut-stretching sittings, finishing it off in the late evening, with the moon already rising through the branches of the surrounding pines.

It was good to be able to relax, resting by the lulling sound of the pounding river. So much of their life in Deathlands was running, hiding and chilling.

The rain clouds had passed away, and the sky was clear from north to south, with the promise of a cool night. Somewhere far off they all heard the howling of a lone wolf, a noise that was picked up by another predator, a few miles closer. Ryan instinctively reached for the butt of his pistol, then relaxed as he realized that the nearer animal was still a good distance away from them, and no threat at all.

He had rarely felt as full, his stomach rebelling at the surfeit of strong-flavored fish. The wind was rising again, moving through the vast forest, coming in from the west, carrying the bitter sharpness of salt from the Cific across the hills.

They had allowed the fire to die down, and it had sunk to a small pile of gray ashes that occasionally flared crimson as the strengthening breeze reached it. Doc had already fallen asleep, lying on his back, gnarled hands folded across his chest like a crusader at his eternal rest on a tomb.

Jak and Dean were also dozing, curled up beside the embers of the fire.

Mildred and J.B. sat close together, hands entwined, whispering to each other. Every now and again one of them would laugh quietly.

Krysty looked across at them, then back at Ryan. They both lay close together, sharing a companionable silence.

Time passed, evening creeping imperceptibly into the darkness of full night.

They heard the keening of the wolf once more, but it didn't seem to be getting any closer.

"RAIN IN THE AIR," J.B. announced, beating his battered fedora into shape.

"Shame no fish left." Jak sat up, honing one of his leaf-bladed throwing knives on a round stone. "Shoot us another, Mildred, huh?"

"Yeah, Mildred. I'm about starved!" Dean added.

She laughed. "Maybe. I still feel kind of stuffed from yesterday."

Ryan stood and stretched, easing the kinks out of his muscles. "Might be best to move on some. Tracks showed plenty of deer around here."

Doc smiled at the thought. "Haunch of venison. With some apple and cabbage and some creamed potatoes. Goblet of a decent zinfandel to wash it down. Followed up with a gut-sticking portion of homemade treacle pudding. And a brimming balloon glass of Napoleon brandy.''

None of them, not even Krysty with her ''seeing'' ability, could have guessed how far off the mark was the old man's sybaritic vision.

THE TRAIL WAS NARROW, winding steeply across the face of a wooded ridge, the ground dropping away to the west toward the river. The water level had fallen during the night, but the river was still a snarling, menacing sight, impossible to cross safely.

There was the threat of rain, though the bank of low clouds had passed over and lifted. Mildred hunched her shoulders and shivered. ''Still cold,'' she complained.

''Spoiled by having such a good fire for two nights running,'' J.B. said with a grin, wiping away the fine mist of condensation from his glasses.

''Warm up once we get moving properly.'' Ryan led the way, swinging along at a good four miles per hour, which was a fair pace over difficult terrain.

They hadn't seen any sign of human life for some time, then Ryan spotted a short wooden sign, almost hidden among a clump of flowering thimbleberries: Beaver Lake Trail, 1.6 Miles. An arrow pointed back and downward. Crest Pine Trail, 8.6 Miles. An arrow pointed straight ahead. The lettering was deeply incised, covered with a thin coating of phosphorescent moss.

''Lots of national parks around here and stuff like that,'' Mildred commented.

They crossed the remains of a wider, edged path,

its surface rippled by some postnuke earth movements. Its tarmac surface was furrowed and cracked, and bright weeds sprouted through in hundreds of places.

"Look at that." Dean pointed into the lower branches of a fire-scarred ridgepole, a little way ahead of them and to the left.

"More of the Children of the Rock," Krysty said as they gathered round the macabre totem.

It was the wind-dried corpse of baby pig, with trotters and head removed, its flanks shrunken and leathery. Two unmatched dolls' heads, plastic and eyeless, had been nailed to the shoulders, staring into each other's face. Threads of blond hair, looking human, were pasted to one of the artificially pink skulls.

Chicken feet had been sewn onto where the forelegs of the pig would have been, the claws painted a faded crimson. And what looked like the legs of a very large rat were fixed to the rear stumps of the hideous thing.

A delicately embroidered waistcoat in rainbow silks had been fitted around the wasted midriff, fastened in place with tiny mother-of-pearl buttons.

"I vow that someone has taken a great deal of time and trouble, bubble, bubble, double trouble, in the caldron.... My apologies, my good and trusted companions, but I fear that my brain took a brief vacation there."

A small white card, about nine inches square, shrink-wrapped in clear plastic, was nailed to the trunk of the tree below the symbol:

The righteous are right and the rest are wrong. We choose life. For you, unless you come to us in abject humility, we choose death and damnation.

It was neatly lettered, signed in scarlet with the stark initials: "CoR."

"Friendly sons of bitches," Ryan muttered. "Religious crazies can be serious trouble."

"Think we should just go back, lover?"

He shook his head hesitantly. "Mebbe not yet."

EARLY IN THE AFTERNOON they reached another cross trail. This one was wider than any of the others and showed distinct ruts from wheeled vehicles and the deep patterns of many horses. Jak squatted on his haunches and peered at them. "Not fresh. Not very. Days not hours."

J.B. leaned over the teenager's shoulders, nodding his agreement. "Yeah. Rain tells us that. But the track's heavy used. Look at the boot marks, as well."

"No gas buggies at all," Ryan offered. "Only flatbed carts. Iron-rimmed wheels. Some ponies unshod. Wonder if they could be the Apaches?"

"Possible." The Armorer looked around them, his head slightly on one side, as though he were listening for some divine message. "Might as well follow them."

"Why not?" Ryan straightened and eased the blaster in its holster. "Just so long as we don't run into the camp of these Children of the Rock."

"THINK SOMEONE'S COMING." Krysty had stopped at a point where the trail wound into a series of hogback ridges, with the trees pressing in thickly on both sides.

"Sure?" Ryan already had the SIG-Sauer drawn and cocked in his right hand.

She nodded, her sentient red hair bunched more tightly at her nape. "Sure, lover."

"Norms or muties?"

Krysty considered the question for a moment, her green eyes squeezed shut. "Norms."

"Many?"

A shake of the head. "Don't think so. Few. But you know that I can never be..."

"Sure," he said, finishing the sentence for her. "Yeah, I know."

Jak cleared his throat. "Can hear something."

"What?"

Ryan knew the albino's hearing was sometimes uncannily acute.

"Bridle. Hooves."

"Right. J.B., you, Mildred, Dean and Doc cover that side of the path. We'll take this side. Keep under cover. Don't make a move unless I do. Best nobody knows we're in the area." As the others began to move, he called out in a penetrating whisper, "But if we need to stop them, then we do it with extreme prejudice." The old killing phrase from the long-gone, distant days before skydark came easily to him.

He crouched in the stygian blackness between two slender sycamores that had somehow seeded themselves among the ranging conifers, his blaster ready, his nerves strung taut.

From where he hid, Ryan could see some distance along the trail toward the north. The sound of a horse coming in his direction was louder, and he heard the soft snuffling of the animal's breath, the noise of the harness and tuneless singing.

It was an old song that Ryan recalled one of the navs on War Wag One used to sing, claiming it was an ancient folk ballad from a hundred years before skydark and that it had at least a hundred verses. And he'd known all of them.

The quavering voice, coming toward them along the trail, could be either an old man or an old woman.

It didn't sound like anything to fear.

Finally the singer appeared, sitting slumped on a sway-backed mule, barefoot, dressed in a collection of ill-fitting rags. It was an elderly man, with shoulder-length, greasy gray hair, tangled and knotted. He held the bridle loosely in his clawed right hand, seeming content to allow the animal to pick its own way at its own speed.

The current verse of the interminable song detailed a biologically impossible encounter between the heroine, Little Betty, and a well-endowed rattlesnake, in a cave filled with long-lost Spanish conquistadores' gold.

Ryan eased his finger off the trigger of the SIG-Sauer. The old man was alone, apparently indifferent to the rest of the world, obviously unaware of any threat to his safety.

It might be worth stopping him and interrogating him about the local region, and particularly about the mysterious Children of the Rock.

Now the mule was almost level with where Ryan was hiding, and the rider still hadn't even looked up, still droning on in a quavering voice.

Ryan made the snap decision to allow him to pass by unchallenged.

When the song stopped, the old man tugged on the reins, bringing the animal to a four-square halt. His head turned slowly toward the fringe of trees, seeming to drill directly at where Ryan was standing stock-still, barely breathing.

He risked a glance around the flank of the tree, seeing to his amazement that the man was stone-blind, his staring eyes both veiled with milky white cataracts.

"Who's there?"

The voice was stronger, and Ryan noticed for the first time that the old man had a blaster tucked into a broad leather belt, a battered Ruger that looked like it had been used for everything from hammering fence posts to stirring mutton stew.

"I can hear you out yonder. If it be one of you brats, then I'll see skin tanned off your asses."

From the other side of the track, Ryan glimpsed J.B.'s face, framed in the low branches of a pine. The Armorer was holding his Uzi at the ready, eyes turned questioningly in Ryan's direction, as if he were waiting for a sign to open fire.

For a dozen slow beats of the heart, nothing happened.

The pale, blind eyes continued to stare toward where Ryan lurked between the pair of sycamores. The mule snickered and lowered its head to graze a clump of long, rank grasses.

"I can hear you. Smell you. By the living God that made me and plucked out my glims, I can *taste* you! If Brother Joshua hears of this…then on your own gob-smitten heads be it. Don't say you wasn't warned!"

There was a note of genuine rage in the trembling voice. Ryan realized that the blind man wouldn't be a person to cross.

"Well enough." His bare heels kicked into the hollow flanks of the patient mule. "Walk on, you spawn of Shaitan. Miles to go before we sleep."

The animal began to amble down the trail, the venomous old man swaying from side to side on its back. Just before they vanished from Ryan's sight, the song started up again, this time with the verse about Little Betty and her meeting with the over-endowed band of traveling monks.

Ryan watched until the voice had faded away in the distance before stepping out from cover.

"Old man was riding the mule stone-blind," Krysty said wonderingly.

"Mean-looking bastard." Jak spit in the dirt and made the finger gesture to fend off evil.

"I wouldn't want him mad at me," Dean added.

Ryan holstered the SIG-Sauer. "Seems to me that there could be a ville close by. Mebbe the Children of the Rock. We'll keep moving, on condition orange. Eyes and ears open. Let's go."

Chapter Twelve

After a half hour, Ryan relaxed the conditions. Blasters were holstered, and everyone walked with a lighter step. Krysty had closed her eyes and concentrated her seeing powers, reporting that she couldn't feel anyone nearby.

"Think we should have stopped the old man on the mule and asked him about the Children of the Rock?" J.B. called from the rear of their rough skirmish line.

Ryan answered him over his shoulder. "Guess not. Could have set him off making a noise. No idea if there was anyone near. And he didn't look the kind of person who'd take to answering questions." He paused, thinking about it for a few more strides. "And there was something triple creepy about him."

Doc nodded his agreement. "I would second that thought, my dear Ryan. I have seldom encountered a less savory individual in all of Deathlands."

Jak laughed. "Love way put things, Doc. Got way with words, ain't you?"

The old man grinned, showing his strong, perfect teeth. "Praise from you, my winged Mercury, is praise indeed. Thought, word and deed. Yes, indeed. Valiant deeds. Prince valiant deeds. Do-dah deeds!"

Mildred tapped him on the arm, making him jump. "Snap out of it, Doc," she said curtly. "You got your mind to wandering off again."

"Ten thousand apologies, my dear sable madam. If only I had my trusty headgear I could remove it to you in token of my deep regrets. But I don't, so I won't."

Ryan slapped his right hand against his thigh. "Enough, people, enough. Let's keep concentrating on where we are and where we're going."

"We going to get something to eat, lover?" Krysty looked down at the muddied state of her chisel-toed boots. "Gaia, but this rain's played havoc with these. Look at them."

Doc had a sudden coughing fit, doubling over, hawking to try to clear his throat and spitting out a chunk of thick green phlegm. "I'm so sorry," he spluttered. "I fear that this damp has gotten onto my chest."

"Could do with somewhere warm for the night," Ryan said. "Place like this should have some old shelters or huts or something like that."

"Most national parks did," the Armorer stated. "Visitor centers and motels and chalets. All kinds of accommodation. Just keep going along this trail here and we're bound to come across something."

THE SIGN WAS crudely painted, white lettering daubed with scant respect for spelling, across a broken hunk of dark blue plastic, about four feet square: Mom's Fyness Jerkiee. Best In Weste. Just The Myle A Long This Trayle.

"'Mom's finest jerky,'" Jak read slowly. "That what says?"

Ryan nodded. "Close enough. A mile along the trail. Hope the cooking's better than the writing."

"We going to risk it?" J.B. pushed back his hat, glancing up at the lowering sky. "Got to be getting closer to the HQ of these mysterious Children of the Rock."

Ryan sniffed. "Step careful. Recce on the way in. We should have enough firepower to take on most hostiles."

"A mile on." Mildred looked over at Doc, who was blowing his nose vigorously into his blue swallow's-eye kerchief. "You all right?"

He turned bleary eyes toward her. "I would be the first to admit that my health has deteriorated a little within the last few minutes, Dr. Wyeth. A closeness of the chest and tightness in the throat." He coughed again. "And a pernicious trembling in the joints."

"You well enough to carry on a ways, Doc?" Ryan asked. "To this Mom's place?"

"I believe so. Let us put the issue to the testing place, shall we?"

Ryan grinned. As long as the old man could still talk like that, then he couldn't be feeling too bad. "Fine. Let's move onto extended skirmish line, friends. Condition red."

A CLOUD OF DRIZZLE swept through the dripping pines, as cold as charity.

Ryan, leading the way, almost missed the second

notice, tipped on one side like a drunkard's dream, half-hidden among some long-thorned brambles: Mom Jerkee. Ahed On Ryte. Soon.

The rain had stopped almost as quickly as it had started, leaving the trail dotted with silvery puddles among the wag-rutted mud.

The sky was like unpolished pewter, dismal and oppressive, casting deep shadows beneath the trees that pressed up against the edges of the track.

The movement caught Ryan's eye.

His hand dropped in a conditioned combat reflex onto the chill butt of the SIG-Sauer as he half turned, crouching slightly, perfectly balanced.

Behind him, everyone reacted fast—everyone except Doc, who was busily involved in blowing his nose again. Blasters were drawn, and everyone stopped, looking around them.

In among the blackness, Ryan caught another flicker of deeper darkness, the glint of golden eyes.

Now his blaster was drawn and cocked.

Doc muffled a liquid cough, fumbling the massive Le Mat from its deep-cut holster.

"What is it, dear boy?" he whispered.

Ryan gestured for silence, concentrating on whatever it was that had snatched his attention. The creature was larger than a beaver and smaller than a hunting dog, short legged with a long scaly tail glistening wetly behind it. It moved slowly, parallel to the blacktop.

His very first thought had been a cougar, but it didn't seem to be making any attempt to conceal itself from him. There was something in the way it moved that put him in mind of a rat, but he'd never seen a rat that size, not even in the mutie rad-cancered hot spots in the bleakest wilderness of Deathlands.

"Other side," J.B. whispered, pointing with the stubby muzzle of the Uzi.

Whatever the creature was, there were two more of them on the left side of the trail.

Ryan stood still and waited.

"By the..." Doc's voice faded into silence, the words vanishing.

Ryan felt his finger tighten on the trigger of the blaster, the barrel of the SIG-Sauer swinging to cover the nearest of the creatures as it came lumbering out from the dark fringe of the forest.

It was a rat.

At least, before the rad sickness burned its way into the genetic codes of its ancestors, it had to once have been an ordinary domestic rat, the sort of rodent that would have skulked in barns and outbuildings and moist cellars.

But several generations over the long winters and the subsequent century had changed it into the monstrous apparition that fumbled its way onto the blacktop, less than thirty yards from Ryan.

It moved slowly, its overgrown claws ticking on the gravel. Its pelt was a bizarre cross between scales and fur, oddly charred. The tail was covered in leprous patches of flaking, infected skin. Its head turned slowly from side to side, trembling with some kind of frightful ague.

The skull was blackened and elongated, earless,

ending in a running sore where the nose would have been on a normal animal. The hooded eyes were pale yellow, crusted with a hard white froth. The lower jaw was underslung, gaping open with a triple row of stained, serrated teeth showing between the swollen, obscenely delicate pink lips.

Ryan guessed that its body was around four feet in length, with an extra five or six feet of twitching tail.

"Look left," J.B. breathed, his voice suddenly hoarse and high.

There were two more of the monstrous rodents, creeping slowly out from the undergrowth to join the other mutie, where all three stood together, their weeping eyes locked to the seven invaders into their territory.

Ryan looked cautiously around, checking that there didn't seem to be any more of the giant rats, trying to decide whether it was best to let them go unharmed, or to wipe the face of the earth a little cleaner by chilling them.

There was always the risk of gunshots attracting the wrong kind of interest.

The mutie rats didn't seem able to decide what to do. Threaten or retreat?

"Let's terminate them," Mildred whispered, a few paces behind Ryan.

"They're monsters, Dad!" exclaimed Dean, unleathering his blaster.

The rats were so disgusting that Ryan felt his instincts taking over from common sense.

The SIG-Sauer had a built-in baffle silencer that

he'd replaced some months earlier. It wasn't as efficient as it had once been, but it was still better than nothing.

"I'll take them," he said. "Mildred, stand ready to pick up anything I miss. Once I start shooting, then there's no turning back."

The three creatures were still huddled together, eyes staring incuriously toward them. The golden eyes were oddly dead, showing no emotion, like a great white shark's. The long, crusted tails were whipping from side to side, as though they were considering making a charge.

"Fireblast!" Ryan said quietly. He leveled the pistol, steadying his right wrist with his left hand, standing in the middle of the blacktop, legs slightly apart, in the classic shootist's crouch.

The first of the powerful 9 mm rounds hit the leading rat through the side of the head, just below the dripping orifice where its left ear would have been. The jolt of the explosion ran clear to Ryan's shoulder, but the noise of the shot was satisfyingly muffled.

The mutie squealed, like a buzz saw slicing through a sheet of plate glass. It rolled on its side, legs kicking up a spray of slurried mud, blood jetting from its shattered skull, shards of bone dappling the ground.

Ryan didn't wait to see how successful his shot had been. He knew that it was a terminal hit.

Shifting his aim a little to the left, he centered the foresight on the throat of the second of the monster rodents, squeezing, steadying the blaster and firing a third round. The full-metal-jacketed bullet hit the last of the vile trio in the chest as it began to turn toward him.

In less than five seconds, all three of the mutie rats were down and done for. One choked on its own sluggish blood, as it scrabbled to try to get back on its paws, but all the lines were permanently down.

The second had simply slumped down, chest and belly in the dirt, dimming eyes staring vacantly ahead into the walls of the dark forest.

The last of them made a halfhearted effort to pull itself deeper into cover, but thick blood pumped from the gaping exit wound. The bullet had splintered the spine, paralyzing the stumpy rear legs. It was making a feeble, mewing sound, like a drowning kitten, its tail lashing from side to side, banging against the fungus-covered stump of a diseased sycamore. Chunks of flesh fell from it, ripped off, scaled and revolting, sending a spray of dull crimson across the trail.

"Pretty shooting, lover," Krysty commented, relaxing her breath in a loud sigh.

Ryan nodded slowly, holstering the warm blaster. "Sound of the shots shouldn't travel too far through thick trees. Not with the silencer."

Doc sneezed, doubled over and sneezed again, groaning as he put away the big Le Mat and reached for his kerchief.

And a fourth rat came rushing out of the shadows of the forest, a little behind the group of friends, heading straight toward Ryan.

The mutie resembled a scuttling, burned log, clawed feet kicking up the slimy mud. Its razored teeth were bared, saliva drooling over the matted hair of its muscular chest.

Mildred was quickest to react. She hadn't holstered her target revolver, but was still holding it by the checked grips, the barrel pointing down at her side.

"Mine!" she yelled, dodging to the right to avoid shooting Doc, bringing the blaster up to the aim. But she hadn't taken into account the treacherousness of the earth under her combat boots, and she slipped over to her left, momentarily off balance. Triggering off a .38 at the charging mutie rat. The bullet gouged up a chunk of dirt six or seven inches from the questing muzzle, making it jink sideways and hesitate for a moment.

Ryan was reaching for his own blaster as he saw his death closing in on him, crazed yellow eyes fixed to his face, greasy fur glistening with damp.

The moment's hesitation gave Mildred the fraction of a second that she needed.

Still unsteady, she snapped off a second round at the giant rat, the bullet narrowly missing the base of the skull, where she'd aimed. But it still hit home in the left shoulder, knocking the creature over, rolling and squealing in the trampled dirt.

It was less than six feet from Ryan, and it was simple for him to aim at the writhing creature and put a big 9 mm round through its spine, halfway along its body, paralyzing it.

"Any more?" he asked, surprised at how calm his voice seemed to sound.

Jak and Dean answered simultaneously. "No."

The last of the vermin was struggling to turn its head to snap at Ryan, and he reached for the big panga on his hip. Shaking his head at the thought of the clean steel being contaminated by the blood and sinew of the vile mutie rodent, he fired another round into the angular skull, chilling it instantly, whistling softly between his teeth as he replaced the SIG-Sauer in its holster.

"Good shooting, Mildred. Thanks."

She nodded and grinned, shaking her head in wonderment at the size of the quartet of massive rats. "Welcome."

"Big fuckers," Jak stated, looking down at the four corpses. "Biggest ever saw."

"Same here." Ryan stood still and quiet, listening for any sound of activity from anywhere around them. But the noise of the shooting and the dying animals' cries had driven the wildlife into silence.

Doc sneezed, blinking as he did so. "Bless me, father, for I have sinned."

"Don't start again, Doc," Mildred warned. "Just seal it in a can, will you?"

"Apologies, my dear Doctor."

"Now what, lover?"

"Head on for Mom's place and try her advertised jerky?" Ryan replied.

Krysty smiled, her teeth dazzling in the gloom of the limitless forest. "Yeah."

THE ARMORER STOPPED, head to one side, taking in several deep breaths. "Now, that smells real good," he said. "Sets the old taste buds tingling."

"Mom's jerky?" Mildred said.

"Gotta be."

Dean grinned. "With baked potatoes or creamed rice or a mess of whipped potatoes or refried beans or—"

Ryan lifted a warning hand. "That's enough, son. But it sure does smell fine."

The taste of cooking meat was drifting through the pines from almost directly ahead of them. There was a faint haze of whitish smoke, hanging at the level of the drooping lower branches. As they stood there, grouped close together, they all heard a sudden burst of loud, raucous laughter, sounding about fifty yards away, along the blacktop.

Ryan looked around at the others. "Got to be Mom's Place. Let's go and see what it's like." He paused a moment. "And let's keep alert out there."

Chapter Thirteen

It was a squat log cabin. The roof looked like it had collapsed several times and on each occasion had been rebuilt with a little less care and attention. Moss grew thick between the heavy timbers, and all kinds of fungus sprouted down along the broken guttering.

There was a hitching rail just outside the lopsided front porch, with three spavined mares and a crookback mule tethered there.

A hand-painted sign nailed to the wall, by the single cobwebbed window, proclaimed the single word Mom. It seemed to have been there for a number of years, cracked and heavily weather stained.

The door was ajar, and they heard another roar of laughter from inside.

Lively conversation stopped the moment Ryan, leading the others, pushed his way inside the small restaurant.

It took a few moments to acclimate his vision to the darkness. There were about six tables, each one with a smoking oil lamp at its center. Half of them were occupied.

At first glance it didn't look like there was a woman in the place.

Two men sat at the table nearest the door, middle-aged, wearing a ragged assortment of furs. The next table had a single man, much older, white bearded, dressed in sober black. The last table had a trio of younger men, all of whom wore white cotton shirts and pants of light brushed denim. Ryan noticed that they each wore identical chisel-toed Western boots in polished black snakeskin.

From habit he also noticed what kind of weaponry was on display.

The pair of hunters had long-barreled Kentucky muskets leaning against the wall by their chairs. The older man didn't appear to be carrying any kind of blaster, but Ryan had a sneaking suspicion that he might be sporting a hideaway derringer, spring-loaded against his forearm. The trio at the last table didn't seem to be wearing any sort of blaster.

"Hi, strangers!" The voice was deep and hoarse, floating out from the darkness behind the bar that ran along the farther wall of the cabin, and carried the flavor of too many black cigars and too much bootleg liquor. It was impossible to tell whether the voice belonged to a man or a woman.

"Hi, there," Ryan replied casually, his hand resting informally on the butt of the SIG-Sauer. "This'd be Mom's Place, would it?"

A throaty laugh. "This downright would, mister, and what's more to the point, I would be Mom."

The figure moved sideways into the light of a gently swinging brass lamp. Mom was close to five feet ten inches tall and looked like she'd tip the scales somewhere around the 250 mark. Her grizzled hair was cropped shorter than of most men, and she wore a plaid shirt about three sizes too small, bursting open across the front. Ryan put her at about forty years of age, with the etched lines around her mouth and puffy, watery eyes that bespoke a heavy drinker.

"Seen enough, mister?" An acerbic note of hostility crept into the voice.

"Didn't mean to stare, lady. Just that you're about the first human we've seen for quite a few days. You serve food here? Jerky?"

"Seen the 'tising signs, have you? Well, I like to say this is the best jerky east of the Cific Ocean. Right here on God's little acre."

"Sounds good. What's it come with?"

"What would you like it to come with?"

Jak answered, from just behind Ryan. "Beans and heap whipped potatoes."

"Christ on a mule, child!" she exclaimed, catching sight of the albino teenager, the fading sunlight spearing through a window into the mane of snowy hair. "When the Lord Jesus made you, he must've been having a kind of an off day."

"Amen to that," added one of the young men, his words echoed by his two companions. All three of them crossed themselves, eyes never leaving the companions.

The pair of trappers both laughed loudly, the same noise that Ryan had heard from outside the isolated eatery. He also noticed that each of them had shifted a little in their chairs, to be that much closer to their flintlock muskets.

"Don't think funny," Jak said, thin lipped. His

hand was a long way off from the butt of the Colt Python. But, Ryan knew, it was near enough to the taped hilt of one of his concealed throwing knives.

"Take it easy, Jak," he said quietly. "No point in forcing blood."

The woman had sensed the sudden tension and moved a couple of steps to her right, hands disappearing behind the bar. Ryan would have staked a fistful of jack that she had a sawed-down scattergun there.

"Everything cool, strangers?"

Ryan nodded to her. "Everything's fine. Dry handed. All right if we set down?"

"Sure. Make yourself at home. Jerky and beans and creamed potatoes all around?"

Ryan glanced at the others, getting nods from everyone. "Sounds fine."

"You come far, mister?" the old man asked as they arranged themselves at two of the remaining tables.

"Enough. We're traders. Travel in clothes of all sorts. Had us some bad luck. Lost our rig into a swollen river about three days back. South of here."

Mom had been on her way through a pair of dirty bat-wing doors toward the kitchen out back. Now she halted. "That mean you're out of jack?"

"No."

"Sure?"

Ryan nodded. "Sure I'm sure."

"We had us some trouble with outlanders. Ate their fill and then sat there calm as sunshine on a cloudy day and told me they can't pay."

"What happened to them?" J.B. asked, assiduously polishing his glasses on a corner of the check tablecloth.

"They paid."

The taller of the trappers finished the dregs of a mug in front of him. "Everyone gets to pay at Mom's Place. One fuckin' way or another."

He laughed, joined by his companion. Ryan observed that none of the three younger men at the table together had shown a flicker of expression since they came in.

"You boys done?" the woman asked. "Want it added on your slate?"

Chairs scraped back, and the muskets were picked up. "Yeah, Mom. Be good. We'll be back in ten days."

"Unless the Apaches get you first," the old man said quietly.

"You got Indian trouble around here?" Krysty asked, absently wiping a fork on the cloth.

The woman sniffed. "Some. Say, that's some right pretty hair you got there, missy. Closest thing I ever saw to a tumble of living fire."

"The heathen are losing their race against the forces of righteousness," one of the young men said.

"Amen," the other two chorused, crossing themselves.

"You fellows anything to do with the Children of the Rock?" Ryan asked.

There was a sudden stillness in the eatery that you could have carved wafer thin.

The hunters stopped, right by the door, faces turned from Ryan to Mom to the trio of men. The old-timer was frozen in the act of sipping at a chipped cup of coffee sub.

"You mean us, outlander?" asked the skinny one of the three. "Us?"

"If the cap fits."

"Meaning…?"

Ryan sniffed. "Meaning that we've been seeing all sorts of signs on walls for the Children of the Rock. Looked like it was some kind of religious ville. You three keep praying and crossing yourselves. So, it seemed more than possible that you might all have something to do with the Children of the Rock." He paused. "Whoever they are."

The woman behind the counter gave a gap-toothed smile. "Good guess, outlander. These young—"

"The prattle of an empty-minded woman is like the shaking of a hollow gourd," said the lean man, who seemed to be leader of the three seated men.

"I was only—"

"'Only' is the first step on the trail to the bottomless swamps of heathen eternity, Mrs. Fairchild. Best you say no more. Go cook the jerky for these folks."

Mom shrugged, halfheartedly wiping at the bar top. A gust of cold air swept into the room as the front door opened and closed behind the two trappers. The old man dabbed at his mouth with a linen kerchief and also made his way out. He hesitated as though he was going to say something, then changed his mind and walked out in silence, leaving behind a handful of small jack on his table.

Mom turned and went out into the kitchen.

Ryan stared at the three men. "Guess my hearing's getting poor," he said. "Didn't catch the answer to my question about the Children of the Rock."

One of them, with a straggly mustache, laughed, but it got nowhere near his pale blue eyes. "You know that the cat found itself burning on the barbecue from asking too many questions, stranger."

"What are you frightened of?" Krysty asked, leaning back in the bentwood chair.

"Frightened? What in the name of the Almighty makes you think that?"

"I can see it in your faces. Sense it in the way you're sitting. Your whole body language speaks to me of a very deep unease."

"No, lady. I'll tell you about the Children of the Rock. Yeah, we're all proud to be members of the flock. We aren't a ville. Not like most in Deathlands. Just some right-thinking folks collected together under the strong arm of the Blessed Jesus Christ and his angelic host."

"Fundamentalists?" Mildred asked quietly.

Again it was the main spokesman who answered her. "A well-honed sword will smite the ungodly better than a whole library of good thoughts."

"None of you carry swords," J.B. commented. "No blasters, neither."

"Not here. We are close enough to our heartland to be safe from the threat of the Apaches."

"Paramilitary survivalists." Mildred's voice was trembling with barely suppressed anger. "You were around in my days. Folks like you. Most of you then were just stinking, redneck racists. All you lack are hoods, sheets and blazing crosses! If you're white, it's all right. If you're black, get back. Hiding hatred behind a blurred version of the gospels. That what the Children of the Rock are up to?"

The three men seemed taken aback at the surge of rage from the black woman. Their leader stammered, face pale, spots of hectic colour dappling his hollow cheeks. "Why, no... That is... Our leader is Brother Joshua Wolfe and he doesn't turn anybody away on account of color. We preach tolerance for those that walk the true path."

The one with the mustache spoke up. "I reckon that before you attack us, you should come see us. See our camp. Meet Brother Joshua."

The third man, who'd been silent, nodded. "The shroud of ignorance is a darkening thing to bear. Come and let us rip it aside. Then you can walk in the bright light of love."

Krysty half smiled. "Sure. Been trying to do that for too many years."

"We are members of the Children of the Rock. Outlanders who are pure in heart are always welcome. Providing, of course, that they prove themselves acceptable. We are going there shortly. Why not walk with us?"

Ryan shook his head at the invitation. "Not right now, thanks. Need a meal and then a bed for the night. This place provide overnights?"

"It does." Mom's voice floated in from the kitchen, showing that she had preternaturally sharp hearing. "Fix a price for y'all, depending on how many rooms you want. Food won't be too long a-coming."

The three men stood with a strange synchronicity, tucking their chairs neatly in place. The skinniest of them smiled at Ryan and the others. "Brother Joshua Wolfe will welcome you, perhaps after the dawning?"

"Perhaps. It's near?"

"Oh, yes. It's only a few minutes walk farther along the winding old blacktop. You can't possibly miss—" His next words were drowned out by a ferocious outburst of coughing and sneezing from Doc.

"My sincere apologies," the old man spluttered. "It's not the cough that carries you off. It is the coffin that they carry you off in."

"Didn't catch the last thing you said." Ryan waited.

"There will be sentries on watch on the road. There always are. The Children of the Rock have many good, good friends and a scattering of hostile enemies."

"Like the Apaches?"

"Yes, brother. Like the spawn of Shaitan. Farewell, then. Until tomorrow."

All three of the young men paused by the door and made a strange circular motion with thumb and forefinger of the right hand. "Be seeing you."

Then they were gone.

The scent of food was growing ever stronger, making Ryan lick his lips.

"Seem friendly," Doc said, wiping away beads of sweat from his forehead. "Very amicable fellows."

Mildred sniffed dismissively. "Yeah, about as friendly as sunwarmed rattlers."

Ryan poured himself a tumbler of water. "Can't say I took to them, myself. But I reckon it could be interesting to go take a look at their ville tomorrow."

"You all right, Doc?" J.B. asked, sitting next to the old man.

"I confess to feeling a little below par, dear friend. A touch of influenza would be my self-diagnosis. But I shall doubtless be myself on the morrow."

Jak ran his long fingers through his matted mane of white hair. "Could do with bath."

"Reckon that could be arranged," Ryan said. "Let's get the meal done with first."

At that moment the bat-wing doors clattered open, and Mom, red faced and perspiring, pushed her way through carrying a big tray loaded with plates of food.

Chapter Fourteen

"That was so good."

Krysty leaned back in her chair and barely stifled a belch, wiping at her chin with a stained linen napkin. She looked at her empty plate, then at the large array of serving bowls that stood in the middle of the table.

One held a few wisps of creamed potatoes, dried and crusted at the edges. Another had a handful of slender green beans, sodden with salted butter. A large gravy boat had the skinned remnants of a delicious creamy sauce. A quarter of a loaf rested on a wooden platter. Its four predecessors had left only a scattering of crumbs.

A flat dish of flower-patterned china had once held a mountain of Mom Fairchild's famous jerky. Now there was only a smear of dark grease against the emptiness.

"Anyone fancy some puddings?" Mom called from behind the bar.

"What you got?" Ryan replied.

"Pecan pie. Pecan pie with cream. Pecan pie and lime jelly. Hot pecan pie."

J.B. gave a thin smile, whispering under his breath. "Pecan pie well-done. Pecan pie medium rare. Pecan pie and grits. Oh, and we got some pecan pie.''

Mom hadn't finished. ''And there's some peach-and-cherry cobbler, hot or cold, with or without.''

Ryan blew out his cheeks. ''Spirit's willing, Mom, but I'm not sure the body can take another mouthful.''

''Try pecan pie, peach-cherry cobbler with cream and lime jelly,'' Jak called.

''Me, too,'' Dean added.

Krysty laughed, shaking her head in disbelief. ''You two are living proof that you *can* get a quart into a pint pot. I seriously don't know how come you don't burst. You must've had at least three helpings of the jerky.''

''Four,'' they replied in unison.

''Anyone else for dessert?''

''I'll have a sliver of the pie with cream,'' Ryan said. ''How about you, lover?''

''No, thanks. I know when I've had enough. And right now I've had enough.''

''Just a glass of water for me, if you please,'' Doc said. ''And maybe some coffee sub.''

''Sure thing.'' Mrs. Fairchild stood in the doorway, sleeves wound up almost to the shoulder, revealing her muscular arms. ''Anyone else? No?'' She turned on her heel and disappeared once more into the steamy kitchen.

''That was the finest damned jerky I ever tasted,'' said the Armorer, leaning back in the seat and easing the buckle on his belt by a notch.

The restaurant was empty, several of the lamps

guttering. Nobody else had come by Mom's Place since Ryan and company arrived.

Ryan felt comfortably relaxed and full. His right hand brushed against the butt of the SIG-Sauer; the Steyr SSG-70 hunting rifle stood upright against his chair.

The great dishes of sun-dried strips of meat, some of them honey roasted and some smoked, had been mouthwateringly good, tender and chewy, with an exquisite flavor that lingered long on the palate.

He'd asked Mrs. Fairchild what kind of meat she used for the jerky.

"Varies. Sometimes I use some prime beef. Hard to get hold of up here in the hills. Goat's real good. Old guy lives down the trail a piece has some he feeds on milk. Tender as hand-reared veal but with a mite more flavor. Then there's often some tasty pork in there."

"Lamb or mutton?" Mildred asked. "Some of it had a real unique texture."

"Not often. Could be venison jerky that you had. Those hunters bring me some now and then. Even tried beaver, but it was kind of tough. Back flavor of fish to it. I often just mix it up and serve it in any order. Kind of potluck, as it comes."

Ryan had tried to pump the woman about the Children of the Rock, but she clammed up and changed the subject, claiming she could smell something burning back in the kitchen and disappearing from the questions.

A little later, when she was actually serving out the meals, she was just a tad more forthcoming.

"Children of the Rock been around here for almost as long as I can recall. Started real small. Brother Joshua Wolfe came with a couple of shootists. Half a dozen women. Some hunting hounds. Now there must be close on a hundred of them. But that's only a guess. I haven't been there myself. Not for years. Fortified ville. Big buildings. They say they got electrics there. Power mill and shock fencing."

She elaborated a little, saying there was a reasonable mix, with a few more men than women, but hardly any children. There were plenty of weapons and they were always on the lookout for recruits. They were at war with the local ranging band of Apaches, and they were seriously religious.

"They leave me alone and I leave them alone. I just take care not to—" She stopped abruptly, as if she'd gone a few paces farther along the line than she'd intended. "Take care not to upset any of them who pass by."

Now the meal was nearly done.

In the end they all joined Doc in steaming mugs of coffee subs, served with plenty of cream and a large bowl of unrefined sugar.

"Guess I'll be closing up soon," the woman said, leaning on the bar counter. "Light's most gone. Won't be any travelers passing through now."

"You get troubled by mutie rats?" Ryan asked.

She whistled between her gapped teeth. "Do I, outlander! I surely do. Biggest sons of bitches I ever saw. They reckon that it's one of the results of the old rad hot spots nearby, among the big trees."

Ryan and J.B. both glanced automatically at the small lapel rad counters they wore, noticing that both were showing somewhere between the orange and yellow. They were some little distance away from the safety of green, but an equal distance from the imminent danger of red.

Mrs. Fairchild carried on, seeming oblivious to their rad counters. "They come for miles after the offcuts from the butchering we do here."

"Can't you poison them? Or just chill them with blasters?" the Armorer asked. "I never saw such mean, sickly bastards in all my life."

"Just keep coming. Think they got some kind of underground nest out in the forest. Wouldn't want to be the one that stumbled on a place like that." She shuddered theatrically at the thought. "Anyway, you folk like some more coffee sub?"

Doc, Dean and Jak both raised a hand at the invitation. The others refused the offer.

"You three goin' to share a room together, tonight?" the woman asked as she poured out the hot, black, bitter liquid from a blue enameled pot.

Dean and Jak nodded. Doc smiled up at the woman. Ryan watched and realized that the old man was entertaining lecherous thoughts. Mrs. Fairchild looked like she could have eaten up Doc for supper and spit out the bones. But there was no accounting for taste.

"I've put you three into the end cabin. Kind of a few steps away from the main building, toward the stream. But there's plenty of bedding. You'll be snug as bugs in rugs. Now drink up, there's good boys.''

Doc sneezed and coughed at the same time, spluttering coffee onto the table. "I am so sorry, my dear Madam Fairchild," he said, wheezing.

"Think nothing of it. Listen up, strangers. Make sure you keep the doors bolted tonight. Windows got armored shutters and locks. Keep them secure. This is a dangerous part of the country, what with the Apaches and all. Also been some trouble with stickies, within the last six months. Plucked folks out of their sleeping beds with their evil suckered fingers and slobbery mouths. Never a trace of them seen again.''

"We've gotten used to looking after ourselves." Ryan stood and stretched. "But we surely thank you for the warning. Old friend of mine used to say that an ounce of warning was worth a ton of regret.''

"Ready for bed," Doc said, wiping his nose with the blue kerchief.

"Take one of the lamps from the table there. You'll find candles set ready by the beds. Plenty of blankets. Extra ones in the closet. Got your own john and washing facilities just off the bedroom. Won't be too much hot water. Plenty of cold. Comes straight from the stream out back.''

"I'd be interested to see the place you store your jerky," Mildred said.

"Why?" The word was snapped like a steel bear trap.

The woman looked up at Mrs. Fairchild, surprised at the vehemence of the reply. "No reason. It was so damned good I just would have liked to have seen the carcasses and the way you dried it. To keep the flavor.''

''Secret.''

Mildred shrugged, palms out. ''That's fine. Didn't want to cause any trouble.''

''Sure, sure.'' A doubtful smile tugged at the corners of her mouth. ''Sorry I snapped. Just that there's always folks sneaking around, trying to find out my secret recipe for the jerky. Get tired of it.''

''I understand.''

''Good, real good. Just so long as you... That's fine, lady. Fine.''

A small part of Ryan's mind was puzzled by the woman's strange reaction to what had seemed an innocuous question. But his stomach was well filled with the fine food, and he was warm and dry, with the prospect of a decent bed for the night to come. Life was rich and interesting, and he set the minor doubt away.

JAK LED Doc and Dean into the gloom, along the eastern flank of the main building, to where a narrow path wound out alongside the foaming stream, among the trees. He held one of the stained brass lamps above his head, the yellow flame turning his hair into a tumbled veil of gold.

Mrs. Fairchild indicated to Ryan and the others where they were to sleep, pointing to a white-painted door that opened into a narrow hallway. ''One room with a double bed on that side. Another one, mite bigger, on the other side. And remember what I said about bolts and locks.''

''Sure. Thanks. We'll take breakfast before we leave in the morning.''

She nodded. ''Sure, sure. Got plenty of eggs and sausages. Running a mite low on jerky. Though I feel sure there's some fresh supplies on the way.'' She paused, smiling to herself, by the heavy steel-lined door to the restaurant's kitchens. ''Y'all sleep well, now.''

RYAN AND KRYSTY TOOK the smaller room. The shutters were heavy, with iron bolts, and he shook them, making sure they were solidly locked.

''She kept on about the danger, didn't she?'' Krysty said doubtfully.

''Yeah. So?''

''Like…like she was almost preparing us for something dark happening.''

''You got a bad feeling about this, lover?'' He had sat on the bed, starting to unlace his combat boots, stopping as her doubts communicated themselves to him.

She stood by the door, reaching up to slide across the top bolt, looking back over her shoulder, her fiery red hair gleaming in the candle's glow.

''There's something that doesn't set right. The way she's out here on her own. With those mutie rats. And the Apaches in the neighborhood. I know she seems kind of tough, but…''

Ryan ran his index finger alongside his nose, easing it up under the patch over the puckered socket of the left eye and rubbing at it. "If she had something planned, then why make such a fuss about warning us?"

"True." She moved over to the other side of the bed, dusting her hand gently over the stained patchwork quilt. "Guess I'm getting paranoid."

Ryan sat, unmoving, thinking. "You got me thinking," he said quietly. "Still, we got our blasters, and the room seems double secure. I can't see where any serious danger's going to come from. Over, under, through or around, like Trader used to say. All seems safe."

She peeled off her white shirt, revealing her magnificent breasts. The nipples were erect, shadowed.

"Got the itch, lover?"

He nodded, grinning. "Seems like I do."

"Then let's get to scratching it."

Chapter Fifteen

The luminous numerals on Ryan's wrist chron showed it was seventeen minutes past one in the morning. Outside he could hear rain beating steadily on the roof of the bedroom.

Ryan stretched, wincing a little at the cool stickiness that he could still feel around his groin. At his side Krysty was sleeping on her back, mouth partly open, snoring slightly. He was aware of pressure on his bladder, and he considered paying a visit to the bathroom that he knew was just along the passage, past the door of the room where J.B. and Mildred would be sleeping.

Perhaps if he lay very still and closed his eye, the feeling would go away.

Ryan tried it for several minutes.

"Fireblast!"

It was no good. He was going to have to get up, unlock the door and walk along the passage to take a leak. It was cold and damp and the middle of the night.

"Fireblast!" he whispered again, swinging his legs from underneath the blankets. After they finished making love, he had gotten partly dressed. Now he had on his underclothes and the blue denim shirt, socks but no boots, and no weapons.

He thought about going just as he was. It would take him only a couple of minutes. Then again, there was Krysty's unease. If you traveled with someone who had a mutie skill at "seeing" and chose to ignore them, then the blood was likely to be in your own face. Trader used to say that a man who took any chances when he didn't have to was a likely candidate for a six-foot plot of good earth and no marker.

Slowly he pulled on the dark blue pants and laced up the steel-toed boots. He buckled on his belt and slid the SIG-Sauer from under the pillow into the holster, making sure that the eighteen-inch steel blade of the panga was secure in its sheath on the opposite hip.

"Time to get up, lover?"

The voice was heavy and muffled with sleep.

"No. Goin' for a piss."

"That's good. Is it raining?"

"Yeah. It is."

"Hear it on roof. Pittering and pattering and…" Krysty's voice faded into silence as she slithered back once more into a deep sleep.

Ryan eased back the bolt and cautiously peered out into the corridor, which was almost completely dark. A flash of bright pink chem lightning made him jump, the clap of thunder following hard on its heels.

It showed him the empty passage, making him blink at the transition from blackness to brightness to dark again. He could have turned and taken the oil lamp off the rickety table by the head of the bed, using one of the box of self-lights provided by Mrs. Fairchild. But he figured there was no need and stepped out of the bedroom into the stygian gloom.

The air was cool and moist. As he went past the door of the other bedroom, fingers brushing the wooden walls to keep himself orientated, Ryan heard the sound of someone coughing, deep enough to be J.B., he guessed.

It crossed his mind to wonder whether the cold that Doc was suffering from was going to turn out to be contagious. In Deathlands, if you were healthy then you were also lucky. Many illnesses could rage through a ville with virulent effect, ailments that he knew from reading about predark days hadn't used to be mass killers. Things like measles and mumps and pink pox.

The next door was the bathroom.

Ryan pushed it open, expecting to find it creaking, but to his surprise it gave with the stillness of recently oiled hinges. There was a narrow window of frosted glass. Another flash of lightning revealed a nest of thick metal bars across it.

"Go to a lot of trouble to keep out hostiles," he muttered to himself, preparing to piss. The thought crossed his mind that the bars might equally easily be designed to keep people in.

The storm was very close, the lightning coming every few seconds, the rolling thunder making the building quiver. After he'd finished, Ryan hauled himself effortlessly up onto the bars, peering out into the California night.

Rain was sheeting from left to right, driven on a

strong northerly wind. He could see that even some of the larger branches on the tall pines were moving violently in the storm. He winced at a great jagged fork of lightning that sliced to earth less than a quarter mile from where he watched. Static electricity made his curling hair stand on end, filling the air with the crackling stench of ozone.

"Fireblast!" It was a storm and a half.

Just as he began to lower himself back to the floor, Ryan's eye was caught by a dark blur of movement at the fringe of the trees, beyond a narrow path that ran along toward the cabin where Dean, Doc and Jak were sleeping. It was impossibly difficult to make out what it was.

Until the next flash of lightning from the chem storm threw the scene into brilliant, stark pink relief, halting the movement so that Ryan could make out what it was.

"Bastard rat!"

It was one of the massive mutie creatures, identical to the ones that they'd run into earlier in the previous day. If anything, it looked even bigger.

The body was bloated, the fur clinging, sodden, to the five-foot-long body. The leprous tail twitched uneasily behind the mutie creature, and the blank golden eyes turned slowly toward the watching man.

Common sense told Ryan that the rodent couldn't possibly see him at that distance in that light, but his grip relaxed and he dropped clumsily to the floor of the bathroom.

He waited, crouched, steadying his breathing, aware that his heart was beating faster than usual.

There was something hideously malevolent about the soaking predator, waiting out in the storm.

Where was it going?

On an impulse Ryan moved fast out of the bathroom, heading to the main entrance. He hesitated a moment, then retreated to their bedroom. He leaned over Krysty and shook her gently awake, his hand pressed over her mouth to stop her from crying out.

"Quiet," he whispered. "Just saw one of those mutie rats, heading toward where Dean, Doc and Jak are. I caught the bad feeling from you." He took his hand away.

"Storm," she said, starting to sit upright.

"Yeah. Bad one." Lightning cracked through a narrow gap at the top of the solid sec shutters, like the slash of a razor-edged knife. "Going outside to recce. Soon as I'm gone out the front, slide the bolts across again. Keep safe. Get dressed. Wait for me comin' back."

"How about the others?"

"Who?"

"J.B. and Mildred."

"Oh, sure. No point in waking them. No need. Just that feeling. Be back in five minutes or so."

"If you're still out there after ten minutes, I'll be waking them and coming out after you."

He nodded his agreement and bent down, kissing Krysty lightly on the cheek, feeling the cool softness of her skin against his lips. "Sure."

THE WIND nearly whipped the heavy door from his fingers, tugging wildly at it. Ryan held on tight, easing it shut behind him. He stood still and waited to try to accustom his eye to the darkness and the turbulent weather, blinking as yet another dazzling flash of purple-pink chem lightning crackled across the forest, followed by rippling thunder. The noise was so deep and so close that it felt like his spine was vibrating in time with it.

The mutie rat had vanished, which was both good news and bad news: good if he never saw it again, bad because he now had no idea where the creature might have gone.

Ryan drew the SIG-Sauer slowly from its holster, thumbing back on the hammer, holding it steady in his right hand, alongside his thigh. He started to move cautiously toward the cabin.

He kept in close to the protection of the main building of the eatery, past the kitchens, catching the lingering scent of the marvelous jerky.

He paused at the end of the block, gathering a breath as he readied himself for the dash into the open, checking once more that none of the mutie rats was anywhere around. But the rain-swept clearing was empty of life.

There was a great temptation to turn on his heel and go straight back to the warmth and comfort of the dry bed. It was almost certain that everything was fine. Dean, Doc and Jak were snug…snug as…

"Bugs in a rug," he said to himself.

Yeah, almost certain.

Almost.

He took a deep breath and moved into the torrential downpour, soaked through to the skin in moments. Ryan didn't make the mistake of trying to run, head down. That way you could easily bump into something profoundly unpleasant and not ever know what it was that had laid you out in the dirt, hot blood gushing from your severed arteries.

Also, the footing was desperately treacherous, with slimy streams of dark mud, mingling with the leaf mold at the edge of the trees.

Ryan brushed rain from his good eye, flicking back his wet hair, keeping a good watch all around as he closed in on the dark cabin.

The iron handle was cold to his fingers and re-sisted any movement. Ryan waited a moment, then tried again, using greater force.

But nothing happened; it was rock solid. He looked around as another great flash of sheet light-ning illuminated the rain-slick slope.

The thought of calling out crossed his mind, but he doubted that they'd hear him anyway. The storm's heart seemed locked in place, directly over that part of the Sierras.

Ryan looked around one more time, shaking his head to clear his vision. He wondered whether he'd actually just seen fresh movement, along a narrow path that he hadn't noticed before, which led past the cabin down toward the stream, flanking what had probably once been a car-parking area.

On an impulse he followed the movement.

The wind was deafening, combining with the con-stant rumbling of thunder to seal him off into a buf-feting world of noise. A gang of stickies could have come up behind him, letting off triple-power cherry bombs as they came, and Ryan wouldn't have heard a single sound.

Branches lashed out at him, making him duck and weave, fending them off with both hands while trying to maintain a tight grip on the blaster.

There it was again!

It was definitely one of the rats, scuttling along about thirty yards in front of him, belly down, scaled tail scooping through the mud. The compensation from the storm was that the gigantic rodent was way too busy to worry about whether it was being the hunter or the hunted.

The trail wound steeply downhill. Ryan could make out faint ruts, despite the streaming dirt, as though some sort of barrow or handcart had been frequently used on the path.

There had been no lightning for several long beats of the heart, and Ryan reluctantly stopped, waiting to gather his bearings again in the swooping blackness. If the rat had stopped, as well, there was the real menace of walking right into it. With predictably unpleasant consequences.

To his surprise the ragged veil of clouds was suddenly torn apart for a moment and watery moonlight broke through, showing that he was on the edge of a wide clearing.

Ryan's mind registered two separate and bizarre images, almost simultaneously.

One was the rat, silhouetted by the stark light, towering on its hind legs, clambering and gnawing away at a mound that stood up against a roof-high deadfall. The other, seen in that frozen fragment of time, like a fly trapped in amber, was what the rodent was eating.

There were bones, glistening, stripped of meat, with just a few shreds of gristle and sinew dangling from them. A small mountain of death was piled high, the smell penetrating to Ryan despite the wind and the rain.

That first hideous glance revealed the presence of dozens of flayed carcasses, all too obviously the source for Mrs. Fairchild's wonderful jerky.

It was the next flash of chem lightning, a triple heartbeat later, that showed Ryan precisely what kind of meat he and the others had devoured so enthusiastically.

There were femurs and clusters of carpal bones, entire rib cages and pelvises. But most of all there were dozens of grinning skulls.

Human skulls.

Chapter Sixteen

Aware of the watcher, the mutie rat turned from its feast and dropped to all four legs.

The few seconds of moonlight were over, the wind blowing the banks of cloud back, plunging the area into total darkness again, with only the scattered bolts of pinkish silver lightning to bring any illumination.

Ryan moved a few steps to his right, feeling with his hand to encounter the rough, streaming bark of the nearest of the immense pines. He sensed the importance of having some kind of solid cover to make a stand against the mutie rodent and pressed his back against the trunk, the SIG-Sauer probing at the blackness like an extension of his right arm.

Part of his fighting brain was locked into the problem of the rats, but another part was wrestling with concern over the grotesque hill of human corpses and what the implications were for himself and the six friends.

And another part of him desperately wanted to throw up and rid himself of the half-digested jerky that seemed to have swollen to near bursting.

It took an enormous effort of will for Ryan to shutter off the thought of what he'd eaten with such delight. It wasn't a good moment to give in to the nausea and double over, vomiting. Not with the rat on the move.

Lightning flashed, a massive display, longer and brighter than any that had gone before, thunder making the centuries-old conifer at his back tremble to its ringed core.

The mutie rat was coming slowly toward him, head moving from side to side, the silver light reflected from the cold gold eyes. Its mouth was half-open, drooling a thick yellowish grue. Ryan noticed that the thing still held a severed limb in its strong jaws, a fleshless arm, bony fingers clacking as the head moved. And it was making an obscene high-pitched squealing sound as it advanced on the man.

Ryan steadied his right wrist with his left hand, aiming the blaster at where he thought the rodent was.

There was a strong wish to cut and run, to get away from the horror that he knew was creeping stealthily toward him.

It would be a doubly bad move to expose his vulnerable back to the monster and risk running pell-mell into some of its brothers or sisters.

He stood his ground, ignoring the clubbing wind and the driving rain, ignoring his own utter discomfort and the worries about his friends.

A staccato burst of short, stabbing lightning strikes burst over the clearing, accompanied by deafening thunder.

The light showed the rat was in midcharge, its movements twitching in the strobing flashes barely a dozen paces from him.

The blaster coughed three times, the explosions muffled by the baffle silencer, the glow of the triple discharges barely visible. Ryan felt the kick of the pistol run up his arm, clear to the shoulder, and saw the bullets strike home, blood flaring black in the lightning.

The first one ripped into the side of the rat's questing muzzle, shredding wet fur and flesh, exiting immediately below the right eye, bursting it from its socket where it dangled in the dirt like a discarded ornament.

The second drilled into the throat as the rat lifted its head in agony from the impact of the first 9 mm round. The bullet dug deep, nicking the spinal column, before coming out at the base of the skull in a welter of blood and bone.

The third round was superfluous. The grossly mutated, rad-cancerous animal was already dying, its legs folding under it, the tail flailing like a demented buggy whip. It lurched as the final round hit it through the right shoulder, toppling it onto its side, dropping its interrupted meal. Sable blood oozed from the parted jaws, the scream of shock and agony muffled by its own arterial flow, which flooded its throat and lungs, choking it.

"Bastard," Ryan said quietly, looking around to see if there were any other giant rats anywhere close by. But the clearing was completely deserted—just the wind, the rain, the lightning and the mortally wounded creature, barely twitching.

Ryan closed his eye for a moment, pressing the blaster to his cold forehead, taking several slow, deep breaths to try to control the sickness that washed over him.

But he kept seeing a vision of the jerky, sitting there on the plate, nestled in its bed of potatoes and vegetables, soaked in that rich, luscious gravy, and Mom's smiling, sweating face, hovering over the plate.

The sickness was shockingly violent, bringing Ryan to his knees in the mud, a thread of bile hanging from his mouth, all the way into the sodden dirt. His stomach rebelled, bringing up every last, bitter morsel of the supper, the watery chunks frothing all around his combat boots.

"Oh, fireblast," he groaned. "Never ever eat at any place called Mom's again."

He remembered now that it had been a part of one of the Trader's sayings. "Never play cards with a man called Doc," was another part of it. And there had been a third part, but it had slipped from his memory.

He knew that—

"Doc," he said, suddenly remembering his original worry about the old man, his son and Jak. He spun on his heel, still holding the SIG-Sauer, and set off back toward their cabin.

IT SEEMED that the storm was beginning to move away, toward the Cific coast, across the next range of mountains. There was a noticeable gap between the flashes of chem lightning and the roiling sound of the thunder, and the rain was easing, as the cold blue norther veered easterly.

Everything was still quiet as Ryan reached the shelter of the overhanging cabin roof, pausing and sniffing, wishing he carried a kerchief. He reached out and checked the big sec lock on the door with his left hand, finding, to his relief, that it was still securely fastened.

If he couldn't get in, then Ryan was comforted by the thought that nobody else would. Even if they had a key, he could tell from the pressure that there were heavy bolts inside, at the top and the bottom of the door.

It had to be well past the ten minutes since he left the main building. By now Krysty would have roused J.B. and Mildred, and they would all be dressed and coming out to look for him.

Ryan started to turn away when there was a dazzling flash of lightning that brought the door and the area on both sides of it into stark relief.

He noticed something very peculiar. The one side was a narrow strip of timbering, the rough ends of the logs overlapping each other. On the other side the strip was wider, almost the width of the door. And the timbers ended in a straight, clean edge. If it hadn't been for the incredibly bright lightning, he would never have noticed it.

Ryan waited, totally still and silent, until the next jagged flash burst around him. He peered closely at the odd architectural feature in that moment and saw something else that he would never otherwise have noticed. The planking held the faint but unmistakable mark of a damp handprint, as though someone had recently pushed at the wood.

Ryan waited again for a few seconds, using the next chem lightning flash to place his own hand precisely in the center of the mark, seeing how much smaller it was than his own spread fingers, and pushing very gently.

It was a cunningly concealed door, matching up to the real, locked and bolted portal, and it swung inward as though greased and counterbalanced.

Ryan felt the short hairs prickling at his nape, thinking again about the excellent supper that he'd just puked up, and the tangle of raw heads and bloodied bones hidden out in the forest. His son and friends were in mortal peril.

Finger tight on the trigger, he stepped inside the cabin.

He had no chance, no warning. Mrs. Fairchild had been waiting in the blackness and she screamed out her hatred, jumping at him, swinging at the side of his skull with a heavy hatchet that glittered in the flare of the next lightning strike.

Chapter Seventeen

No chance, no warning, only razored combat reflexes that had kept Ryan Cawdor alive through long years of hardship and danger.

He was already deeply suspicious of the dark entrance to the log cabin. The open door and the rain-smeared handprint had warned him of imminent potential danger. So, when it came grinning and howling out of the blackness, Ryan was ready for it. As ready as anyone could be.

He lifted the powerful pistol and used it to parry the murderous attack with the ax, blocking the singing edge in a shower of sparks, feeling the lethal impact. The force knocked him three paces backward, staggering off balance.

"Shit-suckin' bastard…"

The voice was high and hoarse, sounding like it could slice through armored sec glass at fifty yards. The woman's breath, rancid in his face, was like the unwashed floor of a charnel house, and she wielded the whirling crescent of steel with a hideous skill, so fast and so furious that it gave Ryan no chance to do anything but defend, unable to bring the SIG-Sauer into use.

Mrs. Fairchild was in a state of murderous frenzy, forcing him back through the false doorway, off the porch, out into the easing rain, the water dancing off the blade of the hatchet, pattering into his face.

Ryan tried twice to close with her, to use his extra strength and height. But she was too fast, supernaturally swift.

He managed to snatch only one shot, taking advantage of a moment when Mom seemed to hesitate, pausing to draw a ragged breath. But his footing was unsure in the thick mud, and the bullet went inches wide.

If Ryan allowed the woman to dictate the course of the fight, then he was likely to go down. Mrs. Fairchild was showing no signs of tiring, and it was only a matter of time—a short time—before the hatchet would slip by his woefully inadequate guard and hack a chunk out of his flesh.

''Bitch fucker!''

He tried the risk of aggression, managing to press her back onto the streaming, shadowed porch. For the next fifteen or twenty seconds, it was like a Mexican standoff. The maniac vigor of the woman held Ryan off, wearing him down, but she was too aware of the threat of the big pistol to be able to step away for the deathblow.

He took a quick step to his left, hoping to snatch a nanosecond that would enable him to take another shot at Mom Fairchild. But some of the planks of the porch were rotten and cracked under his heel, sending him toppling away to his right. The woman whooped with obscene delight as she saw him suddenly vulnerable, and swung down with her ax, sending the SIG-Sauer spinning from his wet fingers, the blaster landing in a deep puddle a dozen feet away.

"Goodbye, you shit-for-brains dickhead!" she roared, the hatchet looping up behind her shoulder, ready for the final, lethal stroke.

Ryan lifted his right hand to try to parry the blow, realizing the futility of the gesture. His mind's eye projected forward, seeing the steel hack clean through his wrist, leaving a blood-jetting stump, when he saw an amazing sight.

Something like a long needle of steel, smeared with blood, glistening in the lightning's fierce dazzle, had emerged from the center of Mom's chest, below her pendulous breasts, tearing a small, neat hole in the check shirt she wore.

"Oh," she said in a little, gasping voice, taking a single, faltering step toward Ryan. Her fingers unclenched the murderous grip on the haft of the ax, allowing it to drop to the boards at her feet.

"Touché," Doc said, his voice overlaid with a note of quiet triumph.

Ryan watched, seeing the rapier's point withdrawn and then thrust in again, penetrating between the ribs, beneath the shoulder blade on the left side of the woman's corpulent body, slicing into lungs and heart.

He managed to free his trapped boot from the splintered wood and stepped neatly to one side, looking for the blaster, which was barely visible in the pitted pool of muddied water. He picked it up, his eye on Mrs. Fairchild.

Once more the heavy clouds had rolled away

from the sailing hunter's moon, flooding the wide clearing with a deliquescent, silvery radiance.

Mrs. Fairchild's little piggy eyes had opened unnaturally wide with the shock of the attack from behind her. Her arms dropped to her sides, and she swayed backward and forward for a dozen long seconds, like a stricken tree. Her mouth opened in a great wordless cry, then she dropped facedown into the liquid dirt, sending a wave of muddy water billowing across the open space in front of the cabin.

"Sic semper tyrannis," Doc said, stooping to wipe the blood-slick steel of his beloved Toledo rapier on the corpse's shirt. "'It was ever thus.' Cast your bread upon the waters and you see what you get?"

"Yeah. Soggy bread," Mildred said from behind Ryan, standing with J.B. and Krysty, all three with blasters drawn.

"All right, lover?"

"Yeah, Dad. Thought you were down and done for," Dean added.

Ryan examined the chipped and scarred metal of his SIG-Sauer. "Yeah, thanks. And a big thanks to you, Doc. I owe you one."

"And I owe you hundreds, my dear friend."

"Mind explaining just what's been going on here, bro?" J.B. asked.

Ryan stepped past Mrs. Fairchild's body and showed everyone the concealed doorway. By now Jak had appeared, shaking his head sleepily.

"Think bit drugged," he said.

Doc patted the teenager on the shoulder. "I

would not be a jot or tittle surprised, dear lad. I confess to feeling a little doped myself.'' He caught Mildred's glance. ''Perhaps I should say that I felt a little more doped than is my usual condition. All part of the murderous plan of that red-eyed trollop.'' He scratched his head and finally returned the slender, engraved steel blade to its ebony sheath. ''But I must admit to bewilderment at what lay behind this scheme. Ryan? What was the ultimate aim of this wicked, wicked woman?''

''You three would have simply disappeared. No way of knowing how or why. Could be she aimed to blame the mutie rats. I chilled another of them out yonder.''

Krysty shook her head. ''I'm puzzled as Doc, lover. What's the point of chilling Dean, Doc and Jak? Just what would she have gained by it?''

''Meat.''

''How's that?''

''Fresh meat.''

''What for?''

''For her famous jerky.''

The storm had moved right away, and the rain had stopped. The clearing was startlingly silent, the six companions staring at Ryan, understanding dawning slowly on each horrified face.

''I cannot…'' Doc began, stopping and swallowing hard. He turned away and leaned one hand on the rain-damp wall of the cabin. In the moonlight his normally ruddy cheeks had assumed the hue of old parchment.

"Dad! I...I..." Dean bent double and puked violently.

Jak said nothing, simply going back inside the dark cabin. A few moments later they could all hear the noise of his being very sick.

Mildred reached out and grabbed J.B. by the hand. "Sweet Christ on the Cross, John," she whispered. "How can anyone be so...so...wicked?"

The Armorer squeezed her fingers so hard his knuckles whitened, moving closer to hug her to him. Rain streaked his glasses, making it hard to see his eyes. "Least we leave things a bit cleaner," he said.

Krysty had also gone pale, her cheeks like ivory. "The jerky was... Oh, Gaia!"

Ryan told them in a few quiet words about the slaughter dump of corpses that he'd discovered along the rear trail.

"So, I guess we won't stay here too much longer. Woman might have friends. Someone supplied her with the...stuff for her jerky. Might even be a colleague of the Children of the Rock. Just don't know."

J.B. looked at him. "Still some time to first light. I reckon it might be a real good thing to go through the place. See if we can find any clean, uncontaminated food. Then, before we set out tomorrow, we drag that—" he pointed with the Uzi at the corpse of the woman "—drag her inside and torch the place. Cover our tracks. Fire purges."

THE SMELL OF KEROSENE lingered in the dawn air like iron on the tongue.

Through the open door of Mom's Place, Ryan could see the feet and ankles of the owner of the eatery, lying by the bar, where she'd been dumped.

Jak was holding a self-light, waiting for the word to set it off.

"Everyone clear and ready?" Ryan waited for the response from the others. They were all packed and eager to move away from the nightmare place.

The first bright light of morning was breaking away to the east, dappling the slopes of the Sierras with the pale golden sheen. Though none of them felt that hungry, Ryan had insisted that they should all try to force down a reasonable breakfast before hitting the road.

There'd been plenty of eggs in the kitchen of the restaurant, as well as a larder with shelves full of sausages and home-cured bacon.

None of them had opted for any of the meat products, limiting themselves to omelets and scrambled eggs. Krysty also whipped up a plateful of buttered biscuits that vanished quickly enough.

Ryan glanced around, taking a deep breath of the clean mountain air, trying to set aside the memory of what they'd all eaten the night before. "Right, Jak?"

"Sure."

"Set the fire."

The self-light spluttered, its flame tiny and feeble in the dawn sunlight. Jak cradled it in his hands against the fresh breeze, stooped just inside the door of the eatery and applied it to a mess of crumpled paper, which flared up, a cloud of dirty gray smoke curling out into the clearing. In moments the kerosene-soaked wood caught, and the smoke thickened and became black.

Jak backed off, dropping the self-light in the damp dirt by his feet, watching, fascinated, as the red-orange flames spread quickly up the rough timber walls, setting the stained plasterboard ceiling on fire.

"Cleansing," J.B. said, holding Mildred's hand. "Like I said."

RYAN PAUSED as they crossed a narrow ridge, looking back down the valley toward Mom's Place. He saw that the column of smoke, shredded by the northerly wind, was already growing thinner, the building beneath it almost totally consumed by the raging flames.

"Be finished in a few minutes," he said to Krysty, who was walking at his side.

"You think our story will prove adequate for the Children of the Rock?" Doc asked, the sentence interrupted by another coughing fit. The old man's cheeks were flushed, his blue eyes watering, his nose constantly running.

Ryan nodded, talking over his shoulder. "Sure. Best kind of lie is the simple one."

Doc smiled, showing his wonderful teeth. "Mom was having trouble with her stove and said it was overheating. But everything was fine when we left." He recited the words in a singsong voice.

"Way you said that reminds me of the way the guides talk who showed you around the old houses in Concord,'' Mildred said, grinning broadly. ''Said it all so many times they can't speak it in a normal way anymore.''

''Shouldn't we be reaching the ville soon?'' said the Armorer, slinging the Uzi across his right shoulder.

''From what those young guys said, there'll be sentries.'' Ryan looked around them. ''Can't be far. Reckon they'll probably see us before we see them.''

They had passed another neat sign, only about a hundred yards back: Pilgrims and Seekers After Truth are Nearly at the Golden City.

And a second line added in a different hand: Come in Peace or Not at All.

''That's us,'' Dean said, giggling.

Doc was doubled over, racked, a thread of greenish spittle dangling from his chin. Ryan caught Mildred's eye, but she only shook her head and shrugged.

J.B. had taken off his fedora, using it to fan away a cloud of persistent small black flies that hung around him. ''How come they only pick on me. Dark-nighted little bastards!'' He brushed at his chest, pausing and staring carefully at the rad counter pinned to his lapel. ''Well into the orange,'' he said. ''Must be a local hot spot someplace fairly close.''

Ryan checked his own counter, finding the same reading. It was very close to the red of imminent danger. ''Shouldn't hang around here too long,'' he said. "And best keep a careful eye on the readings. Real careful."

THEY SAW A SMALL HERD of deer, with flecked skins, bounding across the trail a little way ahead of them, moving fast and elegant, down the hill toward the west. Ryan automatically unslung the Steyr rifle, picking up the head of a young stag in the laser image enhancer, easing his finger off the trigger as he changed his mind about opening fire. In any case, they didn't need food.

The track had widened, showing clear evidence of heavier use—hoof marks and furrowed wag wheels, the muddied scars filled with water.

Just as Ryan stopped, the others gathering around him, a blaster fired from the cover of the trees to the right of the old blacktop. The bullet gouged up a gout of spray that splashed over Ryan's pants and boots, missing him by less than a yard.

The voice from the shadowed pines was flat and unemotional. "Wrong move buys you eternity, outlanders."

"Keep real still," Ryan said.

Chapter Eighteen

The echo of the shot was still bouncing off the steep rocks to the left.

"You got a lot of blasters there, outlanders."

There didn't seem to be a question, so Ryan chose not to answer.

"You triple stupe, stranger?"

Ryan looked up the hill toward the sound of the voice, trying to detect some sign of movement. But the dense wall of pines was impenetrable.

"You got us cold, brother," he said. "Not the sort of charitable welcome we were led to expect from the Children of the Rock."

"Who told you about us?"

"Don't know their names. There was three of them, eating supper last night at a small place run by a lady called Mom. Made the finest jerky I ever tasted."

Silence.

J.B. was still holding the Uzi at his hip, finger on the trigger. Ryan noticed that the blaster was set on full-auto, ready for a lethal burst of fire. "You letting us in, or do we keep on walking?"

"Keep your dick in your pocket, mister. No need for too much rushing."

"You said about you'd been at Mom's Place, stranger?" another voice said.

Ryan nodded. "Sure have."

"Was things snug when you left?"

"Snug? Don't—"

"We seen signs of fire. Big column of smoke. Seemed to come from roundabouts where Mom has her place. You didn't see nothing at all?"

"Don't look back that much. Just forward." He turned and looked behind them, scanning the horizon. "I don't make out any fire. The place stood all right when we left. Had us an early breakfast and left around dawn."

"We got a patrol heading out that way later on this morning. Check it out."

Ryan waited. There was a tension and a suspicion in the air. It was unmistakable, lying on the tongue, bitter and cold. And that wasn't so unusual in frontier pesthole villes. But he didn't feel any serious imminent threat. The short hairs of his nape stayed flat.

The first voice came back. "There any more in your party, mister?"

"No. What you see is what there is."

"You aiming to visit or stay?"

"Who knows? My old father used to say that you had to walk that lonely valley by yourself."

There was a sound of a muttered conversation from among the trees. J.B. shuffled a few paces to his left, coming closer to Ryan.

"Think they're going to let us in, bro? Sounds like they run a tight ville."

"Not a bad thing. They sound like bottom-line sec men, guys who think with their blasters."

The first voice came again. "Yeah. We found out the brothers you saw yesterday. They filed a report with us, last night, on a half-dozen outlanders at Mom's Place. Said you might be along here this morning."

"Good."

"Sure. Also said to watch you. Wondered if you was mercies on the hunt. Or bounties?"

"Not these days. Just traders who've had some hard times. Lost our rig. Been traveling across Deathlands, here and there, picking up what we can. We'd appreciate being able to stay a few days with you."

"What you got to offer? Trade them blasters for some food and beds?"

Ryan shook his head. "Not the blasters. But we can trade some of our time. We heard you had troubles with some local Apaches. Long way off their hunting lands."

"Mescalero. Been trouble for a while to the Children. Brother Joshua's named them as wolf's-heads. Means we can chill them when and where we see them. It's a real bitter mort-feud. You run in with them?"

Ryan considered telling the unseen guards about their bloody confrontation with the Apaches, deciding on balance that one of the Trader's maxims about telling what you had to and not a word more was appropriate.

"No. Heard of them. We'd lend a hand in exchange for bed and board."

"Have to put it to Brother Joshua. He's the voice of the grail up here."

"Grail?"

Doc hissed an answer to Ryan's question. "Grail, Holy. Reference to the drinking cup of Christ. As used at the alleged Last Supper. Then utilized by legendary figure of Joseph of Arimathea to catch drops of Savior's blood after crucifixion. Taken, allegedly, to England and has strong links with King Arthur, mythical ruler of part of Britain during dark ages. A very potent symbol of religious power."

The long explanation brought on another of the old man's coughing fits, doubling him over, hands on knees, his whole body racked by the effort.

"Thanks, Doc," Ryan said.

"What was he saying, there?" demanded the second of the hidden voices.

"Nothing to signify," Ryan replied. "Getting sort of cold standing here. If you don't want us, then that's fine. We'll be moving on."

"Sure are fucking hasty, friends," said the first speaker. "Come ahead, but just don't make any sudden movements to get us nervous."

THEY FILED along the trail. There was still no sign of the watchers, but Ryan was aware of being checked out from both sides of the track. One thing that he noticed was the size of the trees. They had been among huge conifers and sequoias for some time, but there seemed to have been a quantum leap in the past half mile or so. From very big to gigantic.

The others had also noticed the change. Dean took in a great, gulping breath, looking up and around.

"Hot pipe! Trees and a half!" he exclaimed, wonderingly. "Biggest I ever saw anywhere!"

Mildred had crooked her arm through J.B.'s elbow, and they were swinging along like a carefree pair of tourists. Ryan considered pointing out that they should all be still ready on condition orange, prepared for any danger. But there didn't seem a threat at all, so he let it lie.

She glanced around at him. "I think I came here when I was a little girl. Daddy had been murdered by the Klan three or four years earlier. His brother, Uncle Josh, brought me up here to King's Canyon with his family. In a big Winnebago camper, as I recall. He told me that the trees reached up to heaven. I asked if I could climb up to the top and meet Daddy. He laughed and said that maybe I could, when I got a little older." Her smile vanished. "Never did," she said quietly.

At that moment the two sentries who'd been keeping them invisible company emerged from the trees.

They both wore a sort of uniform. Both were in matching white shirts and maroon jackets, with some kind of silver insignia, while one wore black pants and the other dark blue. Both men had heavy-duty boots and were bareheaded, hair neatly trimmed to their collars. Neither of them had any beard or mustache.

Automatically Ryan looked to see what kind of blasters they were carrying. Both of the men, who looked to be in their late twenties, had belts with a holstered pistol in it. But it wasn't possible to make out what they were, beyond the fact they looked like revolvers rather than automatics. Each of the guards also had a long blaster slung across his shoulders.

"Winchester 94s," J.B. said. "Looks very much to me like the Magnum model. Holds ten rounds of big .44s. Dates from the late 1960s."

At a first glance it looked like the firearms were all in good, clean condition.

The taller of the two guards nodded in a friendly manner. "Welcome to the Children of the Rock, brothers and sisters. You understand that we have to be a little suspicious about letting any strangers in."

"You sec men?" Jak asked.

"No. Everyone takes a turn on all the duties. Tomorrow I might be in the kitchens. Not the way we run the ville to have sec men, kid."

Jak's face tightened. "Don't call me kid. Got name. Jak. Use that."

"Sure thing. Jak it is. I'm Josiah Steele. Partner's called Jim Owsley."

The shorter of the pair nodded tersely, not speaking, his face showing little sign of welcome. Ryan noticed that Owsley had a poor complexion with weeping sores around the mouth.

"You all got names?" Steele asked.

"Ryan Cawdor. This is Krysty Wroth. Young man's called Jak Lauren. This is my son, Dean. Fellow in the hat's J. B. Dix. Lady's name is Mildred Wyeth." He thought about giving her the proper medical title, and decided at the last moment against it. The less people knew about you, the better. "And the old guy with the nasty cough's called Dr. Theophilus Tanner."

"He a real doctor?" Owsley asked. "Don't get many of them to the pound, these days, these parts."

"I am indeed a real doctor," Doc said in his finest, roundest oratorical voice. "But not of the followers of Hippocrates. I am of the philosophical and scientific persuasion, my dear fellow. With degrees from some of the finest centers of learning in the known world. Or, even, the unknown world, as well. Of the heartland of Christendom and of all Jewry. Harvard and Oxford are among the several educational establishments that have been honored by my presence."

"I don't understand but one fucking word in ten," Owsley said, his mouth set like a line trap.

His partner, Steele, touched him on the sleeve. "Watch the language, Brother Jim. You know that our leader, Brother Joshua, likes not profanity."

Owsley scowled at him, obviously parroting the words of their chief. "'An obscene word in the mouth of a profane man is as unpleasant as maggots in a fresh wound.'" He sniffed. "Sure, I know it, Josiah."

Now they were close enough for Ryan to be able to make out what the silver badge was that both men wore on their chests. It was a cross, with another crooked cross laid over it, one that he knew was called a swastika, making it into a strange sort of a double-cross.

He could also now make a reasonable guess at the revolvers in the matching holsters. They were unusual blasters, very powerful Hawes Western Marshals, .357-caliber, single action, holding six rounds. Then the sun glinted off the brass-grip frame, and he slightly changed his opinion. The revolvers were actually the Montana Marshal model.

"Seen enough, outlander?" Owsley snapped, catching him staring at the weapons.

"Yeah. Nice blasters. Look in real fine condition, too. Like to see such good weapons well cared for. Where did you all manage to find them?"

Steele answered him. "Brother Joshua came across them in a hidden closet at the back of a burned-out blaster store. Out beyond Muir Pass. Years back. There were the long blasters, as well as two dozen of the Hawes hand blasters."

"Anything else?" asked J.B., unable to conceal his own interest.

Steele shook his head. "Guess not. We got a few blasters that we've gotten...sort of acquired over the years. Few self-mades and patch-ups from the Mescalero."

The trail rose slowly over the next hundred yards, then reached a point where the massive trees had been cleared well back on both sides. Beyond the crest the whole area opened right out into a very large, sunlit clearing, a good three hundred yards across, roughly circular.

"This is called Hopeville," Steele said, holding his arms out wide to encompass the settlement of various timber buildings. "Welcome."

Ryan made a quick count of the scattered ville, making it around thirty of what looked like basic log cabins, rather similar to Mom's Place. They weren't laid out in any particular pattern, jumbled with no recognizable layout of streets. There was also what looked like a frontier church, though the windows had heavy, barred shutters that were clearly designed to be used as fire ports. Ryan also spotted a much larger, fortified house, near the center of the colony.

Most of the buildings had short chimneys, all with covers to stop any attacker gaining access that way. And roughly one-third of them showed smoke.

About a dozen men were visible. A couple carried rifles and seemed to be on a regular patrol, on the northern flank of the camp. One was chopping wood while another was skinning a large pig that had been slung up on a makeshift scaffold over a vat of boiling water. Two more were leading a pair of plow horses through the heart of the ville.

Ryan also spotted about five women, every one of them busily engaged in washing or cooking activities. None of them took much notice of the arrival of the group of outlanders. A few lean dogs scavenged around the backs of the houses, several of them hanging around the man working on the pig's carcass.

He noticed immediately that there were no children at all to be seen in Hopeville.

"How you defend the place against any hostiles, like the Apaches?" J.B. asked.

Jim Owsley ignored the question, walking on toward the largest of the houses. But Josiah Steele seemed happy to answer anything that was asked.

"I wasn't here back in the early days of the Children of the Rock." Ryan saw the sec man's fingers stray to touch the silver double-cross on his chest as he mentioned the name of the community. "But I know that Brother Wolfe tried to build a wall, defensive to the ville. But it was impossible."

"Why?" said Ryan.

Owsley stopped and swung on his heel. "You ask too many fucking questions, outlander!"

Steele held up a cautionary hand. "Now, now," he said quietly. "A friend in Hopeville is worth an hundred enemies. You know that's what Brother Wolfe preaches."

"Sure."

The taller of the men grinned at Ryan, turning to allow his smile to take in everyone in the party. "Impossible because of the terrain here. Too many trees. Too big to man a perimeter. Too few of us."

"Heard that there was about a hundred of you," Krysty said.

Steele looked worried for the first time. "I don't think Brother Wolfe would like—"

"Fuckin' sure he wouldn't," Owsley interrupted grimly. "I'd button the flap, Josiah."

"Not trying to spy on you," Ryan said calmly. "Just interested."

Steele sniffed. "I guess—" He stopped speaking as Doc suffered another of his violent sneezing, coughing fits. "Hope he's recovered for the testing," he said.

"What's the testing?" Mildred asked.

"Brother Wolfe'll tell you all about that. I was saying about defending the ville. I reckon that we're sort of out of the way up here."

"What's altitude?" Jak was staring around him with undisguised interest.

"Varies around here. Average about twelve thousand. Some serious up and downing during skydark and through the long winters after."

Owsley was moving on again. Now they were in the middle of the ville, approaching the large building that stood at its core. Ryan walked with Steele, the others close on his heels, all of them finally stopping a few paces from the open front door of the main house.

A figure loomed from the shadows inside, and an echoing voice carried out to them.

"By the blessed saints! It's my old friend, One-Eye Cawdor. I always swore that I'd chill you next time I saw you. And here you are!"

Chapter Nineteen

Suddenly Ryan was aware that they were surrounded by armed men.

There were at least twenty, most in clothes similar to those worn by Steele and Owsley. Most were clean shaved, though Ryan spotted a couple with neatly trimmed mustaches. He thought one of them was the youngest of the trio that they'd run into back at Mom's Place, but he had other things to worry about.

They had been waiting for their arrival, setting them up. That was all too obvious.

The men, mostly looking middle-aged, were in doorways of houses, some with the barrels of their Winchester 94 rifles protruding from windows. Others had circled behind the outlanders, standing in a rough skirmish line. Most with long blasters, a few with revolvers.

"Don't even think about it, Cawdor," urged the voice from the darkness.

"Wasn't thinking about a thing. Except that this was a fireblasted sort of a welcome to the Children of the Rock. Not friendly, Brother Wolfe."

The man still lingered just inside the doorway of the house. "It's Brother Wolfe, is it now, Cawdor?"

"What else should it be?"

The laugh was warm and friendly, the kind of laugh that sent a finger of ice down the spine.

"What else should it be? I can recall the names that I got called by Trader and his renegades."

So. That was it. The Trader had ridden the length and breadth of Deathlands, and for many of those years he had been accompanied by his two lieutenants, John Dix and Ryan Cawdor. Some of the time they'd left good, warm feelings behind them in the villes they'd visited.

Some of the time they hadn't.

Ryan blinked away the thick red mist of half-remembered blood and sighed.

"Times long past, Wolfe."

"Not worth forgetting," Doc added in his usual runic, inconsequential manner.

"Don't know you, old man," the voice said. "I heard word of all of you, here and there."

"You going to show yourself? Or just give the sign to have us gunned down?" J.B. asked.

"Hold your tongue, Armorer. Think I don't know you, Dix, with your gleaming glasses and your favorite hat? Carrying an Uzi, I see."

"Take some of you whoreson bastards with me, Wolfe. If it comes to that."

"Not the place for a firefight, outlanders," Owsley said at their side. "Be your blood spilled in the dirt. Best way with strangers. Dead man won't betray you."

Ryan looked coldly at him. "Any shooting and I swear I'll take you with me."

"Big talk for an old one-eyed man," said the

voice from the doorway, followed by the laugh again.

Ryan was suddenly angry, irritated by the ambush they'd walked into like wet-eared stupes and not ready to play games any longer with the hidden man.

"You come out now, Wolfe, or I promise you we'll start shooting."

"You've come to talk, then talk. If you've come to shoot..."

It was one of the Trader's favorite sayings.

A spavined, brindled mongrel had crept, belly down, toward the group of strangers, sidling in closer to Ryan. Its teeth were broken and jagged, its eyes red rimmed, panting jaws dripping clotted foam. When it considered it had crept in near enough for its sneak attack, it snarled its hatred and lunged toward the groin of the one-eyed man.

Ryan had been watching it, readying himself for the attack. His SIG-Sauer was safely holstered, the Steyr rifle slung across his shoulders. The hilt of the panga was close to his left hand.

It didn't look like he'd have a chance of fending off the vicious animal.

There was a blur of sudden movement, the pallid sunshine blinking off the honed and polished steel, the whisper of the eighteen-inch blade as it flickered into sight from the soft leather sheath. The hiss of whirring metal overlaid the growl of the charging dog.

There was a dull thunk, like a swung ax blade biting deep into a thick log of sodden wood.

The deep-throated bark was cut off into instant silence. The dog's lean skull dropped in the dirt, washed with a gout of bright arterial blood. The body, paws still scrabbling, fell alongside it, moving a couple of yards nearer Ryan, with the impetus of that final charge.

"Holy shit!" Steele breathed.

"Shep!" cried a woman, standing on the other side of the big smoldering fire at the center of the open square. "That stinking bastard outlander's slaughtered poor old Shep!"

The man in the house clapped one hand against the frame of the door, in sarcastic applause. "Fast as ever, One-Eye. Age hasn't wearied you."

Finally, as though sensing Ryan's building rage, Brother Joshua Wolfe stepped out into the morning air.

Ryan recognized him, the years flooding back at the sight of the man.

"I remember you," he said.

"Me, too," J.B. muttered. "Yeah. Me, too."

"And I remember both of you, oh, so very well. This is always here to remind me, should my memory become lax. With *this* I can never forget."

The man held out both arms, like a huckster displaying his wares—two arms, but only one hand.

The left hand was missing, ending in a neat stump, just above the wrist.

Ryan looked up from the mutilation, recalling the man who now called himself Brother Joshua Wolfe. He was around six feet three inches in height, weighing close to 240. He was broad in the shoulder and narrow in the hip, wearing the same kind of uniform as most of the men in the ville. His hair was graying, where it had once been as black as a raven's wing.

His black cord pants tapered down into a pair of mirrored black Western boots with a silver rattler embroidered across the toes. He had a Mexican rig, ornately worked in silver-and-gold thread, strapped low on the right thigh, holding a revolver like most of the men carried, the big .45 caliber Hawes Montana Marshal. Only Wolfe's had gleaming pearlized grips.

"Remember, One-Eye?"

He turned toward J.B. "Remember me, Four-Eyes?"

"Sure. Didn't have the Hawes back then. If I recall it right, you had a matched pair of Iver Johnson Cattleman pistols, .357s. And a hideaway? Now, what...? Dark night! I remember it. Shoulder rig. Harrington and Richardson vest-pocket model. Smith & Wesson .32. Five rounds. Real short barrel. Pretty little toy."

Wolfe shook his head admiringly. "By the saints... You sure got a memory for a blaster, Dix."

The Armorer nodded, unsmiling, the muzzle of the Uzi covering the leader of the Children of the Rock. At his side Doc gave a raucous sneeze, tugging out his swallow's-eye kerchief to blow his nose.

Ryan's memory was carrying him back. How long? Good ten or fifteen years? Could even be as long as twenty years. Memory for things like that was notoriously unreliable.

But he recalled where it was that the Trader had run into Joshua Wolfe.

"Near Spearfish, up in the old Dakotas. We'd been trading on the site of the old Little Bighorn battlefield. Then we were heading along toward the east. Beaver skins, collected from the Oglala. Ville where you lived was called..." He hesitated a moment. "Pine Fork."

Wolfe nodded, smiling broadly. "Good, very good, my old friend. Go on. Let the memories flow free as fine-graded flour under the millstones."

"You were the sec boss."

"They had shirts the same color as your men's jackets," J.B. said.

Ryan nodded. "Right, they did. Baron was called Tsin Lao. Way-back Chinese warlord."

"Leper," Wolfe said. "You remember that? Tough old bastard had half his face gone."

"That's right." He'd had no nose, just a snuffling hole, fringed with a ragged cuff of snot-dripping gristle. One eye had been pulled down toward the ravaged cheek. His upper lip had been missing, showing his tombstone teeth, like houses in a ghost town.

"You tried treachery," J.B. said accusingly. "Drugged the meat for supper. One of our dogs ate some first. Died right there and then, in front of us. Trader had you questioned."

"Baron let it happen. Scared of losing his whole ville. Trader in his pomp was a shit-scaring sight."

Ryan grinned mirthlessly at the memory. "Most folks he asked questions got around to answering them."

"Sometimes I wake in the small hours of the night and I'm crying." Wolfe reached up and touched the network of old scars that seamed his face around both eyes. "He used a needle, heated up white. Held it in thick gloves and threatened to blind me. Why'd he do that to me, Ryan?"

"You got a strange memory, Wolfe. Kind of picks and chooses, doesn't it?"

"How's that?"

"You planned to murder everyone on War Wags One and Two."

He turned toward J.B., his eye not moving from Wolfe. "We have Two in those days?"

The Armorer sniffed. "Can't remember. Think so. Either way, it was a coldheart plan to butcher us all. Trader needed to know who was behind it. So, you ask the sec boss."

"And I told him it was me." Wolfe took a long shuddering breath, his dark eyes closed. "He hurt me bad. Then, when I'd admitted what I'd done, he had me held fast and took a cleaver. Took it and swung it and hacked off my left hand, clean as whistling. And I swore I'd have revenge if I ever got the chance. And here you are. Both of you. Plucked chickens on my table. Delivered by the good Lord."

Ryan had always known, in his heart, that it might end like this.

The years with the Trader had been awash with blood. So many dead. So many left living, hearts filled with a bitter grudge against the Trader and the men who'd ridden with them.

Deathlands wasn't big enough to expect to run and hide for all your life. In the end you'd bump into someone at the turning of a dark corridor, in a narrow alley in a frontier pesthole, at a desert watering hole, in the kitchens of a gaudy or on a mountain pass above tumbling meltwater.

In a quasireligious, military commune among the tall trees of the Sierras.

"It's me and J.B. you want," Ryan said. "The others had nothing to do with Trader."

Wolfe smiled at him. "Now then, One-Eye, I never thought to hear you talk stupe. We all know that you ride with someone, then you live and die with them. No division of that. Even the boy, who by the looks of him is your kin."

"We take them out and let them have it, Brother Wolfe?" Owsley asked, licking his dry lips eagerly. "Or mebbe peddle them all to Mom?"

Wolfe shook his head and sighed. "From that smoke we saw, I'd be astonished to find that Mom's Place is still functioning."

He turned to Ryan. "No point in asking if you knew anything about that?" When there was no answer, he smiled his glacial smile again. "Now, why am I not surprised at that?"

"Let's get on with it," J.B. said, half turning so that the Uzi pointed directly at the leader of the ville.

Ryan sensed that a lot of the men of the Children of the Rock weren't comfortable at the standoff.

There were enough of them, and they were well enough armed to be confident of massacring the handful of strangers. But unless they were blindly stupid, they had to have also realized that Ryan and the others wouldn't go on into the dark land alone and unprotesting.

Wolfe stepped forward, holding up his mutilated hand in a kind of benediction. "No," he said.

"No, what?" Ryan's hand rested flat on the butt of the SIG-Sauer.

"It says in the Good Book that to err is human and that to forgive is to follow in the steps of Our Savior. It is truly to be divine."

"So?"

"So, my dear Ryan Cawdor. Long years ago you and others erred. Caused me great grief. But I wish for divinity. So I propose to forgive you. All of you. Both the guilty and those plagued with guilt by association."

Ryan was ready to trust Wolfe just about as far as he could have thrown him. "So, what's that mean?"

The first few words of the religious baron's reply were almost smothered by a fit of coughing from Doc. "It means that you are welcome here. If the testing goes well, as I am sure it will, then you will be accepted and may stay here, in total safety, under my personal protection, for as long as you wish."

Chapter Twenty

"So, what's testing?"

Josiah Steele had been appointed by Joshua Wolfe to show the newcomers to their accommodation, a hut that smelled like it had been empty for several months, but was dry and spacious. There were seven single beds and a table and several upright chairs. A decent little kitchen was located out back, as was an outhouse at the bottom of the overgrown garden.

Krysty had run her finger across the table, holding up the gray smudge of dirt. Steele had sniffed, promising to get some women in to scrub and clean it, as well as provide them with some fresh-laundered bedding.

He had also told them a midday meal would be served up, communally, around one in the afternoon, and supper would be at seven.

Now he stood in the doorway, silhouetted by the late-morning sun, his shadow spilling across the dusty planks.

"What is testing?" Jak asked.

The sec man shrugged. "Nothing to worry about for the likes of you."

"Cemeteries are full of folks who thought there was nothing to worry about," Mildred objected.

Steele turned toward her. "Could be that you've got... No, can't say that. Just that the Children of the Rock always welcome strangers, as long as they measure up and fit in. Best Brother Wolfe tells you more over the noon meal."

"Noon or one?" Krysty asked.

"At one. But it's always been called the noon meal. Kind of tradition."

He turned, ready to leave, when Ryan called him back. "One last question, Brother Steele."

"Yeah, Brother Cawdor?"

Ryan touched the tiny rad counter fixed to the lapel of his coat, seeing that it still showed high orange close toward the top-risk red.

"What's the hot spot?"

Steele's jaw dropped, like he'd been gut shot. "Who's told you? Where did you get that?"

"The rad counter? Been carrying it more years than I can remember. If my memory serves, we found a stack of them near Topeka. That it, J.B.?"

The Armorer was sitting on one of the beds, polishing his glasses on a linen kerchief. "Topeka? Yeah, that's where we got them."

Steele had recovered his balance. "I guess that we're so used to it that it doesn't bother us."

"What is it?"

"Hot spot. Not so bad as those little gizmos show. Doubt it's anywhere near to red."

"Near enough," J.B. said. "How far away from the ville is it?"

"Two, three miles. Brother Wolfe found it when he was picking this place for the home of the Children of the Rock. Lies north and east.'' He cleared his throat. ''It's an old complex, built just before skydark. Earth-shift exposed some part of the central nuke core. Leaks.''

Ryan sat on one of the beds, testing the mattress for springiness, looking at the man disbelievingly. ''He knew there was a rad spot that close? And he still picked this for the ville. And you've all been here for all that time. I just find that real hard to—''

''There must be some side effects from the radiation,'' Mildred said. ''Skin problems. Fertility...'' She stopped as a thought struck her. ''Hey, I haven't seen many children around this place. Not for the numbers of men and women. Should be more.''

Steele didn't reply, half turning to stare out through the open doorway.

Ryan pressed him. ''I've seen about four or five little ones since we arrived. There's no school...nothing like that. Is there, Steele?''

''No. No school. Not for years. Not enough children to make it worthwhile.''

Doc cleared his throat, coughed and tried again. ''Might I be permitted a small observation, ladies and gentlemen? On the subject of infants.''

''Go ahead, Doc.''

A half bow of the leonine head. ''My thanks, Master Cawdor, for your courtesy. It is just that I have a great affection for children, having so tragically lost my own two dear little doves. They were so tender and so...but let that pass. The milk is spilled and spilled forever. You cannot ever go back, when you are always moving on. They were only cities, but they're—''

"Doc!"

The old man jumped at Mildred's interruption. "I was wandering, was I not?"

"You was. I mean, you were, Doc. You'd been talking about children...."

"Yes. Have any of you noticed that the majority of inhabitants of the settlement are what one might once have called white Anglo-Saxon Protestants?"

"Sure are," Steele said, not hiding his irritation. "Where's this leading to, Doc?"

"The children all looked remarkably to me as though they came originally from Native American stock." He sneezed violently. "Bless me!"

Ryan blinked. "Fireblast! That's right, Doc."

"Mescalero." Jak punched his right fist into his left palm.

"Is that right?" Krysty took half a dozen steps across the cabin to confront Steele. "Gaia! That's it, isn't it? You're all sterile from the rad hot spot. You can't have your own little ones, so you steal them!"

Without a word the sec man stalked quickly out of the cabin, vanishing into the heart of the ville.

BEFORE GOING OUT to share the noon meal with the rest of the Children of the Rock, Ryan and friends had a long discussion about their situation.

The first problem to face up to was Brother Joshua Wolfe. Could he be trusted?

"Mebbe we should just up and get out," J.B. said. "Out of sight's out of range."

Ryan was in favor of staying. "Keep our eyes open. Course. But I reckon that if Wolfe had wanted us chilled, he could have simply raised his hand and that would have been it. I'm kind of interested in the setup here."

"How about the rad hot spot?" Mildred shook her head, the beaded plaits chinking against one another. "Remember that guy, Owsley, with his skin? Nasty complexion. More spots than a leopard. I would lay money that it's a lupus-linked condition. Got its roots in a rad cancer. I wouldn't want to stay here longer than two or three days."

At that moment there was a hesitant knock on the door. Jak was nearest and opened it, revealing a couple of women holding buckets, brushes and mops.

"Can we come and clean?" asked the older of the pair, a skinny woman with sparse gray hair.

"Sure. We'll move out of your way." Ryan got up from the bed where he'd been resting, leading the way from the cabin. Doc was the only one who didn't move. He had suffered another dreadful coughing fit that had racked his body. Now he slept, uneasily, tossing and turning, muttering to himself, hands opening and closing like claws.

"Can leave him there," said the other woman, a pretty, washed-out blonde, who looked painfully anemic. "Won't bother us none. Need to rest up for testing."

Ryan nodded. "Sure. Not long until the meal. Rouse him for that."

Krysty paused in the doorway. "How long since there was a child born here in the ville?" she asked.

"Child?" The women looked at each other doubtfully. "Born here?"

The older one wiped the back of her hand across her face. "You mean a norm?"

"Sure. Why? You had some mutie births?"

"Don't say anything," the younger one urged. "Brother Wolfe doesn't like blabbing."

"No, won't hurt none. Not a secret, is it? Half the folk of the Sierras know about our problem."

Doc coughed and stirred in his sleep, rolling over onto his right side.

"Go on," Krysty prompted.

The woman hesitated, reluctantly proceeding as though the words had been drawn from her heart. "Last natural-born baby here was a good four years back, and that was a weak sickling. Lived a scant brace of months. Been others." She pulled a grimace of disgust. "Been others."

"Others? Muties?"

"Worse than that." Her eyes had narrowed, and her voice dropped. Her companion looked nervously out the door, as if she feared their being overheard. "Sickly, ailing creatures. Devil's spawn. Head and legs. Body like a girt spider. Another with claws, like a crab, but with a cluster of eyes across its little forehead."

Her friend crossed herself. "Poor wee mites. That one with a tangle of arms from its tiny chest. And the one with kind of feathers all over its misshapen skull.''

"The goat child.''

"Aye, Jesus save it.''

"And the one that bit a finger clean off Goodwife Biddy at its birthing.''

"By the saints! That was one of the worst of them all. Took three bullets to dispatch its hideous scaly body all the way to Paradise.''

"Hopeville to Paradise.''

She addressed Krysty again. "Rightly said, outlander. This is a poor, blighted place for raising children.''

"Why not move from the hot spot?'' Mildred asked. "You'd have been spared much of this.''

"No,'' they said in chorus. The older one wrung out her mop to indicate that the conversation was almost over. "Brother Wolfe says that it's all a part of our suffering. Suffering like He suffered. Our own cross to bear.''

Doc had jerked awake from sleep, lying still, listening to the women talking. "Golgotha!'' he said, very loudly. "Not Hopeville. Golgotha, the place of the skull.''

"Stay loose, Doc.'' Ryan had come back from the sunshine to stand next to Krysty. "How many of the Mescalero children have been taken?''

"Can't rightly say, Brother Cawdor.'' The older woman shook her head. "Not our place to say. But I'd figure the answer is close on twenty.''

"They still living?'' Ryan asked.

"Some. Most of them don't take to our ways and

food and all. Some get sick. Sores around the eyes and mouth. Shittin' disease. Piss blood. Only about four or five actually what you might call left living. The Apaches take it hard.''

The other woman nodded eagerly. ''That's true, Sister Helen. Like bein' at war, it is.''

Jak reappeared. ''Food near ready,'' he said.

IT WAS A CASUAL MEAL, no tables, with the food served on an assortment of home-fired dishes and wooden platters. Big bowls of food sat on one trestle, to be taken away and eaten while sitting on the cropped grass around the huts.

Wolfe was in a jovial mood, ladling out venison stew, reassuring them this was better-quality meat than what they'd eaten back at Mom's Place. He told them that sec scouts had gone back along the trail and found the smoldering ruins of the eatery and a charred skeleton in the glowing ashes.

''And a stench of kerosene,'' he said, grinning broadly, the smile puckering his scars. ''Looks like she disagreed with someone who ate there.''

Ryan figured that the leader of the Children of the Rock strongly suspected their involvement in the slaying and arson, but didn't seem to be particularly worried by that, letting it pass, unchallenged.

Which was fine with him.

But it was another good reason to keep checking over his shoulder.

The rich stew came with an assortment of fresh vegetables, well cooked and flavored with a mix of local herbs and spices. Josiah Steele had brought them straight to the head of the self-service line, where Wolfe was already waiting for them, holding a rough-cut goblet of reconstituted glass filled to the brim with spring water.

He had greeted them cheerily and joined them when they had all loaded their plates and sat down to eat.

Doc was the only one whose platter didn't groan under the weight of food. He had selected a few tender pieces of venison for himself and a small spoonful of the buttered, whipped potatoes, picking at his food between noisy snuffles and outbreaks of phlegmy coughing.

Ryan noticed that the old man looked pallid and was sweating profusely, though the temperature under the shadowing mammoth trees couldn't have been much above seventy.

"Tell us about this testing," J.B. said to Brother Joshua.

"Nothing for anyone to be concerned about," the leader of the ville replied.

"Who gets tested and how?"

"All of you, Brother Cawdor," he replied. "All of you, by all of us."

There was a snicker of laughter from somewhere along to their left, a sound that seemed to come from the general direction of Jim Owsley.

Joshua Wolfe ignored it and carried on speaking. "Nothing for anyone to worry about. If they are pure of heart and fine of spirit, then the Blessed Jesus Christ, Our Savior, will stand at their shoulder and guide them through the gins and snares laid down by the Evil One.''

''Blessed is the light of the world,'' called a shrill woman's voice.

''Amen,'' in a scattered chorus from all around the center of the ville.

''Verily, amen to that.'' Wolfe put his head to one side, like a quizzical crow. ''Enjoy your repast, and give thanks to the Almighty for its preparation.''

''When testing start?'' Jak asked, helping himself to another two sourdough rolls.

''This very afternoon, if we can arrange it. I can see that you and the boy will have skills to offer to us. Young men, Brother Lauren and Brother Cawdor, agile and lithe. And I have no doubt that having walked the walk with Brother Ryan Cawdor and Brother Dix will have set you both up for their sort of living.''

Ryan had finished his meal and given the empty plate to one of the women. He felt comfortably full and relaxed, though a little concerned about the state of Doc's health, which seemed to be still deteriorating.

At least they were in what seemed a snug and secure ville, with warm fires and food and stout walls. If Doc was going to be ill, then there were lots of worse places.

Weren't there?

Chapter Twenty-One

"Brothers and sisters!"

Joshua Wolfe clapped his right hand against his thigh, drawing everyone's attention. "After that wonderful meal, provided by the kindness of the Almighty, prepared by the sisterhood, it is time for a short service to welcome the newcomers into our midst."

Ryan glanced at the others to see if anyone had any obvious objections to the idea of participating in a religious service. Personally he had no sort of belief in any kind of orthodox faith. Trust yourself a lot and your friends a little, and nobody else at all— It was the creed according to the Trader, and Ryan went along with that.

The heavy shutters that had been covering the windows of the squat church of Hopeville had all been thrown back, revealing some surprisingly beautiful stained glass, its bright, rich colors glistening in the early-afternoon sunshine.

Gradually, like fall leaves carried on a light wind, most of the inhabitants of the settlement made their way toward the heavy building, the shadow of its tower stretching across the trodden turf to welcome them.

The overwhelming color was the maroon of the

men's jackets, matched by the blouses and skirts of the women.

Ryan noticed that all of the men carried their blasters with them wherever they went. It was something that he approved of, if it was true that they were in a state of permanent armed conflict with the local Mescalero.

If you met up with hostile Apaches, then you best be carrying all the weapons you could manage. There was no such thing as too many blasters.

Wolfe shepherded them along. "Come, my dear outlanders. You shall face the testing with the love of Jesus Christ as your shield and buckler."

"Sword," Doc said, his booming voice sounding unexpectedly loud.

"How's that, old-timer?" Wolfe asked, his benevolent smile still pasted firmly in place, though Ryan noticed that it didn't seem to quite reach the slightly thyroid eyes.

Doc coughed, covering his mouth with his hand. "My apologies, friends." He half bowed to the leader of the Children of the Rock. "I simply thought it fit to correct your error, Master Wolfe. That was all."

"Error? I think you should know that I am not in the habit of making any errors."

There was a cold edge to the man's voice, like a hacksaw buried in ice.

"Forgive me, dear sir, but indeed you did. You spoke of shield and buckler, did you not?"

Wolfe hesitated for a moment. The men and women of the ville were all pressed around him, hanging on the exchange. It was all too obvious that it was unusual for anyone to contradict something said by Brother Joshua Wolfe.

"Let it lie, Doc," Ryan said quietly, so quietly that the old man didn't hear him above the murmurs of the crowd outside the church.

"I said shield and buckler, Brother Tanner. That was what I said."

Doc laughed croakily. "My point, my point, sir. That is a plain tautology."

"What the fuck you blatherin' about, you triple stupe?" Owsley snapped.

Doc didn't hear, or ignored, the hostility in the sec man's voice. "A shield is a buckler. And a buckler is a shield. They are one and the same thing. I believe that what you meant to say was sword and buckler." A long pause. "Or, mayhap, you might have said sword and shield. One and the same thing, Brother Wolfe. They are one and the same."

"That is *so* interesting. By the cherubim and seraphim, Brother Tanner, but I am *so* pleased that you saw fit to correct my foolish error."

The sarcasm was tainted with a red-mist anger, barely under control.

Mildred sensed it, stepping between Wolfe and Doc. "That's enough of errors, Doc," she said, taking the old man by the arm. "Let's go and have us some churching."

"But of course, madam. I shall mark your footsteps, goodly page, and follow in them closely. And the wolf and the moth shall not corrupt us. While the rabid wolf shall lay down with the lion. I could wolf down some good communion wafers and wine. Wolf them, Brother Wolfe.''

Owsley moved in on Mildred, his eyes tight with rage, the tip of his tongue flicking at his suppurating lips like a rattler tasting the air. His hand was on the butt of the Hawes Montana Marshal. ''You just shut—'' he began.

Ryan's fingers closed on the SIG-Sauer, and he expected the whole afternoon to erupt into gunfire and bloodshed.

But Joshua Wolfe controlled the moment.

''No!'' he snapped, gesturing with the stump of his missing hand. ''No, Brother Owsley. It doesn't signify at all. I'm interested to learn about my mistake.''

The hair-trigger instant came and went. There was a whisper of conversation, overlaid with a touch of disappointment, and they all went inside the church.

THE INSIDE DECORATION of the building wasn't like anything that Ryan had ever seen before.

Most churches he'd encountered had religious pictures on the walls. Saints at their labors, or resting, in all styles and patterns. One near Zuni had Christian imagery pictured through Native American art, the apostles as kachina figures.

This was different.

''Dad, this is something else,'' Dean breathed as he slid along into one of the front oak pews, on the right side of the narrow, maroon-carpeted aisle.

Josiah Steele sat next to Ryan at the end of the

row. "Not many churches look like this, do they, Brother Cawdor? You could walk the length and breadth of all Deathlands and never see its like in any ville."

Ryan nodded. "Can't argue with that."

Joshua Wolfe had gone to the front of the building, standing with arms folded, hooded eyes watching as his congregation settled into their places.

"Welcome to the first Church of the Children of the Rock in the holy sanctuary of Hopeville." His voice was deep and solemn, the words sounding as though they had been dragged out of some cold underground catacomb.

"Amen."

"The Church of Jesus Christ the paramilitary fundamentalist welcomes all."

That was the motif repeated endlessly around the walls and windows of the building. The same theme even decorated the arched ceiling.

Christ was portrayed as a white man in his thirties, with neatly trimmed hair and a small goatee beard, his blue eyes glittering fanatically. In most of the paintings He was wearing a smart set of camouflage fatigues and carried a whole range of weaponry. The main stained-glass window behind the altar—which was made from ammo boxes riveted together—showed him hefting a Kalashnikov, flames spitting from the muzzle.

In one of the side windows, highlighted in garish reds and yellows, the Savior was carrying an antique Lee-Enfield bolt-action rifle, with a bayonet fixed. Blood dripped from the steel blade.

Spread all across the ceiling was the military Jesus, complete with a halo of golden barbed wire, leaning from the cockpit of an unidentifiable tank that was driving over a mountain of pulped corpses, most of which were clearly of different, nonwhite ethnic origins.

Another picture showed the Christ-figure slitting the throat of a huge, red-eyed grizzly, a jet of arterial blood spurting out over the faces of a group of worshipping acolytes, all holding Smith & Wesson automatics.

"Not like any Blessed and Merciful Jesus that I've ever seen, lover," Krysty whispered. "More like a kind of military Conan the Barbarian."

"Gentle Jesus, meek and mild," Doc croaked, sitting next to the scarlet-haired woman. "I see precious little evidence of either meekness or mildness."

Joshua Wolfe held up his remaining hand, waiting for silence. "Enough, brothers and sisters," he said. "We are here in the name of the Lord Jesus, armorer over all blasters. Watcher of ammo and hammer and bolt and cartridge. Master of the full-metal jacket. Upholder of the razor-steel blade."

On the other side of the church, Ryan noticed an immensely tall and powerful woman, eyes closed behind layers of fat, strangler's hands clasped, mouth open in adoration. She wasn't someone he cared to go up against in a dark alley after midnight.

"We worship gladly, O Lord, at thy feet. We welcome thy blessed aid in all manner of chilling. Thou art there at the shooting and the stabbing. At the strangling and the drowning. At the poisoning and the flaying. The hider and the hunter and the tracker. At the slitting and the hacking and the brother with the switchblade knife. At the burning, the night's ambush and the final shuddering breath.''

He paused, and the congregation came smoothly in with their well-rehearsed response. ''Let thy rain and burning embers fall into our open, staring eyes. For we are without all grace if You are not with us.''

''Hallelujah! Come heal the sick and trample down the weak!'' roared the giantess, arms held up above her head, fingers almost touching the ornate wrought-iron chandelier.

Ryan heard J.B. whispering to Mildred. ''Looks like she done her fair share of trampling the weak.''

Mildred sniggered. On the left side, in the second row of pews, Jim Owsley turned and scowled across at the sudden noise, glaring at Mildred.

Wolfe ignored the minor interruption. ''We listen and note all Your teachings, Master-at-arms Jesus. Keep the sun at your back and allow for windage. Lay off the shot if you're firing down a hill. And never hit seventeen when you're up against the dealer. Never give your real name to a gaudy hooker. Keep your powder dry and your blaster clean and oiled.''

The solitary ''Amen'' came from J.B.

Ryan leaned back uncomfortably, thinking that he'd actually never sat in a comfortable seat in any church, anywhere in Deathlands. It seemed to be an inevitable, integral part of any religious ceremony.

Krysty insinuated her strong hand into his, squeezing his fingers.

"All right?" she breathed. Ryan responded by tightening his grip on her hand.

Wolfe was still fulminating on, painting a bloody picture of Christ the guerrilla fighter and survivalist. "We are as one with Him. One with the double-cross and the flame. One with all who are at one. And against anyone who opposes Him or stands against the Children of the Rock."

Another chorus of "amens" was even louder than before, seeming to make the roof beams quiver.

"We have here, Lord, seven outlanders. Two known to us from the olden days when they walked a different path. Now they seek the light and we welcome them. All that remains is the testing, and this shall be done before all brothers and sisters at noon tomorrow."

There was a pedal harmonium in one corner of the church, played by a stout woman in her thirties, with hair almost as red as Krysty's. The hymn, bellowed lustily by the entire congregation, was an old frontier tune, familiar to everyone there: "Guide My Bullet, Precious Lord."

When it was over, they all filed out into the clean, pine-scented afternoon.

Chapter Twenty-Two

Mildred decided that Doc would be far better off, in his sickness, spending the afternoon warm under a pile of blankets in their hut. She arranged for one of the ville's older women to look in on him, and provide him with plenty of drinks of hot lemon and honey.

"Dehydration," she said. "That's the biggest danger when you're running a temperature. I think it's some kind of Sierra influenza. You got all the symptoms that I'd expect—trembling and stiffness and soreness in the joints, feeling hot and cold at the same time. Sweating."

"Perspiring, madam, if you please. Horses sweat and men perspire."

"While ladies merely glow." Mildred grinned at him. "Sure. I know that. Couple of days feeling like death and you should start getting better."

"How about the testing?" Dean asked. "Doc'll let us all down if he's sick."

He was greeted with an angry harrumphing sound from the old man. The boy was eager to be out into the fresh air. Ryan had agreed that they could carry out something of a recce. They'd checked with Wolfe, who'd been happy to grant them his permission. He'd offered them a half dozen of his finest sec men to escort them among the monstrous trees.

"No. Be fine, thanks," Ryan replied. "Be back here before dusk."

"Watch out for Apaches," Josiah Steele warned. "Constant thorn in our side."

"They'll likely see you, before you spot any sign of them," Owsley added. "Nobody like Mescalero for hiding."

Ryan laughed, untroubled. "Lots of them are good as the Mescalero at an ambush—Cheyenne, Oglala, Pawnee, Huron, Creek, Arapaho. You name me any rad-blasted tribe, and I'll have been attacked by them. Dense forest like this, any stupe stickie could hide well enough."

"Hide a cavalry regiment," J.B. added, slinging the Uzi. "Herd of buffalo. Platoon of grandmothers. Township of deaf beavers. Whole army of par-blind priests."

Owsley spit in the dirt and turned away from them. Steele watched his colleague depart. "Not a good man for an enemy," he said quietly.

"I already figured that," Ryan stated tersely, instantly regretting it. "Sorry, Brother Steele. Didn't mean to snap at you. Grateful for the warning."

"Sure. Take care out there, now. Get back and eat well and sleep good. Need to be at your best for the testing tomorrow afternoon."

"GOD'S COUNTRY," Ryan said, sucking in several deep, chest-filling breaths.

They'd gone about a mile and a half from the

center of Hopeville, leaving behind the oppressive, crazed fanaticism of the Children of the Rock. The weather was perfect, with just the faintest breeze from the north stirring the smaller branches of the great pines. After starting along the ribboned blacktop, Ryan led the companions toward the west, up a spur trail that showed only the hoofmarks of a herd of deer.

"Seems like the hot spot's in this direction," he said, checking with his miniature rad counter, which had shifted imperceptibly from orangy red to a reddish orange.

A tiny mountain quail, followed by eight bundles of downy feathers, scampered across the narrow side track, ignoring the interlopers into its territory.

"Looking for game?" Jak asked.

Ryan shook his head. "No need. Seem real well supplied back at the ville."

They crossed a vivid strip of open meadow, surrounded by the towering black corpses of burned-out trees. The grass was lush, speckled with a va riety of colorful plants. Krysty identified mimulus and collinsia, with the delicate orange of columbine and the flaming daggers of the Indian paintbrush.

"God's country," Mildred said, stretching her arms out wide, smiling broadly for sheer pleasure of being alive. "Air like this should be nectar for poor old Doc."

"You worried about him?" Ryan asked.

"Not exactly. There's this bizarre temporal anomaly about how old he really is and how old he seems to be. Two totally different figures."

"I always think of him as being old." Dean waved his hand to disturb a swarm of tiny gnats that had gathered around his head.

Mildred nodded. "Sure thing. Looks to be somewhere around the middle of his seventies."

"Eighties on a bad day," Krysty said.

"No. Nineties on a real bad day," Mildred insisted.

"How old is he? There was all that time-jumping fucked up his body and mind."

Ryan had often thought about that particular puzzle and had the answer ready. "Born Theophilus Algernon Tanner, South Strafford, Vermont, February 14 in the year of Our Lord 1868. Married his beloved Emily in June of 1891. Children came along for them in 1893 and 1895."

"Rachel and Jolyon," J.B. added, fanning at the warm air with the brim of his fedora.

"Right. Then those sick whitecoat bastards time-trawled him forward to 1998, 102 years into his future."

"Not surprising his brain's gotten scrambled." Mildred took a drink from one of the water containers that they'd been given by Steele.

Dean cursed at the insects. "Are we moving on?"

"Sure, Dean, and there's no need to curse. From my rad counter, it can't be that far to the source of the leak."

Krysty bit her lip, worried. "Is that a good idea, lover? Going on? What do you think, J.B.?"

"Reading's not really high enough to present us with a serious, immediate health threat." J.B.

checked the small counter on the lapel of his coat again. "It looks like a long-term, slow-leak hot spot."

"Men exposed at Chernobyl—that was a deadly serious Russian meltdown toward the end of the twentieth century—were only out unprotected for a minute or so, trying to do some instant repair work. And they were nearly all dead within months. Weeks, some of them."

Everyone looked at Mildred, startled into silence by her information.

Ryan sniffed. "That so? Heard the name. Didn't know it was that ferocious."

"There are different kinds of radiation sickness." She stared at the towering trees all around them. "Some's quick and some's slow. Noticed quite a few of the men and women in the ville showed signs of slow—hair loss, sores on their faces, especially around the mouth, bleeding gums, joint stiffness and problems in mobility. And, as we already know, there's sterility for men and for women. So, no kids in Hopeville."

"And then they have to steal from the Apaches," Ryan said. "Sounds like what we remember about Joshua Wolfe. Trust him about so far—" he held his thumb and index finger an inch apart "—and no farther. He wouldn't have an urge to take young Dean, I'd guess."

"I'd shoot him, Dad. Already lost one parent, and I didn't like being away from you when I was at the Brody School."

"No one will ever take you from me—you know

that, son.'' The light of love glowed brightly in Ryan's eye.

"You think we're safe visiting this old 'complex,' lover? And how about hanging around in the ville, so close to a hot spot. Might be safer to move on.''

Ryan turned to Krysty. "We aren't staying long. Couple of days or so. With Doc being ill, it's mebbe better to keep to where he can be looked after.''

"Still not happy.''

Jak had wandered a little way ahead of where they'd all stopped, calling back, "Think see it!''

IT WAS MUCH SMALLER than most of the other redoubts that they'd encountered, scattered throughout Deathlands. Any thoughts that it might have concealed a gateway were immediately dashed. There was every sign it was a place that had been hastily built in the last days before skydark.

The overgrown remains of a tarmac roundabout, edged with disintegrating concrete posts about three feet high, stood in long grass, reminding Ryan of the grave markers that he'd once seen dotting the abandoned battlefield of the Little Bighorn.

The entrance to the redoubt gaped open, one of the double sec doors lying, rusting, in the dirt. The other hung by only one of the set of massive hinges. Even from thirty yards away, they could all smell the dank air.

Krysty sighed, closing her eyes in an expression of distaste. "Almost feel the wickedness here,'' she said. "I know it's imagination, but I swear that I can actually see the radiation poisoning seeping out of the black cavern, like a great slow cloud of evil.''

Ryan left her, walking to stand in the cold shadows of the entrance. He peered into the blackness, listening to the dismal sound of water dripping from the arched roof, some distance inside.

J.B. joined him, taking off his glasses to polish them on his sleeve. "Dark night! Smell of death. Not sure there's much point in going on to recce much farther. Reckon we've seen most of what we need to see.''

It was obvious that the redoubt had been completely stripped when it was abandoned. The inside was bare and empty, glistening with a fluorescent green moss that seemed to cover all the walls and stone floor.

Ryan pointed to a place higher up the side of the hill, where there had been a vast earth shift, probably dating from very early in the days after the heavens were clouded with thousands of missiles and the people died. Dead trees leaned sideways, their rotting roots exposed to the sunlight.

"Quake probably broke it open inside. Set the main nuke-power source to leaking. If we went exploring, we'd probably find it cracked wide.''

Jak, Dean and Mildred joined them, leaving Krysty standing alone in the bright sunshine.

"Going in?" Dean asked, his high voice muffled by the echoing space ahead of them.

"No." Ryan studied the contours of the land above and around the entrance to the old redoubt. "Shame, really," he said. "Look at that.''

J.B. read his mind. "Yeah. It would have been real easy to do."

Mildred smiled at him. "You two are like identical twins, some of the time. Symbiosis. Knowing precisely what the other one's thinking even before you speak. It's kind of irritating to a mere outsider like me."

"I was thinking how simple it would have been to have brought down the whole mountainside with a handful of plas-ex," Ryan explained.

The Armorer put his arm tenderly around Mildred's shoulders. "If they'd done it years ago, they'd have sealed off the rad leak."

"Oh, I get it. And then none of them would have been sick. And they could have carried on breeding. How different life could've been for them."

"No fighting Apaches," Jak added.

"Thriving community, instead of one hanging on the edge of extinction by broken fingernails." Ryan turned away. "All too late now."

Krysty called out to them. "I really don't like this place, friends. Can we get away now?"

Even as she spoke, as though nature were sympathetic to her feelings, a great bank of cloud came sweeping over the tops of the pines, from the north, veiling the sunshine, dropping the temperature and bringing the threat of rain

Chapter Twenty-Three

It was still pouring. The cloudburst had begun almost as soon as they left the deserted ruins of the redoubt, a cold, driving, penetrating downpour that slanted in from the north. The sky had turned leaden, all trace of blue vanishing, the sun disappearing behind a great bank of cloud. The temperature fell by twenty degrees in as many minutes.

A dank mist appeared, clinging to the upper branches of the enormous trees, so that the sky-scraping tops became totally enveloped in gray white.

By the time they caught the scent of the cooking fires of Hopeville, Ryan and the others were completely soaked through to the skin.

They found that Doc was fast asleep. The woman bidden to care for him was sitting, dozing, by a smoldering pile of embers, her breath smelling of whiskey. She woke with a start as they came dripping in, blinking at them.

"Old gentleman's been a tad poorly," she stammered. "Slept some after...after he'd taken a nip of something to fight the fever off from him."

Mildred leaned over Doc, laying a hand on his forehead, wincing. "He's burning up," she said. "It's not the kind of fever to take you up the hill on the death cart, but enough to make you feel pretty damned rough.''

"Anything you can give him?" Ryan asked. "Mebbe Wolfe has some drugs."

"Could ask. I guess that—"

"I'll go ask," Jak said, having roughly toweled some of the rain from his parchment hair. "Back in minute."

He slipped out into the murky cold, vanishing like a wraith in the darkening mist.

The woman was sent scurrying out of the hut, and Krysty piled some fresh, dry kindling onto the fire, bringing it back to a healthy blaze. They all quickly peeled off their sodden clothes, drying themselves by the flames, shrouded in blankets as they stood around the fireplace.

The noise and light dragged Doc back from his sleep. He sat up in bed, looking startled and surprisingly fragile. "By the Three Kennedys! What malign, monkish figures are foregathered here at their vile ministering?''

"Only us, Doc," Ryan said reassuringly, seeing the fear depart from the wrinkled face. "How goes it with you?"

"Ah, it passes, dear Ryan." He coughed. "Would there be any liquid refreshment of any sort available? My throat resembles the front garden of Death Valley, Scotty. Did I ever tell you of the occasion that I was stranded out near Sweetwater? I recall a wheel had come off our trusty Conestoga. No…?" Another rasping cough. "I fear that I am dry, barren, arid, parched. Do you begin to get the picture, my good friends?''

"Yeah, we see," Mildred said, pouring some water from an earthenware jug into a chipped goblet of colored glass, which she handed to Doc.

"Thank you, madam." He took several deep gulps, spilling some down his chest. "Ah, that is so much better. I confess that I feel a few notches below my usual effervescent best. Perhaps a little rest would be of benefit?"

"Sure." Ryan was checking his blaster, sitting cross-legged on his bed. Jak reappeared in the doorway, empty-handed. "Anything to help?"

The teenager shook his head, the strands of snowy hair clinging limply to his etched cheeks. "Found him in big house. Think drunk. Eyes like poached eggs. Red cheeks. Said regretted that ville didn't have medical skills or drugs. Hoped Doc got better quick. Ready for testing. Tomorrow."

Ryan bit his lip. "Yeah, I haven't forgotten. Fireblast! Surely they won't expect a sick old man to have to take part in this testing."

"Think will," Jak said, huddled under a mottled gray blanket while he shook off his wet clothes. "Yeah. Afraid that think will."

"Mebbe he'll be okay by then and be able to take part," Dean suggested.

"Doubt he'll be in much shape to take part in anything for a couple of days," Mildred said. "Children of the Rock can't be that insensitive, can they?"

None of the others answered her.

SUPPER WAS BROUGHT around to their hut by a brace of the younger women, one of whom had a vile cancer disfiguring her face, a rotting hole of fringed flesh, where what remained of her nose joined her mouth. The upper lip was already consumed, showing the line of her rotting teeth.

She tried hard to keep her head turned away from the gentle golden light of the two oil lamps that smoked on the table by the side window, concealing the worst of her hideous scarring from the outlanders.

There were bowls of thick soup, with chunks of carrot and parsnips floating in it, followed by some tough mutton chops, with whipped potatoes that had been grievously undercooked, leaving hard lumps. The bread was good, fresh-baked rolls, with a dish of salted butter. Mugs of frothing, creamy milk completed the meal.

"Soup tasted bitter," Krysty commented. "Recognized some of the herbs in it, but I don't know what it was that gave it that sour aftertaste."

Mildred drained her drink, wiping a white mustache from her upper lip. "Didn't notice. Potatoes were lumpy enough to match the tough mutton. Mustard took away the worst of the flavor from that."

Doc had been awakened and had sipped at the soup, but hadn't felt like facing the meat, drinking the milk and asking for more to combat the dryness of his sore throat.

Within minutes he was fast asleep again.

RYAN YAWNED. "Dropping off," he said, puzzled at how his voice seemed to be coming from a vast distance away, echoing inside his skull.

"Could go for a walk, lover. Fresh air do us good. It's real muggy inside here."

Ryan opened the door of their cabin, looking out into the late evening. The rain had almost ceased, still dripping noisily from the overhanging branches of the towering trees. The cloud cover was being lashed away in the rising wind, showing an occasional glimpse of a sliver of moonlight.

No signs of life were visible outside the buildings of Hopeville, though all the huts showed lights through the slitted shutters. There was a burst of laughter from the big house where Brother Joshua Wolfe lived, and the sound of someone playing a piano, loudly and badly.

"Someone's having a good time," Krysty said, joining him, her warm body pressed against his.

He glanced behind them. Doc was snoring loudly, mouth gaping open. Dean and Jak were lying on their beds, fully dressed again, as they all were. The youths' eyes were closed tight and their chests were moving rhythmically.

J.B. and Mildred were locked in each other's arms on a double bed that they'd contrived by pushing two of the singles together. They also looked like they were asleep.

"Only us chickens awake," Ryan said.

Krysty yawned, leaning up against him. "And it's only a matter of time before..." The rest of the sentence muffled by another massive yawn.

Ryan burped, wincing at the bitterness that came flooding into his mouth, reminding him of the flavor of the thick soup. The odd flavor of the soup.

A loose shingle was rattling on the roof, distracting him from what he felt had been an important chain of thought. He'd remembered something that really mattered, but he couldn't now recall what it had been.

"What was it?" he muttered.

"What? Didn't hear you, lover."

Her voice was indistinct, like it came from inside a suitcase. Ryan steadied himself on the frame of the door, feeling the roughness of the hewed wood.

"Didn't hear you, lover."

"Said that before."

"Did I?"

"We going for that walk?"

A flurry of rain dashed into his face, making him blink. For a moment he was worried. Something was definitely wrong. He shouldn't be feeling this tired.

Krysty hadn't answered him, leaning more heavily on his arm, making him reach around to support her slumped deadweight. The odd, cold realization that she had fallen asleep, standing up, registered. That wasn't right, either.

"Krysty?"

The piano had fallen silent, and Ryan had the strange, familiar hunter's suspicion that someone was watching him from the pools of the dark shadow around the ville.

It had gone very still.

HE WAS LYING on the bed, one arm jammed underneath him. Ryan squinted from his good eye, seeing that Krysty lay on the bed at his side, her bright hair illuminated by the flickering flames of the fire.

A pulse pounded in his temple, like a deadening hammer blow. With an enormous effort he turned his head, seeing that the door of the hut stood wide open, a few drops of rain falling, tinted red by the fire. The door shouldn't be open at night; it should be locked and barred.

"Bolted," he said, his tongue feeling swollen, filling his mouth.

He should swing his legs over the side of the bed and walk the few paces across the floor, push the door closed and slide the heavy bolt. But the idea of so much effort was cataclysmically impossible, so far beyond the realm of possibility that Ryan laughed at the thought.

There wasn't a bolt on the door. Funny. He never noticed that before. Anyone could walk in out of the night.

Ryan burped again, the taste of bitterness seeming stronger, almost making him gag.

The odd flavor of the soup.

Odd flavor.

"Odd," he said.

Ryan closed his eye.

Chapter Twenty-Four

Ryan dreamed, a clogged, dark dream, one that carried him into deep waters and vaulted caverns.

He was the chaser, pursuing a nameless, faceless creature along the slippery corridors. Damp streamed down the rough-hewed walls of what seemed like an ancient mine. His own steps echoed all around him, distorted, making it sound like he was surrounded, behind and before.

He was wounded.

In the biting chill of the caves, Ryan could feel an ominous warmth clotted around his groin and lower stomach. He touched himself, reaching inside the coat. His fingertips, numb with cold, touched hot stickiness.

There wasn't much pain.

A throbbing, pounding feeling lanced across his temples, and a sick dizziness. Two or three times Ryan felt that he was going to lose his balance and fall in the slimy passages. But if he fell, then his prey would escape him.

Or he would find that he had suddenly, inexplicably, become the prey himself.

The shafts kept forking and dividing, yet he somehow always knew which trail to follow. Onward and downward, once having to use the rotting length of braided rope that clung to the one wall like a handrail.

His hand gripped what he had thought was his big SIG-Sauer pistol, but a feeble, guttering lamp had revealed that the blaster in his right fist was really only a single-shot, bolt-action .22. It was a Chipmunk Silhouette, a heavy, long-barreled pistol, almost unique in the bolt action, for a handblaster. It wasn't the kind of weapon that Ryan had ever carried before, hardly the sort of man-stopper that he needed for this subterranean chase.

A black plastic box was hooked to the wall just ahead of him. It made a sinister crackling sound, and then a calm voice came from it, a voice that sounded like the man who ran the legendary Children of the Rock.

"You have four minutes and thirty seconds to complete the testing."

Ryan stopped and doubled over, being violently sick, his mouth flooding with the bitter taste of golden bile. He dropped to his hands and knees, pressing his forehead to the seeping walls of the corridor.

It felt like someone had a fist knotted down in the soul of his guts, tugging and twining, trying to rip out the greasy loops of intestines. He moaned out loud, feeling warm tears streaming down his stubbled cheeks, leaking under the eye patch, the salt stinging his skin.

For a moment he stopped, battling the sickness. He paused in the dark stillness, waiting for his prey to give him some clue where it was lurking.

But there was nothing.

The blackness was filled with complex, shifting shapes. It was like being locked into the heart of a huge puzzle that had a simple solution. Once he had found the missing shapes—or were they symbols?—and slipped them into the correct places in the puzzle, then everything would be all right. Just like that.

He heard the soft sound of someone sniggering with laughter, a vile, triumphant noise, a cruel merriment that began to swamp the tunnels all about him, flooding and welling up, louder.

"Fireblast!" he whispered. There was a bitter anger in his heart that threatened to become a scarlet mist that would shroud his brain and imperil all sense of balance and harmony.

Things were getting worse.

The sickness and dizziness pressed down on the unprotected surface of his brain.

Blood trickled down his thighs, into his combat boots, an icy feeling that seemed to be spreading from the gaping wound in his stomach.

The floor dipped, suddenly, and Ryan dropped, a jolting fall that felt like fifty feet, but that common sense told him was probably no more than eight or ten feet. It was hard enough for him to lose his balance and to bang his elbow, a painful, bone-scraping blow that triggered the reflexes in his fingers. They opened, and the unusual blaster spun away out of his grip.

He stayed where he was, crouched on hands and knees, slowly recovering from the shock of the fall. He reached out around him on the wet granite for the blaster, but it had totally disappeared in the blackness.

Shakily Ryan stood. He felt for the walls, finding one, then, four or five paces off, the other one. Both were hacked from stone, both streaming with melt-water, as cold as whispered sin. Cautiously he reached up into the singing space above his head, but there was no roof to be felt.

He knew that he could never climb back up to the previous level, which meant that there was only one way to go. And that was onward.

But now he was weaponless, and the tumble had stretched the torn lips of his gashed belly. The blood was flowing more quickly, and he had no way of checking it. You couldn't put a tourniquet on your own stomach.

"Lonesome, low-down," he muttered to himself.

He wished that Krysty were with him in the cat-acomb. The Trader always used to say that in a tight spot, two were ten times as good as one.

Ryan blinked again, reaching to rub at his good eye. He pressed hard with his palm, expecting to see a dazzling array of silver-and-gold sparks flash-ing across the retina. But there was nothing. No re-action.

Just all-over sable.

It felt like he was losing it; his senses were be-traying him. Now the pain in his stomach was burn-ing hot, making him cry out in shock. The steady dribble of blood from the wound was bitterly cold, making it difficult for him to lift and lower his feet.

But when he did, it was like walking across an

infinite pavement of human eyeballs that squished and rolled under the soles of the boots, making him lose his balance.

When Ryan brushed against the invisible wall, it wasn't hard stone like it had been before. Now it was just like plunging his fingers into the rotting body of a flayed corpse. He had the horrible sensation of hundreds of blind maggots, writhing in both hands.

"Ryan?"

The word sounded so far away.

The dizziness swept over him like a great wave of nausea, bringing him again to his knees.

"Come on, Ryan."

He couldn't form the words of a reply.

"Ryan Cawdor?"

His mouth was dust dry, and when he tried to speak, there was no sound, not even the faint mewing of a drowning, newborn kitten.

Doom.

The single word pounded in his brain, like the beating of a slack-skinned drum, heard shimmering through the heat haze of a luxurious summer meadow.

"Ryan!"

It was louder, meaning that he was going to have to open his eye again, which didn't seem like the best idea in the world. It would be uncomfortable and painful.

Better by far to sleep and die.

"Give...drink...."

Cool liquid flowed into his mouth, over his swollen tongue and into his parched throat.

"Good," he mumbled.

The other voice said, "What'd he say?"

Another man, whose voice was vaguely familiar, replied, "Said it was good, Brother. Shall I give him more?"

"No. Sit him up. Slap his face if he won't come around. Need him awake."

A blow jolted Ryan's cheek, making the vertigo worse.

"Open your eye, Ryan."

"Soon."

"Not soon. Now."

"Others are coming around. Except old man and the albino kid. Both flaked out."

"Kid had two helpings of the soup, and the old-timer's got Sierra flu. Drug was bound to work a deal harder on him than on the others."

Ryan knew that he was learning something important, something that he somehow already knew.

"Odd flavor," he said.

The men laughed. "Bet it did, Brother Cawdor. Not odd enough to stop you pigging at it."

"Drugged." That was it. That was the missing shape in the puzzle.

"Did he say something about the soup being drugged?" There was more laughter. Ryan felt his whole body moving, as though someone were rocking the bed he lay on.

"Drugged me." He heard his own voice, now louder and much clearer.

"Right. Now it's time you got yourself up and walking good, Brother Cawdor."

The words came from Joshua Wolfe, leader of the ville. Ryan took a deep breath, allowing his right hand to wander under the pillow, feeling for the familiar butt of the SIG-Sauer, ready to wipe away the smiles and laughter.

"Don't think so, outlander." Jim Owsley sneered at him.

Wolfe spoke again, insistent. "We've waited enough. Open your eye and get up. There's much to talk about before you and your colleagues entertain us at the testing."

Ryan opened his eye, feeling an instant tsunami of sickness washing around his skull.

All he knew was that they'd been tricked by the Children of the Rock. All of their weapons had been stolen, and there was this repeated talk of the testing.

It was time to fight back against the drugs they'd been given. Now.

Chapter Twenty-Five

The tiny flickering digital numerals showed Ryan that it was seven minutes from noon.

He was sitting cross-legged on his own bed, holding his aching head in his hands. Sunlight shone through the narrow gap where the door of their hut stood ajar. The air was heavily scented with the fragrance of the surrounding pines, freshened by the heavy rain of the previous night.

To his right, Krysty was also sitting up, her hands laid flat on her thighs. Her emerald eyes were closed, and her sentient red hair was coiled protectively about her nape. She was meditating, calling silently on the powers of the Earth Mother to help them out of this deep, deep hole.

J.B. stood, looking out of the window of the cabin, Mildred at his side, running her fingers through her beaded hair. Neither of them had spoken much in the past hour or so, locked into their own thoughts.

Ryan noticed that Mildred was holding J.B.'s hand.

Jak rested on the floor in a corner of the room, staring at the hewed logs of the wall.

Dean sat on his bed, quietly staring at the ceiling, completely still.

Doc lay on his back, blankets pulled up to his stubbled chin, eyes closed. He was breathing slowly and heavily, with a faint, whispering croak at the end of each intake. From where he was sitting, Ryan could make out the sheen of perspiration that dappled the old man's pallid forehead.

The main thing that had struck Ryan on his recovery was that all of their weapons were gone—all of them, including the panga.

"They get all your knives, Jak?" Ryan asked quietly.

The white head shook slowly. "Some," was the whispered response. "Not all."

That was something.

"Doc's Le Mat's gone, as well," Krysty said. "And his trusty sword."

"Why fuck done this to us? All fucking words friendly shit! What's game?" Jak asked.

A shadow filled the doorway, and the answering voice came from Brother Joshua Wolfe.

"No game. Oh my, not at all a game! We are being careful, young man. I learned from your wonderful and wise Trader that a man who takes a chance that he doesn't have to take, doesn't often live long enough to take any further chances. Well, something a lot like that."

"What's the danger? If we wanted to cause you trouble, then we could have done that from line one, page one. We had all of the firepower we needed." Ryan closed his eye at a shaft of pain from his headache. "Like Jak says, all your words were just a load of bullshit."

"Possible."

Ryan raised his voice, feeling the red mist of anger swooping over his mind. "Probable!"

The leader of the community wasn't in the mood to be provoked. He shook his head and smiled. "Patience and forgiveness are great virtues, Brother Ryan."

"You drugged us and stole our weapons."

"But of course. Did you believe that it was the fairies and elves of the great trees that had crept in while you slumbered and took your blasters? Goblins and gnomes of the high mountains and the rushiest of glens? No, I rather think not, Brother."

"Cut the crap." Ryan got up off the bed, managing to conceal his dizziness. "What about the testing you talked about? That still on?"

Owsley was at Wolfe's elbow, and he laughed, an unpleasant, abrasive noise, like sandpaper drawn over the edge of a piece of crystal.

"Course it's on, outlander. That's just what all of this is about."

"Drug us and take our weapons? Why not just chill us all?"

Wolfe smiled gently. "That is not the way of Our Lord, the military fundamentalist. We have simply taken precautions. Made sure the testing will go well. And fairly."

"Fairly?" It was Ryan's turn to smile cynically. "Not a word I'd link to you, Brother Wolfe."

"Then you would be wrong, Brother Cawdor. Hopeville is built upon the strong foundation of fairness."

"Hallelujah, brothers and sisters." The cry came from the large woman, who clapped her meaty hands together with a noise like distant thunder. Krysty looked across at her, and was surprised at the glance of bitter hatred that she received in return. The woman spit in the dirt to show her contempt.

"We shall all eat at God's own table," Wolfe said, lifting his hand to silence the people around him. "A time to remember things past and to look forward to things that are soon to come. Let us go dine."

JOSIAH STEELE WAS TRYING to explain the purpose of the testing to the six outlanders. Doc was still very unwell, with a scorchingly high temperature, and Mildred had insisted that the old man had to stay warm and snug in his bed, with plenty to drink to fight off the real dangers of dehydration.

"Everyone who comes here has to prove themselves worthy of acceptance to the Children of the Rock. That's why we all have had to face the testing."

"What if a woman arrived with half a dozen little children?" Krysty asked.

Steele hesitated. "Guess that the rules can always be bent some."

"But not for us," Ryan stated, munching away at a crusty bread roll. "One child doesn't count."

"Guess not. Seems there's too many aces on the line between you and Brother Wolfe." Steele helped himself from a small iron caldron of thick pork-and-lentil soup. "Too many rivers for you both to cross."

The food was very good, satisfying to the palate and rich, well flavored, without the oppressive bitterness of the previous evening's meal. Also, Ryan had watched carefully, taking the precaution of checking that he and the others ate out of the same cooking pots that the members of the Children of the Rock had dined from.

Mildred slipped away to go back to their cabin and check on Doc's progress, returning with a worried look on her face. She squatted alongside Ryan, putting her mouth close to his ear, speaking fast and low.

"I think he's about at his worst," she said. "At least that's what I hope. Temperature's sky-high, but his heart and respiration are steady."

"Conscious?"

She pulled a doubtful face. "Sort of."

"Recognize you?"

"I think so. But he's away on the far side of knowing where he is and what's going on."

"At least they won't be making the old buzzard take part in this stupe testing."

Mildred nodded. "No, I guess not."

THE MEAL WAS SOON OVER, the dishes taken away by the women, the scraps devoured by the lean mongrels that scavenged around the ville.

"Testing time is nearly upon us, my beloved brothers and sisters." After a significant pause, the leader of Hopeville added, "And outlanders."

There was a hum of excitement around the open area that had the central fire at its heart. It seemed like the whole settlement was there, with the sec men all armed with their Hawes Montana Marshal revolvers, many of them also hefting their Winchester rifles.

Ryan suspected that the display of arms was for their benefit, not to hold off any potential attack by the Apaches who lived among the trees.

He stood and stretched, savoring the powerful scent of the surrounding pines. "We're ready as we can be, Brother Wolfe," he said.

"Then let's get at it."

RYAN AND THE OTHERS stood together near the smoldering fire, feeling oddly naked without their weapons.

After the meal they'd been allowed to go back to their log cabin to clean up and get ready for the afternoon. And while there, they'd had a short but bitter conversation about what they should do.

J.B., allied to Mildred, had urged very strongly that they should cut their losses and run for it.

"Leave the blasters?" Ryan had asked in disbelief.

"Why not? Dark night, Ryan! We can always replace the weapons. Much as it hurts me. But I'm real triple unhappy about the setup here."

"I'm not delighted with it, friend. I'm not comfortable when anyone takes away my blasters. But it seems best to just go along with the flow."

"We can jump a guard or two. Grab their blasters. Try and retrieve our own weapons and blades and be out of here. All in ten minutes flat.'' He replaced his fedora. ''Less.''

Ryan shook his head against the idea. ''Haven't thought it through, J.B. Close on a hundred souls here in Hopeville. All the men are bristling with blasters, thicker than fleas on the back of a hog. No chance.''

''But it could be a trick.''

''They had us all out cold. Drugged and helpless. All they did was take our weapons off us. It would have been child's play to butcher us there and then. One dull-edged knife and seven slit throats. If that was what they wanted to do. I don't see that as Wolfe's plan.'' He paused and stared at the others. ''But if anyone else has a different view on this, let's hear it.'' He waited, but nobody spoke. ''Krysty? You got any sort of a feeling about what's going down?''

''Not really, lover. Can't say I like it.''

Ryan became angry. ''I don't bastard like it, either. Thought I'd said that. Talking to my fucking self! But you have to look at the way the dice lie.''

''The lice die,'' Doc muttered from his crumpled bed. ''Fly like a flea or flee like a fly. If I fly like a flea, then you won't catch me.''

Everybody ignored him.

After a few more bitter exchanges between Ryan and J.B., they all agreed to go for the testing and give it their best shot. And then see, that evening, how things looked.

WOLFE SLAPPED his good hand against his thigh, calling out for quiet. "Now we can begin," he said, voice ringing out among the scattered buildings. "Will the outlanders all stand before us now?"

Ryan took Krysty by the hand, leading the others into the center of the ragged circle of men and women.

"Tell us all your names and where you come from," Wolfe commanded.

"Name's Ryan Cawdor. From the ville of Front Royal, up in the Shens. This is my son, Dean." Dean stepped forward.

"I'm Krysty Wroth and I come from the ville of Harmony."

"Jak Lauren. West Lowellton."

"Where's that?" someone yelled. Ryan suspected that it was the giantess.

"Near Lafayette, Louisiana."

"Swampie," shouted a man's voice, reedy and thin. "Look at his hair. Mutie and a swampie!"

Jak ignored him, though Ryan saw the teenager's knuckles whitening.

"I'm John Dix, originally from Cripple Creek. Since then I've been all over Deathlands."

"And my name is Mildred Winona Wyeth. Father was a preacher man. I was born in Lincoln, Nebraska."

"How about the old man?" Jim Owsley shouted.

"Doc's ill," he replied.

"Doesn't signify. Need to know who he is and where he comes from."

Krysty patted Ryan on the arm and replied to the

questioner. "Dr. Theophilus Algernon Tanner. Degree in science from Harvard and in philosophy from Oxford in England. Comes from the ville of South Strafford up in the green hills of Vermont. Anything else you want to know?" she asked, challenging Owsley with her flashing, bright emerald eyes. The sec man looked down at his feet and wouldn't meet her stare.

Wolfe laughed, a natural, friendly country laugh that set Ryan's teeth on edge. "Well, I guess we know about all we need to know about these folks. Nothing out on the surface to stop them being accepted by us here in Hopeville. So, we rest things in the hands of the Blessed Lord Jesus. He can decide if they are meet to join us as Children of the Rock."

There was a moment of stillness, broken by the sound, drifting through the open door of the cabin, of Doc having one of his rending fits of coughing.

Joshua Wolfe addressed himself once more to the group of outlanders, his hand resting on the pearlized grips of the big revolver.

"The testing is carried out alone, one of you against the best we have to offer in the ville. The choice of combat is yours. Who goes first?"

"Combat?" Ryan repeated.

Chapter Twenty-Six

"Combat," Wolfe stated.

Ryan felt the short hairs prickling at his nape. Combat! Their best against the best from the Children of the Rock. "Who goes first?"

"Up to you, Brother Cawdor."

Ryan had been about to step forward himself, when he was beaten to it.

"Me," said a familiar female voice at his elbow, which brought a stir from the crowd.

Mildred smiled at J.B. and kissed him lightly on the cheek. "Don't worry," she said.

"You want to go first, lady?" Wolfe asked, his face splitting into a broad smile.

"Yeah, I do."

"Very well. But what kind of weapon do you choose to use here?"

"Can I have my blaster back for the testing? Is that permitted?" Mildred asked.

"Surely. You want to shoot against our best man? Or woman?"

"Man. Who claims to be the finest sharpshooter in Hopeville?" Mildred challenged.

There was a confused hubbub, with several names being put forward. But gradually Ryan was aware that a single name was being repeated.

Wolfe heard it, as well, keeping a thin smile pasted in place. "Sounds like Brother Carlo Caitlin. Step forward, Brother Caitlin. Will you accept this woman's challenge?"

Caitlin looked to be around thirty, with long, light brown, shoulder-length hair. Ryan noticed that both his hands lacked any fingernails, and the skin around his mouth was puckered with old scarring.

He smirked as he moved forward out of the crowd with a slight swagger. A .44-caliber Winchester 94 slung over his shoulder, with a telescopic sight fixed to the barrel that Ryan didn't recognize.

"Take her on anytime. Not like a real testing, Brother Wolfe. Shootin' against a woman."

Mildred addressed the leader of the ville. "I can definitely use my own blaster? Check the load myself, have a little time to go over it, sight it in? No weasel-word trickery?"

"Surely. The lord of all armaments will pronounce the verdict for us."

Caitlin was already becoming irritated. "Time's wasting, brothers and sisters. I say we set to it here and now. Why not, in the name of gentle Jesus?"

"Get her blaster, Brother Steele," Wolfe said, keeping his patient smile pasted firmly in place. "I imagine that Brother Dix might wish to go over it out with you, Sister Wyeth. You may have fifteen minutes from now."

"IT'S FINE," the Armorer said, quickly and neatly clicking the weapon back together, having given it a lightning field-strip and clean. He wiped a layer of thin gun oil off his fingers with a length of cotton rag.

Mildred took it, automatically checking the load, feeling the familiar balance as she weighed it in her right hand. "Wonder what they'll want us to shoot against."

"That man Caitlin," Krysty said, lip curling in disgust, "had a beady little red eye like a rabid ferret. Looks to me just like a classic redneck shootist. Put one through the belly and leave it to suffer."

"You happy with your blaster against his long gun?" Jak asked.

"Guess so. Unless they set up the match at a half mile or over. Then I'd struggle."

"Be little point in this testing they have if it was all a cheat," Ryan said, hearing the layer of doubt that hung there in his voice.

"STANDARD MATCH TARGET of nine inches across, graded in regular circles from ten through to one point. Shoot just four rounds at each distance, beginning at twenty-five yards, then fifty, then one hundred. Finally at two hundred paces."

"Long range for a big pistol," said a voice from the watching crowd.

Wolfe half turned. "Anyone object to it? How about you, Sister Mildred?"

The woman shrugged, the beads in her hair tinkling softly. "Doesn't matter to me," she said.

Mildred walked calmly to the mark scratched in the dirt at the end of the ville's main street. The heavy Czech revolver was at her side, her thumb already on the short-fall cocking hammer.

The targets had already been nailed to pine trees, one above the other, out at the agreed distances. Brother Wolfe called out that the outlander would aim at the higher target and Caitlin at the lower. "We'll spin a silver coin for the right to shoot first or second."

"Heads," Caitlin called as the glittering coin whirled in the air.

Wolfe neatly caught the coin, peered at it and then quickly pocketed it. "Heads it is," he called loudly.

Ryan glanced at Mildred, questioning whether she wanted to object to the blatantly unfair tossing. But she simply shook her head.

"I'll go first," Caitlin said, readying himself on the mark, slowly bringing the rifle up to his right shoulder, squinting two-eyed along the barrel.

The big .44-caliber blaster was as steady as a rock. The man licked his lips and held his breath, finger creeping onto the spur trigger.

"Open fire at will, Brother Caitlin," Wolfe said quietly. "And may Blessed Jesus the marksman guide your bullets to their target."

The crack of the Winchester was flat, the echo of the shot instantly swallowed up by the vastness of the surrounding forest.

A tall man, as skinny as a lath, stood at a safe distance from the target, holding a tiny brass folding telescope that looked like it dated back into the

1800s. He raised it to his left eye, hesitated a moment, fiddling with the delicate adjustment.

"Looks like a ten."

Caitlin fired again. Again a ten.

The third and fourth shots were also dead-center bull's-eye, bringing a round of hearty applause from the watching Children of the Rock.

"Forty from forty," Wolfe announced. "The saints be praised, Brother Caitlin. Your turn now, Sister. You may shoot at will."

Mildred stood sideways on, her whole body relaxed. Ryan knew that the woman's skill with her revolver was unparalleled. It was the sort of skill that had died out after the long winters. He had no doubt that she could outshoot anyone he'd ever seen in all Deathlands.

Caitlin was better than adequate with his rifle, but so he should be at only twenty-five paces.

Mildred aimed and fired quickly, all four shots seeming to run into one another, giving an odd quadruple echo that quickly faded into silence.

The elder with the scope took some time. "Looks like all four through the same hole," he called, bringing a buzz of excitement from the spectators.

"Good shooting, Mildred," Dean shouted, clapping his hands and jumping up and down excitedly.

"Fish in a barrel," she snorted.

Both of them scored maximums at fifty yards.

Attention shifted to the hundred-yard target, a tiny square of white pinned to a ponderosa.

Caitlin hawked and gobbed, the greenish lump of

spittle striking a stunted larch to his right, dangling there, catching the sunlight.

"Me first, I reckon," he muttered. Ryan had always been a keen student of body language, and he noticed that something of the spring had gone from the shootist's step. He moved a little more slowly, as if his confidence had been eroded by Mildred's performance so far.

He was firing more slowly at each distance, taking around fifteen seconds at the hundred-yard marker, giving the skinny man time to check each shot.

"Ten."

Applause.

"Ten again, Brother Caitlin."

More applause from the Children of the Rock. Mildred watched impassively.

There was a long delay. "Nine."

"What?"

"Sorry, Brother. Clipped the line between eight and nine, but I call it a clear nine."

The last shot hit the bull's-eye again, giving him 119 out of a possible 120. It was pretty fair shooting, though Ryan reckoned that he could have probably matched it himself.

Mildred stepped up, quickly and easily scoring bull's-eyes with her four shots.

"On to the last set of markers," Wolfe announced, pointing into the distance, at two hundred paces, where the target seemed almost invisible.

"Sweating," Jak whispered to Ryan.

The teenager was right. A thin sheen of perspiration lined Caitlin's forehead, trickling down the side of his nose onto the stubbled chin.

"When you're ready, Brother," Wolfe said, holding up his good hand for quiet.

"I'm ready."

"Nine."

A hum of excitement ran through the crowd.

"Take your time," Wolfe urged, biting his lip anxiously. "Just take all the time you need."

"Puts more pressure on the son of a bitch," J.B. said quietly.

They heard the crack of the rifle, and the faint hum of the .44 round as it sliced through the pine-scented sunlight between the tall trees.

Another long pause.

"Eight."

Caitlin muttered a colorful curse under his breath. He walked around his mark in a small circle, kicking his heels into the damp ground.

"Two more shots left," Wolfe said encouragingly. "Make them count, Brother."

The barrel of the rifle was visibly trembling as the man took aim for the penultimate time. With an effort he lowered it, wiping sweat from his forehead. He sighted again, squeezing the trigger, the Winchester 94 kicking against his shoulder.

"Four."

"You sure about that, Brother?" Wolfe shouted, his voice rising above the gasp of dismay.

"Fear so. Aye, fear so. Just a four. One round remaining. Brother Caitlin's score stands at..."

There was a moment's hesitation for the mathematics. "From one hundred and fifty, his score is 144."

"One hundred and forty," the Armorer called without a moment's pause.

"No." Wolfe stared at the man with the telescope. "Check your numbering, Brother."

"It's 140," Krysty agreed. "Missed one point up to this last round of shots. And he scored a nine and an eight and the last four. That's nine. Plus one makes ten. One hundred and forty even."

Nobody argued.

"Woman won't hit fuck-all at this range with her toy!" yelled a man from the back of the crowd. "Nothing to worry about, Carlo."

He scored a seven with his last round, making 147 out of 160.

Mildred hadn't missed a single shot yet, putting them all into the center of her target with a monotonous regularity. Now she stood there on the mark, calm and unflurried, the light wind tugging at her beaded hair, the long-barreled Czech revolver seeming an extension of her body.

"Ten."

That gave her 130 out of 130, meaning she needed only seventeen from the last thirty to win.

There was a tense silence, broken by Wolfe dropping his own hand-blaster onto the dirt with a sudden, loud clatter that made everyone jump. The interruption coincided perfectly with Mildred's fourteenth shot.

"Bastard!" Jak spit.

"Sorry," Wolfe muttered. "Slipped."

"How many?" Mildred asked, the most serene person there.

"Take that again," Ryan said.

But the woman only smiled back at him. "No worries, friend."

"Nine," said the marker.

Eight to tie from the last two shots, and nine to win it.

Everyone's attention was focused on the minuscule square of white card. Ignoring the excitement, a tiny copper-winged scarab moth had landed on a branch just above the mark, its poisonous tendrils tasting the air.

Mildred aimed and fired.

"Miss," brayed the man with the scope too eagerly. "Yeah, a miss."

"I want..." Ryan began, stopping at the collective sigh of wonder as the venomous little insect fluttered lifelessly to lie pulped on the ground below.

Mildred fired her last shot without even seeming to sight, instantly starting to reload her blaster, not paying any attention to the marker's call.

"How many?" Wolfe yelled. "Did she miss the target again? Did she?"

"Ten," Mildred said very quietly.

"Ten," the skinny man echoed. "She scored a ten with her last shot. Woman wins."

Caitlin spun on his heel and stalked off, ignoring Mildred's outstretched hand.

Wolfe raised his voice above the hubbub. "Outlander wins the first part of the testing. No quarrels with that. Finest shooting I ever saw. Now we move on to the second part. Not over yet.''

He turned to Ryan. "I say that it's not over yet.''

Chapter Twenty-Seven

Jak was next for the testing.

He and Ryan had discussed what weapon the albino teenager should choose. The youth's first instinct was to go for his beloved throwing knives. Ryan had seen him in action with them often enough to know that nobody in Deathlands could touch his uncanny skill.

"But they don't know you got them, Jak. Still got any of the knives?"

"What?"

"They got all our weapons off us. But you said you still got two or three blades concealed, didn't you?"

"Yeah."

"So? Best to keep them hidden, don't you reckon? We don't have many surprises going for us on our side."

"Could ask for one blade they took."

"Yeah." Ryan considered that possibility. "But how about if you choose hand-to-hand?"

Jak's red eyes glinted at the idea. "Like it, Ryan. Show them fucking testing."

"Then that's decided."

THE CHOICE THREW Wolfe and the senior members of the religious community.

"Not proper testing," Jim Owsley complained in his customary whining voice.

"Don't see why not," Josiah Steele argued. "It's a genuine skill."

Wolfe nodded his reluctant agreement. "Guess that's so, Brother."

Caitlin had rejoined the group. "Probably some sort of trick. Like that bitch with her freaky-deaky blaster! A cheat."

One of the older men laughed out loud. "Not sure that bein' a better shot is cheatin', Brother Caitlin. Not by any of the Lord Jesus's definitions. I vote we let the kid try his hand at close combat."

There was a general agreement.

But a fresh problem sprang up as soon as they tried to select who their champion would be in the testing against Jak.

Ryan and the others watched as a bitter argument developed among the Children of the Rock. It came down quickly to a straight choice between a pair of siblings—Bull Burrows and his almost identical brother, Lee.

Both were big men, weighing in, Ryan guessed, close to three hundred pounds, with hands like platters of raw ham. Both had lost all of their teeth, with bleeding gums, probably owing to the rad sickness. Both were in their middle twenties, close to six and a half feet tall, with long, greasy hair that was flaking away from their narrow skulls in places.

"I can lick my little brother, Lee, blindfolded," Bull Burrows protested.

"That'll be the day, pilgrim," mocked the younger of the pair. "Not, not, not!"

"Make them tussle to pick a winner to lick the whitey kid," someone shouted.

"Let the outlander pick which one he wants to whale the tar out of him!" was another suggestion, which seemed to be greeted with general approval.

"Sounds fair," Joshua Wolfe said, turning toward the silent, watching youth. "How do you feel about making the choice yourself, sonny boy?"

"Both," Jak said flatly, the single word lying there like a shovelful of graveyard dirt.

"Both?" Wolfe repeated, shaking his head as though he'd misheard. "You say that you'll take both the Burrows boys on? One after the other?"

"Both at once," Jak said.

RYAN COULD HAVE written the script for the coming hand-to-hand conflict, and he'd have been pretty close to the final, predictable outcome. J.B. could have done the same.

Just as Mildred was, possibly, the finest shot in the whole of Deathlands, so Jak was very probably the finest exponent of hand-to-hand lethal fighting that Ryan had ever known.

His lean 120-pound body was almost unbelievably agile, his fighting reflexes acutely honed, like a fine, ivory-hilted cutthroat razor.

"Won't last more than a short minute," Ryan whispered across to Krysty.

Jim Owsley overheard him and gave out a raucous, bellowing laugh of derision. "Right there, outlander. Inside a minute and the kid'll be dead meat.''

Ryan didn't bother to reply. He knew what he knew, and it wouldn't be long before Jak proved him right.

To an outsider the fight looked absurdly unbalanced and unfair.

Two huge men were stripped to the waist, in belted jeans and knee-high boots. Their hairless bodies showed signs of running to fat, with a number of deep purple, weeping sores dappling them, but their jowled faces were wreathed in eager, anticipatory leering grins, and they were flexing their massive hands as they both dropped into a half crouch.

Jak, facing them, looked like a starving waif. He had taken off his canvas camouflage jacket and chose to fight in his ragged, short-sleeved, gray fur jacket.

Even Joshua Wolfe looked uncomfortable, glancing at Ryan. ''You sure about this?''

''Sure.''

''Well, may the Lord Jesus, Blessed Savior of the merciful stranglehold and the knee-drop pick the winners of this combat. Go to it, boys.''

Bull and Lee weren't particularly triple stupes. It was just that they hadn't traveled all that much around Deathlands and had little experience of serious fighting outside their secluded enclave. It was easy enough to beat the crap out of some of the younger men living in the ville, and the fragile youth with the mane of tumbling white hair had to be just there for the taking.

And the first few seconds of the "fight" confirmed what nearly everyone expected.

The moment the word was given by Brother Wolfe, Jak turned away and ran from the two hulking men, his feet barely seeming to brush the earth as he glanced back over his shoulder to see if he was being pursued.

He was, the brothers splitting up and readying themselves to close in slowly on him from both sides.

"Yo, catch him!"

"Stop runnin' and turn and fight, kid!"

"Shoot him if he tries to break out of the ville," Wolfe ordered.

Jak opened up a gap of about forty yards, stopping before he reached the edge of the settlement. He paused for a moment, facing the heavily built pair of brothers, his arms dangling loosely at his sides.

Lee and Bull paused in their pursuit, grinning at each other, fingers clasping and unclasping. Ryan could smell the rancid odor of their sweat from where he watched.

"Nigh on a half minute already, outlander," Jim Owsley said with a sneer.

Ryan said nothing.

Jak gave the brothers a mocking half bow, then exploded into movement, powering across the clearing toward them, his legs a blur of white speed.

Suddenly he changed direction, reversing his attack, going into a series of snapping back handsprings.

"Look out!" Joshua Wolfe called, but his warning was drowned out by the roar of the spectators.

Jak was so much faster than the Burrows boys that neither of them managed to lay a hand on him. He whipped between them at extraordinary speed, and everyone heard a double cracking sound, like two dry branches being crushed at once.

Very few people had good enough eyesight to make out precisely what had happened. All most of them heard was the snapping noise, followed immediately by a double scream, high and thin like a boar being gelded.

Lee and Bull Burrows were down in the dirt, both clutching at their knees.

They rolled over and over, their faces contorted with a twin rictus of rending agony, a feeble, mewing cry erupting from their bloodied lips, eyes squeezed shut.

"Did he...?" Mildred said wonderingly. "Damned if I could make out how he did that."

"Kicked out both sides as he went past them," J.B. grunted, clapping his hands approvingly. "Hit them smack on and smashed their knee joints apart."

"Jesus!" Owsley breathed. "That ain't..." He let the sentence trail away into the sudden stillness.

Jak had done a final double somersault, landing agilely on both feet, perfectly balanced, hands still at his sides. His chest was barely moving.

"Finished?" he called, not even a little out of breath.

"You finished them both, kid," came a voice from the crowd.

Wolfe swallowed hard, clearing his throat. "Help them up and take them away," he ordered.

"Two to us," the Armorer said, taking off his fedora to wipe his forehead. "Sure you want to keep this going, Brother Wolfe? Can you afford to lose good men?"

"Who goes next?" Ryan asked. "How about me or J.B. taking our turn?"

For once the leader of Hopeville seemed to be quite lost for words.

"How about me takin' on the redhead slut? Yeah, me, Sister Sprite."

It was the giantess, her voice as deep as a thundering torrent through an abyss.

She pushed to the front of the crowd, standing with her hands on her broad hips, staring aggressively at Krysty, her face contorted with a violent hatred. She wore a cropped, short-sleeved white blouse of bleached leather over torn and faded ancient denim cutoffs, leaving a gap that revealed her belly button, sticking out like a chameleon's eye.

Her hair was hacked short, teased into sharp spikes. The wide leather belt carried a knife nearly as long and broad as Ryan's panga.

At a guess he put her at just over six-three and way above the 250-pound mark. And there didn't look to be an ounce of fat on her body.

"Well now, Sister Sprite," Wolfe began doubtfully, "I don't know if—"

"Fuck you and the wag you ride on, Brother Wolfe! I don't see anyone here, woman or weakling, who's going to stand agin me on this."

Ryan glanced at Krysty out of the corner of his good eye, looking for some reaction. But she was totally still and impassive, arms folded across her chest, eyes half-closed against the bright sunlight.

"Sister Sprite challenges the outlander woman, Sister Krysty Wroth, to a testing, as under the laws and gospels proscribed by the Children of the Rock."

"What weapon?" Krysty asked quietly.

Behind Ryan, somewhere deep within the mighty pine forest, a flock of crows rose squawking into the sunlit air, circling around, their black shadows etched on the cerulean blue of the sky. He half turned, wondering what might have startled the birds, watching them as they weaved around one another before, at a soundless signal, they flew off southward.

He was distracted by the crows from what was happening right at his side.

"What weapon you like? Blaster or blade? Best would be to get my fingers round that scrawny neck and choke the fucking life from it. Watch your tongue swell, purple, and your green cat's eyes pop out their sockets like the knobs on a mission-hall harmonium."

"Not hand-to-hand, lover," Ryan whispered to Krysty. "She looks to be—"

She turned and laid a hand on his arm, as gentle as the brushing of a butterfly's wing. "What has to be, has to be, lover," she said so quietly that nobody else heard her.

"You see this?"

"Yes. I see this, lover. Like I've known this moment for all of my life. Seen this woman. These trees. These people. Yeah, I know them all."

Ryan felt the chill of layered ice, gripping around his heart, seeming to paralyze him. There was a grim note of doom in Krysty's voice that he'd never heard before in all the time that they'd ridden together.

"No," he said, so hushed that he couldn't even hear himself speaking.

"You ready for this, Sister?" The aggressive, grating voice was like a ragged fingernail in the eye socket.

"Guess so."

Maybe if they all acted together they could grab some weapons from the watching sec men, taking advantage of their fascination with what was going down in front of them, open fire into the heart of the crowd and hope to be able to make a run for it amid the panic and bloody confusion.

In the stillness he suddenly heard the sound of violent, muffled coughing, as Doc, in the cabin, had another of his bad turns.

They couldn't try any sort of an escape with Doc, not in his present sickly health, and they surely couldn't run for safety without him.

The bones had to lie where they fell.

Krysty was speaking, her words sounding like they came from an infinite way off.

"I'll do what you want, Sister Sprite. And all the gods, yours and mine, can decide who has the right."

"To the death," the huge woman shouted.

Krysty nodded. "If that's what you wish."

Ryan knew that this was terminally serious, and that he should try to stop the fight.

But Krysty's hand was still on his arm, the touch of her flesh on his warm and reassuring.

Reading his thoughts, she half smiled into his face. "No, lover," she breathed. "Not this time."

Chapter Twenty-Eight

It wasn't like it had been with Jak and the Burrows boys.

Ryan would have wagered a panful of jack against a dead skunk that the teenager would easily take out the two bulky, muscle-bound good old boys. And he'd have accepted odds of fifty to one for Jak.

This was something else.

The big woman emanated a genuine aura of power and midnight evil.

The name of Sprite conjured up a picture of someone light, blond, blue eyed and delicate, small boned and skinny with flounced hair and a rose pink complexion.

Sister Sprite, Hopeville's finest, was the exact antithesis of that.

Ryan was as good a judge as existed in Deathlands of someone's fighting potential. It wasn't necessarily the biggest and strongest that won the day. Jak's lethal performance against the gigantic Burrows boys had shown that only too clearly. But Sister Sprite was something else.

Her whole body breathed violence, and her small piggy eyes flared with the desire to torture and murder. Her strong, stubby fingers, with chipped and jagged nails, clenched and unclenched as she waited for Wolfe to give the signal of approval for the testing with Krysty to begin.

"Come on," she grated impatiently.

Ryan tried one last time, touching the redheaded woman on the arm, but she shook her head and pulled away. "No, lover," she said firmly.

"Combat between Sister Sprite and the outlander woman, known as Krysty Wroth. No blasters or blades to be used. Anything else allowed. That includes kicking and gouging, hair pulling and thumb twisting. May the blessed apostles all watch and lend their support for a clean fight. With the right to lie, as always, with the winner. Ready?"

Krysty nodded solemnly. "Ready."

Sister Sprite spit in the dirt, rubbing her booted feet back and forth to ensure a good grip. "Yeah, I'm fuckin' ready."

"Then get to it. No quarter to be asked or given. To the death."

Sister Sprite didn't come rushing in, charging in a clumsy manner at the slighter build of Krysty Wroth. She edged in toward her adversary, her arms held loosely at her waist, ready to grip or to counter.

The shouting was all for the big woman, though Ryan led a countercheer from J.B., Mildred, Dean and Jak.

Sister Sprite spit again. "Come on, you ginger bitch! Come to Momma."

Krysty saved her breath, circling counterclockwise, keeping out of reach of Sister Sprite. She was so much outweighed that she knew to try to fight at close quarters could, literally, prove fatal.

The champion of Hopeville made several feints at Krysty in the first few minutes of the mortal combat, once nearly managing to grab her slender wrist and draw her into her embrace.

Ryan's heart leaped to his throat, his breath whistling between his parted lips at the narrow escape.

"Keep off her, lover," he shouted.

"Mind your own business," Jim Owsley yelled, fingering the butt of his Hawes Montana Marshal blaster.

Krysty tried an attack of her own, feinting to lunge, straight armed, stiff fingered, at Sprite's face, altering the angle at the last nanosecond to try to kick at the woman's knees. But Sprite laughed mockingly at her attempt, moving easily out of range, like a huge cat, perfectly balanced.

"So far, so bad," the Armorer muttered.

It was difficult to see how Krysty was going to beat her larger, stronger opponent.

In the front row a skinny young guy, with a heavy mustache, wearing the tall white hat of a chef, called out in support of Krysty, but was instantly hushed by all his neighbors.

Sprite pretended to stumble, landing on hands and knees in the piled leaf mold close to the footpath through the ville, waiting a moment and shaking her head as if stunned. Ryan was about to shout a warning, but it wasn't necessary. Krysty wasn't a person to let herself get faked out just like that.

She backed away, half turning to grin reassuringly across at Ryan.

And Sprite struck.

The breath died in Ryan's chest, and his good eye blinked shut in a reflex of utter dismay.

Nobody that big, especially a woman, had the right to be that fast.

As she straightened, Sprite had thrown two handfuls of the powdery leaf mold, mixed with sharp pine needles, directly into Krysty's face, following it up with the frightening speed of a charging buffalo.

Krysty staggering backward, stumbling clumsily, hands trying to clear her blinded eyes, opening and closing them to try to see through the sudden flood of tears.

Too late and way too slow.

Sprite was on top of her, screaming with a fervid delight, clasping her muscular arms around Krysty's chest, crushing her to her own body as both women fell to the earth. There was a dull thud as Krysty's skull hit the dirt, followed almost simultaneously by a sickening crack as Sprite drove her forehead into her face. Blood gushed from Krysty's nose and cut mouth, and she lay still and helpless.

"Chilled, bitch!"

Sprite straddled the inert body, her knees gripping Krysty's chest, holding her motionless, while the woman's big butcher's hands grappled for a hold on her throat.

There was a collective sigh of delight from the watching Children of the Rock. Out of the corner of his eye, Ryan noticed that Jim Owsley's right hand was caressing the tight front of his jeans and his mouth sagged open with a morbid, obscene delight at the killing spectacle.

"Krysty!" Ryan yelled, his voice cracking. He took a step forward, stopping as he felt the sharpness of the barrel of a pistol jammed into his spine, not even seeing who held it. He was aware that several of the ville's sec men had leveled their revolvers and rifles at the outlanders, preventing the possibility of interference from any of them.

"Watch and enjoy," Wolfe whispered to Ryan. "Payment of debts."

Sprite grinned at her shrieking supporters, showing her broken, stained teeth. She leaned forward, putting all her weight into the strangulation, her fingers digging into the soft flesh of Krysty's neck.

Krysty thrashed her head from side to side, her emerald eyes staring wide, white rimmed, threaded with blood. Her mouth was open, rasping breath struggling for release, her tongue protruding and purpled.

Brother Wolfe was rocking back and forth, his hand on the butt of his blaster, grinning broadly, his eyes locked to Ryan's face.

"Yes, Brother Cawdor," he crowed. "A dish best eaten cold, wouldn't you say?"

Ryan didn't say anything. If there hadn't been so many blasters trained on him and his friends, he would have made a grab for Wolfe's pistol and risked holding him for ransom—the life of the leader of the Children of the Rock in exchange for the life of Krysty. But it would have been a hopelessly suicidal gesture. All that seemed left to him was the ultimate possibility of wreaking a bloody revenge.

Sprite was toying with her victim, releasing her grip and allowing Krysty to draw in a couple of tortured breaths, then closing off the air passage again.

"She's dying, bro," J.B. said very quietly.

Mildred turned to face Wolfe, her fists clenched tight with anger. "She's butchering her," she said accusingly.

"So she is, Sister Wyeth, so she is."

Krysty was fluttering in and out of consciousness, her hands beating feebly at Sprite's broad shoulders, making no impression on the woman.

"Use the power, lover," Ryan shouted. "Use Gaia! You fucking well have to."

It was a grim decision.

Krysty had been taught a number of arcane skills by her mother, Sonja, a woman wise in the old mystic traditions. It wasn't just the power of seeing. It was the ability, in times of extreme need, to transform herself with almost supernatural forces, giving her an inhuman strength.

But it always drained her energy so deeply that it often took her to the brink of the grave.

"Use it!" Jak and Dean yelled in unison.

"Do it!" Ryan shouted as loudly as he could, trying to make sure that his words carried to Krysty over the screams of the spectators.

There was no sign that she'd heard them. It

looked like she'd passed out and was well along the dark road from which no traveler ever returned.

Sprite sat back once more, taking a moment to release her victim, clasping her meaty hands above her head in a gesture of triumph.

"Now, lover! Call on the Earth Mother! Krysty! Fireblast, lover, do it now!" Ryan's voice was breaking, ragged, high and desperate.

He saw the bloodless lips moving, but it was impossible to hear what Krysty was saying. Her eyes had closed, and she seemed to be concentrating all of her mental energy on taking herself to another place.

"Gaia!" she was saying, focusing inward, hands opening and closing.

Ryan realized that he was holding his breath, watching what was going to be, one way or the other, the terminal scene in the brief drama.

Sprite seemed to sense that something was going on, that there was a bizarre change happening in the helpless body clasped below her.

She reached down and resumed her grip on Krysty's throat, fitting her fingers onto the dark bruises that marred the soft skin of her victim's throat, smiling in triumph as she began to apply what everyone recognized was going to be the final pressure.

But Krysty seemed to have grown.

Her eyes snapped open, and the rictus of hopeless agony on her face changed into a gentle smile. It was something that Sister Sprite saw immediately, and the watchers gradually recognized as being an ominous development.

"Sprite is plucking defeat right out from the jaws of victory," Mildred said.

Krysty reached up, almost lazily, and laid her hands on the muscular forearms of the huge woman. She flexed her entire body, with a visible surge of the Earth Mother's power.

Sprite screamed, once.

The piercing sound rose above the double snap of the bones of both her arms, radius and ulna, both breaking like fragile frosted twigs.

For a moment Ryan saw the whiteness of jagged ivory, as the broken bones tore through muscle and skin, bright blood spilling into the sunlight.

Sister Sprite screamed again, trying to throw herself clear of Krysty. But the smaller woman, the gentle smile scarily unchanging, clung to her, twisting and crushing.

The whole settlement of Hopeville was utterly silent.

"Crippled me...done for..." she moaned, hanging like a helpless rag doll in Krysty's inexorable grip. Everyone could hear the harsh grating sound of the raw ends of bone rubbing against each other.

"To the death?" the redheaded woman questioned, pushing Sprite away from her with an unforgettable gesture of contempt. "That what you said, Brother Wolfe?"

"I said...that...I didn't...not..." Wolfe stammered.

Sprite was hunched over, her ruined arms clasped

under her, her face in the dirt, sobbing. Krysty paused to wipe sweat and leaf mold from her own face, standing over the disabled woman, holding her steady with her knees.

For a moment Ryan had a vision of Krysty astride a broken stallion.

The wind was rising, whipping up a minitornado of circling dust, obscuring the tableau.

"Do it, lover," Ryan called.

"Oh, I will..." Krysty answered in a voice that was barely human.

The dust cloud blew away and everyone saw that the redheaded woman had stooped over the hapless Sister Sprite, gripping her skull between her hands.

She started to twist it.

"Jesus!" Mildred breathed. "Nobody could..."

Krysty Wroth, in thrall to the Gaia power, could. And did.

Ryan watched, unable to avert his eye from the macabre sight. Sprite's bull-like head was revolving on her thick neck, the bulging, blood-streaked eyes staring sightless into the sky, toward the pitiless face of her tormentor.

It didn't seem possible for the skull to turn any farther without the spine cracking.

When the crack came, it seemed surprisingly quiet, almost insignificant.

The body jerked and relaxed, vacated, the spirit gone. There was a dark stain appearing at the crotch of Sprite's pants, as her bowels and bladder emptied.

Krysty stood a frozen moment, then opened her

hands and staggered away from the twitching corpse. She took three tottering steps and fell like a hewed log to the earth.

Ryan ran to her, kneeling at her side, seeing that the use of the Gaia power had, as always, exacted a dreadful toll. Krysty lay completely still, unconscious, her breath rapid and shallow, her heart pounding at twice its normal speed.

"You said to the death, Wolfe," he said. "If she dies, as well, I swear on the grave of all my friends that I'll take your bastard life."

But the leader of the Children of the Rock wasn't listening. He'd turned on his heel and walked away, his head drooping, toward his own hut.

Chapter Twenty-Nine

Krysty was still deeply unconscious.

Mildred sat by her, chafing her wrists, dabbing a water-soaked rag on her white forehead. There had been no sign of life since Ryan had carried her into their cabin, placing her on the bed with an infinite gentleness.

And that was nearly four hours ago.

"Any change?" he asked.

Mildred shook her head. "Not really. Though her respiration's better than it was, and the pulse is slowed some. But she's still way out of it."

Jak stood in the doorway, staring out over the settlement. Sister Sprite's body had been dragged away by half a dozen of the sec men, her heels digging twin furrows in the soft earth.

"Nobody moving," he said, terse as ever.

Doc was propped up on one elbow on his bed, sipping at a mug of hot water and honey, held for him by Mildred, who had left Krysty for a moment. He had managed to stop coughing for several minutes, but he still looked desperately frail. Krysty lay on the adjacent bed, her eyes tight shut.

Mildred had been seriously worried for the first few minutes, but now was much happier. She decided that it had been using the power of the Earth

Mother that had stricken her friend, and that time and rest would probably see her recovered in a few days.

"If we have a few days," had been Ryan's response. "After all that's gone down, I'd like us to be away from here as soon as possible."

After the death of Sister Sprite, the ville had been quiet. A dog had started yapping, then they had heard the sound of a blow, and the animal had become silent.

"What do you reckon happens next, bro?" J.B. asked, standing next to Ryan, by Krysty's bed.

"No idea. You?"

The Armorer pushed back the brim of his battered fedora and shook his head. "Bones might fall either side of the line. By their rules we all passed the testing."

"Except you, me, Dean and Doc."

"Baron's coming," Jak said, moving away from the doorway. "Alone."

A shadow fell across the floor, and Brother Joshua Wolfe walked into the hut.

"Good afternoon, outlanders," he said quietly. "How is Sister Wroth?"

"She'll be real fine," Mildred replied. "How are the Burrows boys?"

"Shaken. Got the wise woman to give them some sleeping herbs. Set the breaks. Should help. We have to do some talking about the rest of the testing."

"Haven't had enough?" Jak snapped. "Want everyone in ville chilled?"

Wolfe looked at him. Ryan noticed that the man was stroking the stump of his amputated arm. "Race isn't over until the fat lady crosses the line, kid."

"Don't call kid."

"Sure."

Ryan sat on the side of the bed, hearing the springs creak under his weight. "What happens next? What do you want me, Dean and J.B. to do for our testing?"

Wolfe shrugged. "The boy's not of age. He's excused. I've seen enough of both of you, personally, to know that there's no need for you to face any trial. You are two of the most dangerous men in all of Deathlands. There's no need for you to be tested."

Ryan was puzzled, not believing that it was going to be that easy. Give Krysty three days or so, and they could head back to the redoubt and make a fresh jump. By then Doc should also be well.

"So, it's over."

"No." The single syllable hung in the dusty air of the cabin.

"No?"

Wolfe shook his head. "I'm deeply regretting this, old friend, but it isn't quite over yet."

The smile was as sunny and broad as the Grand Canyon in August. The eyes and the voice were like a cascade of Sierra meltwater in April.

Doc suddenly sat up, his pale eyes blinking open, and he stared directly at Joshua Wolfe. "Just send my mail to the Tijuana jail," he said firmly, then pushed the mug of water aside and lay down again.

"Not good." Mildred laid a cool hand on the old man's fevered forehead, wincing at the fiery heat. "No, not good at all. Wish the temperature would go down. Set him on the road to recovery. Still, with rest..."

Ryan was still staring at the leader of the ville. "What do you mean?"

Wolfe shook his head gently. "Not who wins the first lap, friend. It's who's first past the tape at the end of the race. You all did real well in the testing."

"But?"

"But you haven't all taken the trials. Still one of you left." He pointed at the recumbent figure of Doc Tanner.

"What?" Ryan's temper was always on a short fuse. Always had been, always would be. The suggestion that the critically ill old-timer should somehow have to prove himself to the sick-brain bastards of Hopeville was so obscene that an instant red mist descended. "You don't—"

Wolfe had the pearlized grip of the blaster firmly in his hand, the gaping barrel drilling into Ryan's abdomen. "One wrong step, One-Eye. That's all I want."

Jak had taken a half step toward Wolfe, his fingers groping for one of the concealed knives, and he barely halted the movement. "Test Doc?"

"Right. Test Doc. Couldn't have put it any more succinctly myself."

"He's real sick," Dean said shrilly.

Wolfe nodded gently. "That's absolutely correct, young man."

Mildred looked for a moment as if she was about to throw the drink in the man's face. "You really are something damned special, mister."

"Why, thank you," Wolfe replied, dropping a low bow.

Ryan could have taken him at that moment, but they would still have been absurdly outnumbered by armed men, all within calling distance. He held himself in check, waiting to see how the cards fell.

"I'm not a hard man," Wolfe protested. "Nor do I wish to be unfair. Blessed Jesus of the cap and ball wouldn't want that to happen."

Ryan managed to control the crimson rage that had brimmed dangerously close to the surface. "Just what are you saying, Wolfe?"

"If he's unwell, we can postpone the testing."

"For how long?" Mildred asked. "Long as it takes for him to recover?"

Wolfe gave out his genuine, friendly laugh, which crinkled the lines around eyes and mouth. "Oh, dear me, no. I'm afraid that's not on at all, lady." He slipped the blaster back into its holster. "Lady, we don't have the time."

"Then...?"

"Doc can have all of the rest of today to recover, and all of the coming night, as well. He needn't face his testing until... Let me see. Until eleven tomorrow morning. No, why pinch the penny? Until noon."

"Noon!" Mildred roared. "Poor old guy'll probably still be unconscious by then. Give him a week and then he might, just might, be able to make a showing.''

"Tomorrow. Noon. Best you don't leave the hut. Food'll be brought to you.''

He turned about and marched quickly out of the cabin, leaving a pool of shocked silence behind him.

THE SHADOWS HAD lengthened around the ville, as the great golden bowl of the sun slipped slowly out of sight, behind the final range of hills that separated the place from the endless stretch of the Cific.

They'd been fed from a black iron caldron of vegetable soup, thick with carrots and parsnips, served with fresh-baked bread and some tender roasted sweet potatoes. There was home-brewed beer on offer, but Ryan gestured for them all to reject it.

Now they were left alone again.

A bowl of the soup stood cooling on the small table under the window, waiting to see if Krysty could be roused enough to try to sample it.

The one slightly encouraging sign was that Doc had been able to sit up, with help from Ryan and Jak, and had sipped at his own helping of the steaming soup, licking his lips after three or four spoonfuls before wearily lying down again.

"We have to get him well away," J.B. said, standing in the doorway, the setting sun flaring off the twin lenses of his spectacles.

Ryan was sitting on the bed, holding Krysty's limp hand. "Fates are against us, bro.''

"You mean her using the Gaia power and it knocking her out like this?''

"Sure."

Mildred was lying on her own bed. "She's hit harder by it than I ever saw before."

"When do you reckon she might be able to travel again?" Ryan asked.

"Krysty's about the strongest woman I ever came across, Ryan, but she's not going to be up and walking good for... At the most optimistic, say three days."

"Just to get back to the gateway?"

"Still, three days."

"How about Doc?" Jak asked.

"Same. Think he's about turned the corner. If it came to it, he could maybe walk a short distance, tomorrow evening. Not a lot sooner."

"If made break tonight? Me, Dean and J.B. help Doc, and you and Mildred take Krysty?"

Ryan sniffed. "Don't know the country like they do, Jak. They got some dogs. And there's the Apaches, as well. One of them'd hunt us down before we got two miles."

The teenager got up from his bed and walked to stand alongside J.B., the dying rays of the sun turning his white hair to a mane of living fire.

Ryan looked at the two slight figures, side by side. His mind flashed back to the long years that he'd known the Armorer, and the shorter time with the boy, all the desperate times they'd faced together.

He wondered if they were all coming close to the end of the line.

"You four could get away," he said hesitantly.

"Looks like a cloudy night. Be long gone into the forest before they started off to chase you. Move fast, a lot faster, without Krysty or Doc to slow you down."

"Dad! You can't mean that. I'm not going, and you can't make me."

J.B. and Jak both opened their mouths to speak, but Mildred was quicker, holding up an accusing finger. "In my time, Ryan Cawdor, we had a good saying. 'Why not go and take a flying fuck at a rolling doughnut.'"

"Come on, it makes sense."

J.B. bit his pale lips. "Never reckoned to hear you say anything like that, old friend. Times to walk away and times to stand. Trader used to say that. And you know what, he was right as ever."

"Tomorrow at noon they'll find a legal way of butchering Doc in front of our faces." Ryan sighed. "And there's nothing we can do to save him. Then there'll be some pretext for chilling you and me, J.B., then the others. Knife in the back? Poison in the cup? We don't all have to die."

"Together," Jak said very quietly, with a calm finality. "What goes down, goes down together."

JIM OWSLEY HAD LOOKED IN just after dark, lighting the oil lamps for them.

The sec man was hardly able to restrain his delight at their hopeless predicament.

"Always said that nobody likes a smart-ass. Specially not mutie, black smart-asses. All that winnin', just so you can end up losin'."

Ryan casually rested his hand on the man's scrawny shoulder, letting finger and thumb bite together. He clipped the nerve ends of the muscle, making Owsley whimper with the sudden electric pain, making him drop to his knees on the chipped planks of the floor.

"Hey, you son of a bitch! Didn't have to do that to me."

"Get out." The voice of the one-eyed man was icy with anger and contempt.

"Just come to bring you light."

"You did that. Now get the hell out of here."

The sec man paused in the doorway. "You should try and reckon on winning some friends, outlander. By the saints of night and fog, but you'll be needing them."

He went out and slammed the door shut behind him, making the whole cabin shake.

"Mean little redneck peckerwood," Mildred spit. "Wish I'd got my blaster with me now."

"Wish we'd got a single blaster between us," J.B. replied. "One'd be a start."

Ryan sat down and picked up Krysty's limp hand. "Talk's cheap, friends, and action costs. And time is passing us by. We got the rest of the dark hours. Then it's done."

Doc coughed in his sleep.

THE CONVERSATION kept following the same circle. There was no hope of Krysty being well enough to make a nocturnal run for it, so they all had to stay. But Doc was irrevocably doomed if he was still in

Hopeville at noon tomorrow. Mildred had awakened him around nine, feeding him some oatmeal gruel that she'd gone and begged from one of the older women. She chafed his cold hands and legs, making him stand and move around, despite all of his protestations, keeping him walking around and around.

"By the Three Kennedys, madam!" he moaned. "To so torture a wretched, dying old man. You must certainly be kin to Tomás de Torquemada, accursed head of the hateful, hated Spanish Inquisition. Give me peace."

Josiah Steele had returned the ebony cane to the sick man that evening, not realizing that it concealed a lethal blade of Toledo steel. Now Doc used the swordstick, leaning heavily on the silver lion's-head handle as he built up his strength, the ferrule clicking on the floorboards.

Ryan bit his lip. Though the old man was much better than earlier, he still had the uncontrollable cough, and he was desperately frail.

"Doc?"

"Dear boy?"

"Let's go through the plan one more time."

Chapter Thirty

Ryan opened the door a crack, peering out into the first dim glow of the false dawn. A huddle of sec men stood by the dying embers of the main camp fire, while half a dozen others were patrolling the perimeter of the ville. A thin coil of gray white smoke rose lazily up between the branches of the enormous pines that lined Hopeville.

"Shit's going to be hitting the fan any minute now," he said. "Best all get up and ready."

Dean yawned and sat up. Like the others, he'd remained fully dressed. "How's Krysty, Dad?"

"No change. Slept quiet."

She hadn't yet recovered consciousness, though Mildred had kept checking her vital signs, finding both respiration and pulse were improving.

J.B. checked his wrist chron. "Doc's been gone for just on eight hours. Should be time enough for him to hole up someplace. Fingers crossed."

Three times during the night, Owsley had peeked in, checking that everyone was still there. Doc's bed was farthest from the door, and they'd made up a realistic mount of blankets. Each time the sec man had left, convinced they were all there.

Mildred was busily washing her hands and face in a large blue-and-white china bowl, using a large tablet of dark brown soap. "Cold," she said. "Went to take a leak—must have been around three—and there was a biting frost. It's not going to help Doc with his cough and all."

"Cough could be the least of his problems," Ryan said. "Uh-oh. Here comes Wolfe and his sec men, taking their early-morning check."

Mildred held up her fingers, crossed. "Good luck, Doc," she said.

THE TRUSTY BLUE swallow's-eye kerchief had been lifesavingly useful.

Doc's mind was never one hundred percent sharp. Mildred, Ryan and J.B. had all tried to explain to him what was happening, what had happened and what was going to happen. But he'd ended up more confused than when they started talking at him.

There was to be a testing. He'd clued in to that. But he still didn't quite understand what it would have involved and why his presence in the ville would be seriously bad news.

And Krysty was ill. She'd had some kind of a fight and she had won it. Doc understood that much. But it had made her very sick so she couldn't travel.

What he had to do was get out of the ville without being seen or heard, make his way through the cloudy darkness and try to keep back along the trail to hide in the burned-out eatery, where the rest of them would join him when they could.

When he'd sneaked out of the back window of the shared log cabin, it had been full dark, with only a sliver of moon visible through some drifting clouds. Ryan had used some fragments of charcoal from the old fireplace to draw a rough map onto a torn linen rag, showing Doc where he thought the guards might be encountered. He showed him the route back in the general direction of the redoubt, to the ruined restaurant, warning him to look out for the giant mutie rats.

"And the Apaches," he'd reminded Doc.

"*¡No problema, mi amigo!*" had been the reply. Doc had to remind Ryan that he'd once spent time with a tribe of Mescalero Apaches and spoke a little of their language.

Doc felt another cough prickling deep in his chest, and he took out the trusty kerchief again.

He'd still been well within the settlement, only a scant thirty yards or so from their hut, when he'd been seized by a racking paroxysm.

He'd hastily pulled out the swallow's-eye kerchief and crumpled it into his open mouth, muffling and cutting off the noise of his helpless coughing.

He crouched, feeling the damp of the sodden pine needles through the thin material of his ancient breeches, squinting to try to spot the sentries that Ryan had told him would be patrolling.

Doc moved on when he'd regained some measure of control, having to stop twice more before he was clear of the perimeter of Hopeville and out onto the winding trail.

"NONE OF YOU HEARD him go?" Disbelief rode high in the angry voice of Joshua Wolfe.

Ryan answered for them all. "Nope. Reckon we

were all totally bushed after the testing and all. Thought Doc was real sick, but the old coot sure fooled us.''

Owsley leaned close to the leader of the Children of the Rock and whispered something in his ear.

Wolfe listened intently, nodding a couple of times. Then he shook his head. ''No. Not yet. Means a sort of delay in the plans. Best is to go after the old goat and bring him back here. Then things'll be back on course.''

''But we—''

''No.'' Wolfe held up his unmutilated hand as a warning to the sec man. ''You heard me, Brother Jim. We play this one like I said. Understood?''

''If you say so.''

''I do. I say it with the backing of the Blessed Lord Jesus, Savior of the gun and the blade.''

''Amen, Brother Wolfe.''

Wolfe managed to claw a smile back into place. ''Small and temporary victory, outlander.'' He pointed at Ryan. ''Trader used to say that he who shoots last shoots finest, didn't he? Think about that, One-Eye.''

''We getting after the old man now, Brother Wolfe?'' Jim Owsley asked.

''Right now. Double the watch on the rest of them.'' He stared intently at Krysty. ''But she doesn't look like she'll be going anywhere. Not for a while.''

DOC HAD TO KEEP reminding himself that he was supposed to be traveling light-footed. The temptation to use his ebony swordstick as a walking cane was very strong, but he realized immediately that the metallic tapping sound would carry a long way at night in the deeps of the forest, and bring any potential pursuers after him at a flat run.

He would have been a whole lot happier if he'd had his beloved Le Mat in the fancy hand-tooled Mexican rig on his hip.

Jak had offered to lend him one of his remaining concealed throwing knives, but Doc had turned down the offer. "Such a weapon would be as much use to me as a chocolate chamber pot, dear boy."

The forest was showing the first signs of the false dawn. The sky above had become fractionally brighter, throwing Doc's shadow on the winding trail. Twice he'd been stopped in his tracks, aware of something moving, ponderously, in the dark depths of the pines. But nothing had come near him, and he hadn't actually seen anything.

He carried a gold half-hunter watch on a fob and he tugged it out, angling the face to try to catch enough light to read it. But it wasn't yet possible.

By his own rough calculation he'd been traveling for five or six hours and was well over halfway toward his destination. The one thing that Doc couldn't know was at what point his escape had been noticed. If luck was with him, he'd still have something of a clear run. If not, then the pursuers could already be closing in on his track.

"I said that the hounds of spring were in winter's traces," he muttered. "But let it pass, yes, let it pass."

There was a whisper of movement, and he turned toward the sound, seeing something white floating toward him, showing a hideous, ghostly face. Great golden eyes seemed to bore into him, and he noted a wing spread of six feet or more and a cruelly hooked yellow beak.

"A wise old owl, swirling," he said, ducking as the apparition swooped low over his head, the beat of the bird's passing disturbing his silvery hair.

Doc was beginning to feel close to exhaustion. The attack of influenza, or whatever it had been, had taken even more out of him than he'd guessed. It was an effort to lift each foot and place it in front of the other. But he knew that if he stopped, he might likely fall asleep and not carry on at all.

He tried to swing into a regular march, whispering the beat to himself. "Left, right, left, right. Left… Left, I had a good job and I left."

On into the early morning.

JOSIAH STEELE TOOK charge of the serving of breakfast brought by two women, each carrying a groaning tray of food, with mugs of buttermilk to wash it down.

Ryan noticed immediately that they had been given only old plastic spoons to help themselves. No forks or knives. Brother Joshua wasn't taking any chances on an armed rebellion from his remaining prisoners.

"Buckwheat toast with jellies and honey," Steele said. "And oatmeal gruel. There'll be some steaming acorn coffee for those who want it, in a while.

At least it'll be hot." He hesitated in the doorway. "How's the woman?"

"Sleeping," Ryan replied.

"Hope she... Well." He paused as though considering saying something else. "You did the right thing getting the old man away. He'd have been cold giblets by noon. Shame you couldn't get away yourselves."

"We could still mebbe manage it if we had our weapons back again," J.B. said quietly.

Steele sniffed, wiping his nose on his sleeve, and looked outside the hut. "Sure, you could, outlander. But the cold fact is, I don't aim to slit my own throat. Nor put a ball through my own temple. Not just yet."

"Where are our blasters and knives?" Ryan asked, seeing the doubt in the man's eyes. "Suppose I just said that I thought that they were likely in Wolfe's own house. You can just choose to say nothing. You don't have to tell us they aren't there. Just say nothing."

Steele half smiled. "Guess I'd best say nothing, Brother Cawdor. Not a word."

Ryan grinned across at him. "Thanks," he said. "Yeah, thanks a lot."

"FRIED BACON, please, Emily." Doc jerked awake. "Upon my soul! What am I saying? What am I doing? Where am I and where am I going? Have I been... I suspect that I might have taken a small rest and closed my eyes for a moment. Most unwise, my dear Theo. Oh, dear, so careless."

He hauled himself unsteadily to his feet, using the trunk of one of the smaller pines to help. He took several deep breaths of the cool morning air, looking around in the half light of the early dawn.

"What is the time, I ask myself?" He checked the half-hunter watch. "And I answer myself that it is closing in on six o'clock. No pursuit yet."

His voice disturbed a pair of pigeons that fluttered noisily away from the lower branches of a nearby larch. They circled once before heading north, still protesting at the intruder in their domain.

He lowered his tone. "What would dear Ryan and the other companions think of me? To be so rash and foolish, falling asleep within a couple of paces of the track through the woods. Though the road through the woods has been undone by the wind and the rain. And there is no road..." He slapped himself hard across the forehead. "Enough, Dr. Tanner. Enough. Set your face toward the path to the redoubt."

He picked up his cane and took a last quick look around the clearing.

"By the...!"

The pair of Mescalero warriors seemed to have literally appeared from nowhere, sprung from the heart of the forest. They stood silently a few yards away from him, leaning against the massive trunk of one of the largest of the sequoias. They were both in their midtwenties, both holding strung bows with a quiver of arrows across a shoulder.

One of them said something in the Apache tongue. Doc dredged at his memory for his scant vocabulary. The nearest translation that he could come up with was, "Greetings, walking man who is already with the spirits."

"Bother," Doc said.

Chapter Thirty-One

Bear Cub Running and Fast Silver Hand were two of the boldest young warriors of the Mescalero band. Their hostility against the numerically stronger Children of the Rock was deep-rooted, going back a number of years. They knew nothing of the rad hot spot, but it was common knowledge that the white Bible carriers had few if any children among their numbers, and those that were born were sickly and rarely lived long.

Which was why the renegade Anglos had so often tried to steal the little ones from the Apaches.

Which was why any white person walking along through the tall pines was fair game.

The old man with snowy hair and pale eyes didn't seem to be carrying any kind of blaster. The two braves had been watching him carefully for over half an hour, at first suspecting a trap. But they had just decided that the old man was truly alone.

Fast Silver Hand had whispered that it would be like shooting fish in a barrel.

"Truly. Should we take him back to camp for the women to show us their skills with knife and fire?"

Then Doc woke up.

Seeing his imminent danger, he fumbled in his

faltering memory for the few ragged Mescalero phrases that remained in the dusty back rooms.

"Greetings, brothers. It is a good day."

"A good day to die, old man," Bear Cub Running replied, sneering. "For you."

Slowly he reached around for an arrow to notch on the string of his bow. His young companion matched him, move for move, very cautiously.

"I have no wish to harm you," Doc said, his arms spread, gripping the silver hilt of his swordstick. "Let me pass through the hunting lands of the Mescalero."

Fast Silver Hand laughed at the clumsy attempt to speak their language. "He is like a coyote who has drunk too much of the winter wine," he muttered so as Doc couldn't hear him. "He will give good sport."

"Perhaps he is mad," the other warrior said doubtfully. "Mad, bad and dangerous to know."

"No. Just triple stupe. As are all whites. See how he stands feeble like a blind baby."

Doc couldn't hear what they were saying, but he was awake enough to know that their body language was a long way short of friendly.

He struggled to remember things that Ryan had tried to teach him over the years. Watch their eyes. Watch their hands. Watch their feet. If you have to strike, then do it hard and fast. Don't wait to admire your handiwork. Watch their mouths. Try to take out the leader first.

"Which one is the leader?" he asked.

But the two young men just nudged each other

and laughed. They both had arrows notched, bowstrings taut, but the bows were still held loosely down at their sides, not yet threatening Doc.

"Get close," Doc mumbled. That was one of the most important things to remember in combat.

He took three hesitant steps toward the Apaches, halving the distance between them.

Another step. He felt sweat on his palms, cold against the metal of the lion's-head hilt. He lifted the shaft of the stick, so casually, now holding it in both hands.

Doc was still a little too far away, but he could see the glimmering of doubt in their eyes, suspicion that perhaps the old cougar still had claws.

"Yes," he said, nodding wisely and reassuringly. "It is truly a good day to die." He took the last step that brought him close enough to risk his move.

His gnarled right hand twisted the grip and pulled, his left sliding the ebony sheath off the polished Toledo steel of the rapier's blade.

A half turn to the left gave Doc the necessary room for the first, devastating sideways cut, followed by the lunge and withdrawal.

The early-morning sunshine glinted like watered silk off the honed metal, giving the two young men a frozen splinter of time to realize the terrible threat they faced from the helpless old-timer. Too little.

Too late.

His aim was true.

The cutting blow slashed through the two bowstrings, severing them both at once, the arrows falling limply to the forest floor, the bows left useless in the shocked hands of the Mescalero warriors.

Before they could even begin to draw breath, the blade was back, the needle point striking Fast Silver Hand just below the rib cage, driving upward and across, Doc giving his wrist the classic duellist's twist as he pulled the blade down and out.

The young Apache's guts spilled to the grounds. The man had only time to take a staggering half step backward before the blade, swifter than a striking rattler, had lunged a second, mortal time.

Bear Cub Running gasped at the sudden, shocking cold chill that spread through his lower body, burning like fire into his chest and lungs.

"He has—" he said, but his throat filled with pounding arterial blood and he began to choke on it, aware of it frothing from his open mouth, dappling brightly down across his naked chest.

Doc stepped back, panting as though he'd just run a swift quarter mile across a plowed field, watching the young men as they sank to their knees, like ruined marionettes, faces shocked, eyes protruding from red-rimmed sockets.

"I am sorry, boys," he said, infinitely gentle. "I did not want it this way."

There wasn't going to be any need for a second strike at either of them. The lines were down, and life was a handful of pumping, failing heartbeats.

They fell simultaneously, Bear Cub Running rolling onto his back, sightless eyes staring up at the waving branches of the nearest sequoia, his hands clenched at his sides. His companion lay on his right, fingers moving slowly through the dirt, the nails snapping, his teeth grinding together for a few seconds before death closed everything down.

"I am truly sorry, boys," Doc repeated.

He was genuinely grief stricken, though his heart told him that he had done the right thing. It had so clearly been their lives or his. Doc stooped and wiped the blood-slick blade in the loose earth.

THE HUNTING PARTY from Hopeville found the bodies less than half an hour later.

"Neat killing for a sick old man," one of them said, examining the corpses.

"That cane of his held a sword," Owsley said, spitting bitterly into the face of the nearest of the corpses. "Should have taken it away from the old bastard. Stupe of us!"

"Think he did this on his own, Brother?"

Owsley spun, nearly biting off the younger man's head in his anger. "Course! Think the Blessed Jesus Christ came down with a cross and a switchblade and gave the old stupe a hand? Bodies are still warm. Can't have been chilled more than an hour ago. Likely less."

He spit again at the dead Apaches, then led the way at a fast trot along the path toward the still smoldering ruins of Mom's Place.

RYAN SAT on the stoop of the cabin, his head thrown back, soaking in the morning sunshine, welcoming its warmth among the towering, dank trees. Behind him, Jak and Dean were sleeping on their beds. J.B.

and Mildred were sitting in the matching chairs, on either side of the blackened fireplace, talking quietly. And Krysty was still lying unconscious, under a pair of striped blankets.

In the past hour there had been some improvement in her condition, and her breathing was steadier.

Mildred had been puzzled by the bleakness of her condition. "Not really like anything that I ever encountered before. Having to utilize the Gaia force has completely drained her resistance. But it's not just physical. Krysty almost seems to have lost the will to live."

And there had been nothing to do for her, other than the usual methods of life support: keeping her turned so that she didn't suffer from sores, making sure that she drank some liquid by dabbing at her parched lips with a damp cloth of torn linen.

Wolfe had looked in once, standing in the doorway of the cabin, silhouetted like an etched shadow. His good hand fondled the stump of his amputated arm, his dark eyes locked to the motionless body of the redheaded woman on the bed.

"She is very beautiful, is Sister Wroth," he said so quietly that only Ryan heard him. "Such a shame that... It could, with Jesus' will, have been different." A small smile played on the cold lips. "But we have little choice in the road that we walk, Brother Cawdor. So little choice."

"That's bullshit, Wolfe. We all have choice. All the time. You pick the road to walk, because that's the one you want to travel along."

Wolfe shook his head and walked away, leaving the friends together.

The community resumed its normal morning life, with cooking and washing going on, the mongrel dogs snapping at one another in the dust, the double-armed sec men patrolling, all of them on triple alert.

And there was still no news of the escaped Doc Tanner.

J.B. stood by the window, glancing down at his wrist chron. "My guess would have put them along-side him an hour or so back. Unless he's gone to earth and they missed him."

"The old fool wouldn't have the sense to conceal himself," Mildred commented, her voice hiding her concern and the depths of her love for their friend. "Probably completely forgotten by now that he's supposed to be running and hiding." She shook her head. "God help him."

THE SMELL OF KEROSENE and burned wood still hung in among the pines, overlaid with the sweet-sour scent of roasting meat. Doc tried to breathe in and out through his mouth to avoid inhaling it, knowing that he was now coming very close to his destination.

The wind was rising, and the sky had grown dark in the past twenty minutes. Clouds swept in from over the Cific in the west, blackening like old pew-ter, banking with silvered edges, forming a solid mass that drowned out the cheerful sunlight, killing all of the shadows.

Doc shuddered, turned up his collar and looked back behind him along a section of the winding trail that ran straight for a quarter mile or so. There was no sign of the pursuit that he knew would inexorably be coming after him. A coughing fit hit him, making him double over, hawking spittle on the side of the path. He noticed that it was still flecked with bright crimson blood from the straining.

As Doc stood, fighting for breath, he suddenly saw a strange apparition. A large white Persian cat padded along the roadway toward him, emerging from the undergrowth. What was odd was that it wore a neat red silken ribbon around its fluffy throat, decorated with a tiny pair of silver bells that tinkled softly as it closed in on the old man.

"Hello, puss." He knew he should be moving, though it had momentarily slipped his mind quite why. He had to be somewhere for some reason or other. But the cat was singularly beautiful, reminding him of a kitten that he and Emily had once owned.

What had its name been?

"Ozymandias," he said, smiling broadly, showing the animal his set of excellent teeth. For a moment it hesitated, then walked right up to him, rubbing its arched back against the stained knee boots.

He stooped and stroked the Persian, feeling oddly pleased as it purred and pushed harder against him, its golden eyes closing in delight.

"You're a beauty, you are, indeed, Ozymandias," he said, totally forgetting that he was a man on the run. "A truly fine fellow!"

The woman's voice startled him and made him jump. "He is a she, and her name is Lucretia. And I wonder what your name is, my fine fellow?"

Chapter Thirty-Two

Owsley was breathing hard, like a hound dog on a hot trail, urging his companions to a fast run through the forest.

"Come on! Got to track down the old fucker, quick as we can. Get back with him."

"Brother Wolfe said dead or alive," one of the sec men panted. "Dead be easier."

"Less sport."

Another of them, trailing, laughed wheezily. "Could have some good sport with the redhead bitch."

They were very close to the ruins of the abandoned eatery, near to where a narrow side trail forked sharply to the left up the hillside, meandering off among some particularly tall trees.

"Hold on here." Owsley doubled over, leaning against the bole of a massive, fire-scarred sequoia. Sweat ran down his chest, darkening his shirt. His face was flushed, heightening his poor complexion.

"Must be close, Jim," said the youngest of the men in the sec patrol. "Don't want to lose him now."

"My guess is that he'll likely be holed up in the burned-out buildings," another man suggested.

Owsley coughed and spit in the rotting pine needles. "Don't want to risk overrunning him. Know what his boot heels look like. Brother Waits?"

"Yeah?"

"See that dark patch ahead of us? Looks like there's some seepage, clear across the track. Go check that the old bastard's still heading that way."

The sec man, as skinny as a picket fence, with dreadful sores clustered around his toothless mouth, nodded. He crossed himself and pattered quickly off, pausing and stooping, straightening, then looking again.

"Well?" Owsley yelled. "Trail there?"

"Nope."

"No?"

"There's no sign."

They all went and looked, ranging round, making sure that their prey hadn't skirted around the damp patch of earth, among the bordering woods. But there was no sign at all of the distinctive marks of the old man's worn boots.

"Think he's backtracked on us? Heading toward Hopeville behind us?" one of the men asked, angrily fingering the butt of his revolver.

Owsley could barely contain his anger. "Only other place he could have gone is up the spur. That madwoman with all the cats lives up yonder. Could be he's gone there."

But the side trail was hard and stony, not carrying any tracking marks. A six-year-old Mescalero child could have followed Doc, but it was beyond the ability of any of the Children of the Rock.

"What's that?" the toothless man said. "Sounds like a steam engine."

"Sounds like it's underground, close by." Owsley steadied himself against the tree. "Dirt's shaking like—"

"Earthquake," the youngest sec man said in a surprisingly calm, conversational tone of voice, as if he were commenting that the coffee was brewed.

"WHAT'S THAT?" Jak said, leaping agilely from his bed, looking around, his ruby eyes wide-open.

J.B. moved quickly to the doorway. "Feels like a shaker on the way."

A row of old predark bottles on a shelf began to rattle and jingle, and dust fell from between the hand-hewed rafters of the roof.

On her bed Krysty stirred in her blackness and suddenly opened her eyes.

"Hey, lover," Ryan said. "Might be a good idea to move out of here."

"WHAT IN THE NAME of perdition is that roaring noise?" Doc asked.

"My loved ones have been restless for days. I should have known they sensed something in the air."

Maya Tennant sat in her rocking chair, unperturbed by the quake that shook the land all around her trim little cabin. Her hands were folded in her lap and supported a brace of tabby kittens, which were just a couple of her forty-seven feline companions.

"You get many tremblers up here, ma'am?" Doc asked, sitting on the stoop, his knees drawn up uncomfortably close to his bony chin.

She put her head to one side. "I've lived here for…let me see now. Twenty-seven years since my dear husband, Albert, passed away. And we shared twenty excellent years together. So, close on fifty years since I came hear as a teenage gal. In all that time I can count the bad quakes on the fingers of both hands. Perhaps as many as twenty."

"Is this a bad one?"

The roaring noise had risen to a howling crescendo and was now beginning to fade away. The trees around the hut were stopping their quivering, and the dust was settling once more. And the cats were becoming quiet again.

Maya smiled gently. "If I may say so, Doc, the things that we perceive when we're younger don't always look the same when we grow a little older. If you take my meaning."

"Indeed I do, ma'am, indeed I do."

She stared out into the wilderness around, and Doc stared at her.

By her own admission Maya had to be closing in around seventy. But she was a remarkably handsome woman. Tall and slender, she moved with the easy grace of someone half her admitted age. She had dropped a kerchief and stooped to pick it up, as limber as a young girl. Her hair was as fine and white as Jak's, tied back in a neat roll at her nape.

Maya was wearing a midcalf-length skirt of patched denim, with a dark blue blouse with long sleeves. Her feet were cased in a fine pair of hand-made sandals with long thongs that tied just below her knees.

She carried no weapon, but Doc had noticed there was a small silver whistle on a red ribbon around her throat. Seeing him looking at it, she smiled.

"My way of passing messages along to my family," she said. "They can hear me calling them a good couple of miles away on a still day."

The kittens on her lap began to play-fight, cuffing each other with their tiny velvet paws.

Doc laughed with sheer delight, the fact of his pursuers almost totally gone from his wavery memory.

"Now, Romulus, stop trying to bully little Remus," Maya said, like an indulgent mother. "Doc, you said about there being some of those crazies from the Children of the Rock coming this way after you."

"By the Three Kennedys! I had nearly—"

"The cats will carry warning if there's strangers around. Just tell me a little of what's been going down, so I can decide on how to play the cards." She carried on rocking. "Sounds like the quake's passed on. Only thing is..." She hesitated a moment.

"What, ma'am?"

"Way the felines are still skittish, I have an uneasy feeling that we've just experienced something of a preshock. Could be a much bigger one lurking just around the next corner. Best be ready for that and all."

JOSIAH STEELE CAME BY a few minutes later, to make sure they were all safe after the earthquake.

"Young Penny Boot broke a wrist when a cupboard came off the wall on top of her. Not serious."

"We're fine. Don't know how Doc got along, out in the woods on his lonesome."

The sec man shook his head. "I have to reckon that you could be hearing some bad news in the next two or three hours. Once that coldheart Owsley and his gang get back to the ville. They won't likely be taking prisoners."

"Is Wolfe planning to chill us all?" J.B. asked, sitting on one of the beds, holding Mildred's hand.

For a long moment Steele didn't reply to the question, then he cleared his throat, looking all around him. "Not for me to try and guess."

"But if you were a gambling man," the Armorer said, "then you wouldn't give good odds on survival."

Steele stared at him, stone-faced. "No odds I could offer you at all."

Suddenly J.B.'s usual icy control snapped, and he jumped off the bed, coming right at the sec man. "You stinking bastard! I'll rip your lungs out!"

Steele hastily drew his blaster and jammed it into the advancing man's stomach. "Hey, just back off," he shouted, his voice thin and high and frightened.

Ryan quickly came between them, brushing aside the Hawes Montana Marshal .45. "No need for this," he said quietly. He placed a hand on his old friend's shoulder, looking him in the eyes, unable to see the true expression behind the glittering lenses of the spectacles.

"All right. Dark night! But I hate…" He turned away, ignoring the threatening blaster.

Ryan also turned away, but his eye had been caught by something glittering brightly on the lapel of J.B.'s coat. The little rad counter was a clear and unarguable red. Not orange. Not reddish orange.

Full red.

THE WIND that had dropped, oddly, during the quake, was suddenly rising again, setting up with a real menace, shaking some of the largest branches on the huge pines all around Maya Tennant's little cottage.

"Could be in for some darned unpleasant weather," the woman said, one hand absently stroking the kittens.

"Hold up the pursuers, mayhap. Indeed, I have a scintilla of hope that the quake might have deterred them from chasing me any farther."

"Not if it's those Children of the Rock, Doc. All the years I've been here, they've been sniffing around and causing trouble. Kidnapping little ones from the Mescalero who arrived here a few years back. Nothing but anguish. They leave me alone, though that miserable one-armed son of a bitch, Joshua Wolfe, tried to have me burned as a witch about three winters ago. Failed. I went up to their poverty-hill ville and defended meself against their charges. Challenged them to burn or hang me."

Maya gave a throaty laugh. "Course he backed off."

Doc leaned back, blinking as the wind blew dust into his pale eyes. "You think it likely that the villains will attempt to follow me?"

"Guess so, Doc." She stood suddenly, brushing the little tabbies from her skirts. She stared across the small kitchen garden, with its neatly tilled rows of vegetables. Coming toward them was a very large ginger cat, stalking between the cabbages, tail held high like a bright orange beacon.

"Here comes Mehitabel," Maya said. "Way she's moving tells me that we're about to have us some company. Best go get hid where I showed you, Doc."

KRYSTY WAS SITTING UP, sipping at a bowl of oatmeal with some wild honey stirred into it. She was still very fragile, but the draining effect of using the Gaia power to save her life was gradually wearing off.

She had sat and listened while Ryan took her quickly through everything that had happened since she became unconscious, explaining why it became necessary for the ailing Doc to flee from Hopeville.

"Couldn't you have tried…tried to get at the weapons? Mebbe it would have been easier. Safer?"

Ryan had argued against that idea, pointing out that Wolfe only needed a feather of an excuse to set in the balance to justify murdering them all. And the odds were way too long against them. It was just a question of waiting a while longer.

Now the wind was rising, making the flames of the big central fire tear sideways in streaks of red and orange, rattling a loose shingle on the roof.

J.B., as taciturn as ever, stood and peered out through the dirt-smeared window. "Some folks putting up storm shutters," he observed.

Dean was on his bed. "Cover for escape?"

Ryan nodded. "Possibly. Need to be a sight worse than this. Now, if there was to be another shaker, then it might give us a chance."

OWSLEY LED his sweating men up the narrow side trail. To his frustration they hadn't been able to find any definite tracks of the old man, but he felt confident that they had trailed him down to the cottage of the mad old cat woman.

"Hey, in there," he shouted, lifting his voice over the soaring wind. "Bitch! We know you got a guest, and we fucking want him out here. You got just thirty seconds to come out with him, or we come in and we come in hard and heavy. Do some damage and mebbe some hurting of your cats. And you. Thirty seconds, witch, and your time starts now!"

Chapter Thirty-Three

Doc could hear the shouting.

He was crouched in a sweet-scented linen chest of carved walnut and cedar. Maya had told him that it had once belonged to her great-great-great grandmother, taking it back way before the long winters and the horrors of skydark. The acanthus pattern around the lid was deeply polished, and the ornate key turned smoothly in the oiled brass lock.

The woman had led him, holding his large hand in her slender, dry fingers, up a twisting cupboard staircase, into a low-beamed attic. It was crowded with antique items of furniture, many of them so old that they actually took Doc back to his childhood, some two hundred years ago.

There was a beautiful mahogany credenza and an elegant pedal harmonium, made in Woodstock, with ivory knobs and keys; a sideboard so big that Doc guessed it had to break down into smaller constituent parts, unless they'd originally built the attic around it; a round table, beautifully veneered, with a pie-crust edge and a single, central claw foot.

And the linen chest.

At first it didn't seem possible for Doc to coil his length into it, but Maya removed some fragile sheets from it, and he was able to hunker down. Cramped and stooped, he heard the key turn in the lock.

For a passing moment Doc felt the frightening taint of claustrophobia, sucking in a deep breath, wondering just how airtight the old chest might be. And just how long that remaining air might last him.

With an effort he controlled his respiration, fighting against the sudden temptation of a violent coughing fit. He'd seen enough of the sec men to figure that they wouldn't deal kindly with Maya Tennant if they found out that she'd been sheltering the object of their anger.

The shouting seemed to be coming from the first floor of the cabin, and he could make out the noise of boots pounding on the stairs. And there was Maya's voice, tense with a barely controlled anger, threatening action if any damage was done to any of her valued possessions. Or if even a hair was harmed of any of her beloved felines.

"Shut that flapping trap. The Blessed Jesus, lord of freedom and detester of government says that the open mouth of a nagging slut is an offense in the eyes of any right-thinking person. I say amen to that." The whining, hectoring voice belonged to Brother Owsley.

"I say that sec men are all either bullies or cowards. And most frequently both."

Doc had unsheathed his rapier and gripped the silver lion's-head hilt in his right hand, though he was only too aware that it was likely to be a futile gesture.

"By the Three Kennedys! But I can take one of

the mongrels with me, Emily,'' he whispered to himself, and to his long-dead beloved wife.

Outside, the whole building seemed to be swaying in the wind, now risen to full gale force. Doc was aware of timbers groaning, and he could actually feel the sides of the chest vibrating against himself.

"This is the attic," Maya said. "I keep telling you, I haven't seen an old man. Haven't seen a man at all for nigh on three weeks. There's just me and my cats here."

"If I have to I'll slit the throat of every one of your fucking cats, starting with this sinister black bastard." There was a shriek of protest from an animal and a yell of anger from the woman, followed by a gasp of pain and the sound of someone falling to the floor of the crowded attic.

"You broke my balls, you—"

"You hurt Astaroth, you devil! You deserve all the agony there is going, trying to wound a poor, defenseless little mite like Astaroth."

"Defenseless! Its fucking claws opened me up from wrist to elbow."

Another voice warned Owsley that he was bleeding from the cat scratch.

"I know it, you triple stupe. And the witch kneed me in the balls."

Doc's fingers were slippery with perspiration. He was trying to do what Ryan had always advised. If there was going to be some sort of combat, then try to ready yourself for it—imagine the opening moves of the fight, so that you had a heartbeat's edge over your opponents.

But that still came down to having a single chance with the rapier.

One lunge. That was all there'd be. Doc thought it through, imagining the feeling of the razored steel as it slid between the fourth and fifth ribs, warm blood gouting along the blade, over his hand and wrist.

Then there would be the crack of blasters. Probably, Doc thought, several of them. He winced, closing his eyes in the perceived expectation of several .44- and .45-caliber bullets ripping into his body, punching great holes in his flesh, smashing bones to white shards.

He wondered how long death would take to come.

"Where is thy sting-a-ling-a-ling," he hummed to himself. "And grave thy victory?"

Now he could feel the floorboards vibrating with heavy boots, feet very close to the chest, and Owsley's complaining voice, still moaning about the grievous injury that Maya Tennant had inflicted on him.

"How about opening up that old chest for us? Or would you rather we smashed it in? Come on!"

Doc clearly heard the clatter of a shingle breaking loose in the gathering storm.

He held his breath.

J.B. STOOD in the doorway of their cabin, bracing himself against the gale, his eyes narrowed. "Bastard rough,'' he said, making two words do where other men might have used two dozen.

Krysty was walking around the room, leaning heavily on Ryan's shoulder, her fiery hair glowing in the gloom of the hut. Her face was pale, emerald green eyes tight shut, lips pinched. A tiny worm of blood inching over her jaw. Ever since she first recovered consciousness, at the beginning of the storm, she had been fighting hard to regather her damaged strength.

''Damn this Gaia weakness!'' she exclaimed, letting go and flopping back onto the bed.

''Without it you'd likely have been butchered,'' Mildred said. ''You know that you can't just use it and hope to get away free. Always takes a dreadful toll from you, drawing on the Earth Mother's power.''

''Yeah, yeah, I know it. But if I'd been fit and able, then we could have pulled together for Doc.''

They hadn't seen any sign of Joshua Wolfe or any of his crazed minions, not since Owsley had led his hunting party off into the deteriorating weather. The shutters had been battened down on all of the buildings, fires extinguished, the ville's dogs gathered in to safety.

''Getting worse,'' J.B. commented, leaning hard against the door to press it shut, softening the howling of the storm. ''Hope Doc's not caught out in this.''

''Hope Doc's not caught period.'' Ryan carefully turned up the wick on the oillamp, pushing the dancing shadows into the corners of the room.

"Reckon they'll bring him back here?" Mildred asked, stretching out on her bed.

Ryan nodded, dropping his voice even though they couldn't have been more private. "Wolfe seems to be the sort who likes showing a good example. Let the Children of the Rock see his authority. Big public execution is likely his style."

"Then us," Krysty said.

He nodded again. "Yeah. Then us."

DOC WAS as ready as he ever could be, the lion's-head hilt gripped tight, his whole body braced to explode out of the chest.

He could almost see the sec man, poised to smash his wooden coffin, hear Maya Tennant protesting in the background. And above it all was the muffled fury of the storm.

"Last chance before I break it in, lady."

"I have a key somewhere. Just give me a bitching minute, will you? If this man you're after is in there, then he surely isn't going anyplace."

Doc grinned, lips tight across his excellent teeth. "Game to the last," he whispered to himself.

"Sounds like the roof's going," said another voice, high toned with the edge of panic. "Mebbe we'd best get out of here, Brother Owsley."

Suddenly Doc felt the wooden walls of the chest start to vibrate, and he tensed himself, thinking that the pursuers were trying to tilt it or lift it.

But it wasn't that.

"WHAT FUCK?" Jak exclaimed, taking a couple of loose, staggering steps to one side, hands stretched out to fight for balance.

J.B. lurched toward the bed, stumbling and falling on top of Mildred, who reached up to check him.

Ryan and Dean were close to the bed where Krysty lay, and they managed to sit down quickly, feeling the floor shifting and rippling, like liquid sand. The timbers creaked and split, unpeeling furrows of white splinters.

And there was the familiar noise, rising all above and around the noise of the massive storm, like a dozen powerful war wags revving their engines at once, somehow directly beneath the planking of the cabin.

"Outside, lover, Dean," Krysty said. "Safer than in here."

He could barely hear her above the cacophony of noise from the twin sources.

There'd been bad quakes at other times in his life, and he recognized the bizarrely disorientating effects, with reality crumbled at the edges. He struggled to focus his mind on what they should do.

"Outside, everyone!" he shouted, agreeing with Krysty's mutie feeling.

Easier said than done.

Ryan remembered being on a sailing ship once through a tornado, and when he stood the sensation was remarkably similar. The whole building was quivering like a frightened animal, and he staggered and nearly fell. He recovered his balance and held out a hand to steady Krysty as she swung her legs off the bed. Dean was up and moving.

Jak was first to reach the door, moving with the natural poise of the skilled acrobat, hesitating with his fingers gripping the handle. "Ready?" he asked, his voice shrill above the raging noise.

J.B. held Mildred by the hand, as they weaved across the heaving floor, looking like a couple of drunks trying to make a decorous exit from a frontier gaudy.

"Door's jammed!" the teenager yelled. There was a ferocious shuddering, and the kerosene lamp crashed off the table onto the floor, rolling under one of the beds, plunging the room into momentary darkness.

But that lasted for only a few seconds. A flicker of orange flame snaked out of the blackness as the dust-dry blankets caught fire, followed by the crackling of the floorboards igniting in the fierce heat.

J.B., Dean and Ryan reached Jak, and they all threw their weight against the opening. But it was obvious that the whole structure of the hut had become twisted by the quake, pinning the door into its warped frame.

Already the place was filling with coils of choking smoke, muffling the climbing flames.

"Windows are all shuttered from the outside," the Armorer shouted.

Already it was hard to breathe.

THERE HAD BEEN a period of total confusion.

Doc's control over his own mind had never been that strong, and times of severe stress tended to create some serious brain slippage. If he'd been presented with a wag load of jack, he could never have told anyone how long the shuddering, crashing, sliding and yelling went on.

It could have been less than fifteen seconds.

It might well have lasted for two or three minutes.

Either way it seemed to Doc to be an endless eternity of terror.

The chest spun as though possessed by its own malevolent demon, crashing across the attic floor, pitching and tossing, the wood of the panels splintering, showing daggers of light through the fresh cracks.

For a few shards of broken time, Doc passed out, slipping into a mysterious blackness.

When he came around, the movement had ceased and there was an uncanny near silence. For a while he lay cocooned in the welcome stillness, luxuriating in the calm.

He couldn't sense the presence of the sec men. They had to have gone. Otherwise they'd have broken in the lid of the chest and hauled him helplessly out.

"Hello," he said cautiously. Doc cleared his throat and tried again, aware of the frailty of his voice.

But there was no response.

"Anyone there? Mrs. Tennant? You out there, madam? Could you possibly unlock me?"

He braced himself against the sides of the chest, pushing with all his strength. Despite the splits in the wood, the bands held like iron.

Doc realized that the storm was still raging, and

that the silence was comparative after the intensity of the massive earthquake.

He also realized that he could smell the bitter, acrid tang of wood smoke.

"Help! Help me...."

THERE WAS a final shock that felt as though the whole building were being jerked sideways, with one end dipping and twisting. Krysty was knocked off the bed onto the floor, and all the others were thrown off their feet.

"Fireblast!" Ryan banged his elbow against the door, blinking in the sudden shaft of light. One of the shutters had been torn off its mounting, the glass shattering in the window, as the wall of smoke opened before his eye.

"Get out!" Krysty screamed, staggering across the rocking floor.

She led the way, risking cuts on the broken windowpanes, followed by Jak and Dean. Then came J.B., helping out a dazed Mildred.

Ryan was last out of the burning building, emerging into a wilderness of destruction.

Chapter Thirty-Four

The grating of a key in the lock jerked Doc back from the brink of total panic.

He had wriggled around onto his side, kicking out with the heels of his cracked knee boots, pounding at the splintered sides of the old chest, conscious that he was making precious little progress and that smoke was filtering in from a substantial fire elsewhere in the cabin.

"Doc, are you all right?"

He blinked in the light, seeing the silhouette of the elderly woman, taking the proffered hand to haul himself upright onto shaky legs.

"I am a little fatigued, madam. But what of your good self? Did those brutish thugs harm you?"

Smoke billowed around her, and he could see a deep cut leaking blood from her forehead. He reached up and gently touched the wound. Maya winced and pulled away.

"Not Brother Owsley," she said. "It was that last severe shock did the damage. Quite threw me ass over tits, and I banged my temple on the dining table."

"Have they gone?"

"Wouldn't know, Doc. Think so. Ran off like they'd messed their breeches."

"I confess that I do not entirely blame them. It was as unpleasant an earthquake as I think I have ever encountered. There is a fire...." He waved his blue kerchief to try to clear the air.

She managed a rather wobbly grin. "I fear the old homestead's done for, Doc. Got my felines out of the way. Looks like they all sensed it coming and headed out into the woods. Collect them together later. Main thing is for us to get our asses into gear and out of here."

"I am with you, ma'am."

The old man had another coughing fit as the smoke thickened, and he could now glimpse the red-gold glow of flames, burning on the first floor.

"Best take it careful outside. Those religious crazies could be anywhere close by," she warned.

The kitchen and living quarters were well ablaze, bright fire dancing along the tumbled ceiling. Doc thought he glimpsed a dead ginger cat, pinned beneath a fallen rafter, but he felt it better not to draw attention to it. He followed Maya toward the open front door.

She hesitated a moment, just inside, glancing behind her, shaking her head sorrowfully. "Best part of a lifetime going here," she said.

Doc took her by the arm and led her gently out, blinking into the light, moving off the veranda to lead her past the cottage garden.

"Least you've got your blessed cats and you also have your life," he said, taking in several deep breaths, savoring the clean freshness, while behind them the flames were roaring into an inferno.

"You're a fine person for looking on the bright side of life, Doc," she said, shaking her head ruefully.

"Better to look in the mud and find a diamond than find mud among the diamonds. Or some such saying. I disremember the details."

One of the sec men suddenly appeared from behind a fallen apple tree, holding his rifle at the high port, eyes wild, bleeding from mouth and nose.

"Hold it there, bastards!"

SEVERAL OF THE BUILDINGS of Hopeville had gone down under the quake, and at least a quarter were ablaze. The gusting wind was whipping up cascades of red-and-orange sparks that whirled into the air, vanishing among the mighty trees. A few men and women, looking shell-shocked, wandered around the ruination of their settlement, one or two making halfhearted efforts to throw buckets of water onto the fire.

"Best get out weapons," J.B. shouted, still gripping Mildred by the wrist.

"Makes sense." Ryan glanced at Krysty. "You manage it, lover?"

"With you. May Gaia aid me."

An elderly man saw the prisoners making a break for it and opened his mouth to yell a warning.

Without breaking step Jak plucked out one of his concealed throwing knives and flicked it toward the old man. There was the distinct click of his wrist snapping with the effort of hurling the leaf-shaped blade.

It struck the brother with a fearsome accuracy, sticking in the right eye, driving through, pulping the liquid orb, penetrating the front of the brain through the optic nerve, beginning the rapid process of dying.

The man's arms flung wide as though he were welcoming an invisible comrade. A watery thread of blood inched over the stubbled cheek. The lines went down in his legs, and he stumbled and fell, fingers scrabbling in the wet dirt.

"Head for Wolfe's house," Ryan shouted. "Over there." The big building was one of the few that didn't seem to have been damaged by the storm and the following quake, standing rock solid at the head of the single street of the ville.

The ground trembled in a violent aftershock, making Ryan stagger sideways, clutching at Krysty to steady himself. Somewhere there was the sound of a woman screaming in terror. Jak had darted over to retrieve his knife from the twitching corpse, resheathing it out of sight.

Nobody else in Hopeville seemed to be aware that the prisoners had escaped.

DOC REALIZED that the sec man was terrified, eyes staring, mouth gaping, breath coming fast. His voice was thin, high and ragged. "Stop there! Don't move."

But the muzzle of the Winchester rifle was wandering from side to side.

Doc let go of Maya's hand and half turned away from the pursuer, masking the movement, reaching for the silvered butt of the little .32 automatic that he'd noticed in the woman's belt. He palmed it smoothly and thumbed back on the hammer, firing from the hip.

The snub-nosed blaster bucked in his wrist, spitting out its flat sound and a tiny jet of flame. The bullet hit the sec man an inch above the big brass buckle on his broad leather belt, driving straight through and splintering the spine. It broke up, distorting, shredding the intestines into ragged loops of bloody tissue.

The rifle went spinning into the mud, and the man dropped like a discarded doll, clutching at his stomach, rolling and kicking, screaming out his shock and agony.

"Got him, Doc," the woman crowed. "Brilliant piece of shooting!"

The familiar voice was from behind them, near a tumbledown shed with all of its windows shattered. "Yeah, fuckin' brilliant shooting."

THE HOUSE WAS SILENT.

There was the smell of wax polish, and banisters glistened, oak paneling reflecting the light of several dangling oil lamps on brass gimbals.

A full-size oil painting hung crookedly on the opposite wall of the entrance hallway, showing a soldier from predark times in a green uniform florid with crimson and gold frogging, holding a drawn cavalry saber. He was a tall, handsome man with a proud, scarred face.

"Find the weapons," Ryan snapped.

J.B. sprinted up the staircase, followed by Jak and Dean, while the others started to check out the ground floor. The lamps swung from side to side as yet another brief but powerful aftershock made the building tremble.

There was every evidence of panic.

The dining table lay on its side, food spilled, glasses broken, the smell of beer strong in the dusty air. Chairs were on their backs and sides, legs in the air. Ryan found a smear of what looked like fresh blood on the edge of the doorway into the kitchen. The stove had slid the length of the room, still lit, with a pot of beans miraculously steaming away, undamaged.

Mildred called from the back room, which looked as if it had once been Wolfe's private study. Dark oak shelves lined the walls, with all of their books piled higgledy-piggledy on the gleaming floor.

"Locked cabinet in here. Seems like it might hold some blasters."

Ryan poked his head into the room, agreeing. "Yeah. Let's smash it open."

He picked up a heavy stool and hefted it over his head, bringing it around with all of his strength to hit the inlaid cabinet just above the ornate brass lock. The wood splintered under the blow, and the door swung slowly open, revealing the rifle, scattergun, machine pistol and a variety of familiar hand blasters and knives.

"Get your blaster, Mildred. I'll take Doc's Le Mat. Hope to give it to him real soon."

Ryan tucked the SIG-Sauer P-226 into its holster,

the balance immediately feeling right. The eighteen-inch panga went into the oiled sheath on the other side, and the Steyr SSG-70 rifle was slung comfortably over a shoulder. He tucked Doc's massive cannon into his belt.

The others came running in, heels ringing on the wooden floors, clattering on the stairs.

J.B. straightened his back, testing the action of the Uzi, a rare glacial smile decorating his sallow face. "Dark night! That feels better," he said, hefting the powerful weapon across a scrawny shoulder.

The others helped themselves to their own blasters, emptying the shattered cabinet.

"We going to spread some chilling around the ville?" J.B. asked.

Ryan shook his head. "Best is to get out clean and fast. That way we can go after Doc. Mebbe get to him in time to do some good. Might pick up the sec gang on the way back."

"Think should take out Wolfe." Jak glanced along the hall, through the open front door. "Evil bastard. Best without him."

Ryan considered the teenager's suggestion, recognizing that there was something in Jak's idea. Brother Joshua Wolfe's presence on the planet would be better terminated.

He shook his head. "No. Think it's better to get out fast, Jak. Time's not on our side."

"I'd like to see that shithead chilled," Mildred said. "Did us some serious harm."

Ryan sniffed. "Decision's taken. We'll get out

the back way, if we can, into the big trees and loop around. Head after Doc.''

Doc STARED at the gloating face of Jim Owsley, feeling a biting pain in his heart at the sickening realization that they were finished. He felt sorrow for himself, and a deep misery that Maya Tennant was also doomed. He'd know the woman for only a few hours, but everything he knew about her was good and positive. Now she was minutes from death.

Owsley was only a few paces from them, holding his Hawes Montana Marshal .45 revolver in his right hand, aiming at Doc's chest.

''Put the blaster in the dirt, you old fuck. Or I chill you and the bitch crone both. Don't much matter to me, one way or the other.''

Doc dropped the little hideaway in the mud by his feet, still holding the cane in his left hand.

Owsley's eyes darted around the clearing, staring at the burning house, glancing behind him.

''You see any mutie rats around? Reckon there's nests of them.''

The woman hadn't moved at all. Now she edged closer to Doc, laying a hand on his arm. ''Don't worry,'' she said. ''You did your best.''

''Rats! I loathe them. You seen them around here?'' The voice was high and cracking.

Doc managed a laugh. ''They're everywhere, Brother Owsley, waiting in the shadows for you.''

''Shut the fuck up!'' he roared, waving the powerful brass-gripped blaster at him.

"Forgive me, but you had asked me the question, had you not, Brother?"

A tawny cat strolled out of the wreckage of the little shed, stalking up to the sec man, tail held high, back arched, purring loudly. It rubbed against the legs of Jim Owsley, who promptly shot it through its angular skull.

Maya Tennant screamed.

Chapter Thirty-Five

Ryan had been struggling to open the back door of Joshua Wolfe's imposing house. But the massive earthquake had distorted the entire frame of the building, breaking windows and jamming many of the doors.

"Fireblast!"

"Let's set our shoulders to it."

J.B. was at Ryan's side, pushing at the stout oaken door, but it was immovable.

"Try upstairs windows?"

Ryan shook his head. "Waste of time, Jak. We'll just walk straight out of the front door. Least we know that it's open. Everyone on triple red."

There was yet another savage aftershock. A long-case clock in the hall, which had been already jarred off balance, toppled with a sonorous clanging sound.

Somewhere outside they all heard an old woman scream in fresh terror.

Ryan paused just inside the front door, peering out. "Right. Head for the nearest cover, then on the trail back toward the redoubt. If we get split up, meet there. Don't stop for anything or anyone. Time to lay down bullets without any questions. Good luck, friends."

He squeezed Krysty by the wrist. "Stay close to me, lover. Close as you can."

The storm had faded away almost to nothing, with an occasional flurry of rain running cat's paws over the surfaces of some vast puddles.

As they huddled together by the door, there was yet another jolting quake that rattled windows and brought the smashing of glass. Ryan grinned reassuringly at Krysty. "Keep the bastards busy," he said.

"Fire," Jak muttered, sniffing the air. "Ville could go like tinder."

Ryan nodded and drew the SIG-Sauer, thumbing back the hammer. "Ready? Here we go!"

THE CAT'S HEAD WAS blown apart by the heavy-caliber bullet, and its body flopped limply in the dirt at the sec man's feet. It didn't have time to make a sound as it died.

Maya stood still, hands reaching up to her face, as though she were about to gouge out her own eyes. Doc touched the woman on the arm, seeking to comfort her, and to restrain her from any violent action.

"Please…" he began.

But it was too little and too late. Maya was launched into a red-mist rage, half running at Owsley, clawing toward the man's face.

"Murderous, coldheart bastard," she screamed.

Doc closed his eyes, not wanting to see what he knew was going to happen.

The boom of the blaster was muffled, the barrel

of the weapon pressed hard into Maya's stomach. The jolt of the .45 round threw her backward, hands clasped over the small entrance wound. Doc blinked in horror, seeing the hideous gaping chasm of blood and splintered bone at the center of her back.

"Oh, dear God, no..." he breathed. His eye was caught by the little blaster glinting in the mud, but he knew that Owsley would shoot him down before he could reach it. His fingers tightened compulsively on the hilt of the swordstick.

The sec man seemed hypnotized by the dying woman, watching her, wide-eyed, as she staggered backward, miraculously keeping her stumbling balance.

"Stupe bitch..." he stammered.

Maya turned her head, her eyes staring blankly toward Doc, as though peering down a long dark corridor. One hand reached toward him, then the lines went down and she dropped to her knees, sliding forward onto her face like a swimmer entering deep water.

"Devil," Doc whispered, hands moving almost without his control. One hand gripped the ebony shaft of the cane, the other twisting the silver lion's-head hilt, drawing the rapier blade in a silent, smooth action.

He was four short paces away from the stupefied sec man, who stood with his Hawes Montana Marshal revolver pointing at the dead woman.

"Stupe bitch," he repeated quietly.

It was like he was paralyzed, squinting at Doc as the old man closed with him, dropping the sheath of the sword, the steel glinting in the watery sunlight.

"What...?"

There was another aftershock, which made the whole forest shift sideways, trees rustling, branches creaking and splitting. The sec man took a half step sideways, fighting for his balance.

Doc felt a fierce, burning exultation as he lunged at Owsley, the needle tip of the blade slicing into the man's belly, two fingers above the belt buckle. Hot blood flowed over the slender steel, down over Doc's hand, dripping to the dirt. A full ten inches penetrated Owsley's stomach, and Doc gave his wrist a savage twist, lancing through muscle and intestines, opening up a great gash. Loops of blood-slick guts spilled out, splattering in the mud by the dead cat.

The blaster dropped from the nerveless fingers, and a thread of blood came worming out of Owsley's gaping mouth. The eyes widened, and his fingers groped for the murderous steel. But Doc had already withdrawn the rapier, stepping away from the mortally wounded sec man.

"The debt is well paid," he said to Owsley in a calm, conversational tone.

Though the man was dying, he was still able to move, tottering away into the edge of the forest, clutching at his stomach, trying to stuff the coils of muddied intestines back inside himself.

Doc ignored him, kneeling in the damp dirt by the side of the dead woman, feeling for her cold fingers.

SEVERAL OF THE BUILDINGS of the settlement were burning well, the wrath of God having finally being visited on the evil community.

As Ryan darted out of the front door, his arm linked with Krysty's, he realized that the big house, Wolfe's own home, was one of those that had caught fire. Flames billowed out of the rear living rooms, smeared with thick, oily smoke.

"Whole place'll go," he said.

"Serve it right. Serve them all right," Krysty panted as they headed for the fringe of trees. "Only wish we could've chilled Wolfe himself."

"No time."

He could see J.B. and Mildred, about twenty yards ahead, following on the heels of Jak and Dean, the youths sprinting toward the forest. So far nobody seemed to have seen them.

Jak was already close to the nearest edge of the dank, dripping forest, where the powerful quake had brought down three of the biggest trees, the giant limbs tangling with one another into an impenetrable maze.

Ryan heard the crack of a rifle and saw a gout of dirt kick up within a yard of Mildred's heels, but he couldn't locate the shootist among the smoke and confusion.

The woman stopped in her tracks and turned, the barrel of her target blaster scenting the air like the tongue of a hunting snake.

She froze like a pointer, and her right arm straightened, pointing almost directly at Ryan, a little to his right and above him.

He saw the tiny crimson flash from the muzzle as she squeezed the trigger, the blaster kicking in her hands, and he felt the warm blast of the bullet as it passed within a few inches of his head. Ryan spun to see the effect of her shot.

Josiah Steele was about thirty yards away from him, standing in the entrance to one of the houses, the Winchester rifle drooping from his shoulder. His white shirt was dappled with scarlet, just above the breastbone. His jaw had dropped with surprise, and he looked as if he were trying to speak.

But the .38-caliber shot was mortal, and he slipped to his knees, the rifle clattering on the porch. Mildred still held the SKR 551 aimed at him, hesitating a moment, considering a second bullet, but she saw almost immediately that it wasn't going to be necessary.

Within a few minutes they'd made their way, unchallenged, to safety, a good half mile from the edge of the settlement, on a rising point in the buckled trail, where they could pause and look back at the smoking ruins of Hopeville.

"Seems like given up," Jak said, shading his eyes with a long white hand.

"Surely do," J.B. agreed, pausing to wipe splattered dirt from the lenses of his spectacles.

"I'm glad we're out of there," Dean added. "Sure hope Doc's okay."

There was activity around only one of the burning buildings, the large house that belonged to Joshua Wolfe. There was a feeble bucket-chain operating, and one man was at the top of a rickety ladder, directing water from a hose into the inferno of bright orange flames.

Coils of dark smoke enveloped him, and it was impossible to make him out clearly. Then the wind suddenly dropped and veered, and everyone recognized him.

"Wolfe," Mildred said.

With his left hand missing, the leader of the Children of the Rock was struggling to hold the hose while keeping himself steady on the swaying ladder.

Ryan stared across the hazy distance, balancing against a small aftershock, squinting at the figure of his bitter enemy. Krysty laid a hand on his arm.

"Said you'd leave him be, lover," she said quietly. "We can walk away."

"Sure, only Trader used to say that when you walked and left an enemy alive, you were storing up future trouble for yourself. Know what? He was right."

He slowly unslung the Steyr bolt-action rifle from his shoulder, then took Doc's ponderous Le Mat from his belt and handed it to J.B. "Mind this for me, friend. Just while I do me some hunting."

The Armorer took it and jammed it into his own leather belt. "Wind's dropped," he said. "Still about ten miles an hour, left to right."

Ryan levered a 7.62 mm round into the chamber, then hefted the rifle to his shoulder and peered through the Starlite nightscope with the laser image enhancer. The scope brought Joshua Wolfe much closer, the crosshairs centering on his chest. Though he couldn't see it at that range, Ryan knew that a tiny red dot would have appeared on the man's shirt, almost invisible.

"Good half mile," Mildred said. "Way beyond my blaster's range."

Ryan remembered her advice on classic target shooting: hold your breath, and keep the rifle well braced into the shoulder. He didn't need to close one eye. Mildred claimed that all great shots fired two-eyed anyway. His finger took up the slack on the trigger, and he readied himself to shoot, taking account of his heartbeat, aiming to fire between beats for maximum efficiency.

At the very last moment Wolfe seemed to sense his danger and turned on the ladder, staring directly toward Ryan. He spotted the red dot on his shirt and brushed at it with his good hand, his mouth opening as though he were about to yell for help.

Too late.

Ryan corrected his aim a fraction, centering the sight on Wolfe's mouth. He then squeezed the trigger, bracing himself against the buck of the walnut stock.

Eye locked to the sight, he saw a crimson rose blossom from the centre of the man's chest.

Joshua Wolfe threw his arms wide, in the pose of crucifixion, and toppled from the ladder into the flaming heart of the inferno, vanishing into the fire.

"That's one of the finest shots I ever saw," Mildred said admiringly.

Ryan grunted. "No, it was one of the worst. I was aiming at his head."

DOC HAD FOUND a rusted shovel in an outbuilding and was already three parts through burying the small body of Maya Tennant, picking a shady patch of ground beneath an ancient, twisted quince tree.

Ryan called out as soon as the old man came into sight, so as not to frighten him.

"Looks like there's been some blood spilled hereabouts, Doc. We passed a handful of sec men on the trail, heading for Hopeville like their asses were on fire."

Doc straightened and sighed, rubbing at the small of his back. "Getting too old for this, friends. I would be grateful for a hand with the interment. A fine woman died here. That scum dog Owsley butchered her down."

"Didn't spot him on the trail," J.B. said, handing over the Le Mat to Doc.

"You chill him?" Jak asked.

"I dispatched him to dwell with his master, Beelzebub," the old man replied.

"How?" Dean asked interestedly.

"Trusty rapier. Gutted him like a landed trout."

Ryan laughed. "And we were all worrying about you! You did good, old friend."

Doc nodded solemnly. "But what a price to pay," he replied, pointing to the woman's corpse.

"I'll help you," Dean offered.

"We'll all help," Ryan said. "Then we'll head on back toward the redoubt."

IT TOOK THEM a little under the hour, during which time there were three more aftershocks, one of them passingly severe, causing some of the excavated earth to slide back into the unfinished grave. But they quickly cleared it out and laid the body reverently into the cold ground.

"Want to say anything, Doc?" Ryan asked as J.B. Dix patted down the pile of gray brown dirt.

"She was a good woman and I scarcely knew her. But what I knew was good and brave and kind. She saved my life from those running dogs."

"Amen," Krysty said, followed by the others.

Ryan brushed muddy earth off his hands. "Time to go now, friends."

"Think that the Children of the Rock'll come after us?" Mildred asked.

Ryan grinned and shook his head. "No. They're finished. From the red reading it looked like the quake opened up the hot spot at max level. Means they count in days."

J.B. picked up his fedora and placed it back on his sallow head. "Yeah," he said. "And the sooner we're out of here the better. Let's go."

Chapter Thirty-Six

Both Doc and Krysty had tired quickly as they picked their way along the trail, through the trees. The quake didn't seem to have been so powerful as around Hopeville, but a number of the pines had come down.

It was nearly dark when they finally walked through the massive sec door of the redoubt, heading for the elevator that should take them down through the buried levels to the subterranean floor of the mat-trans unit, past the notice that they all remembered from passing by on the way out.

The elevator worked smoothly, carrying them silently into the deeps of the military complex. Nobody spoke, all of them sharing the usual apprehension about the pending jump.

Ryan was thinking back to their last glimpse of the outside world before the sec door slammed shut. A magnificent sunset blazed away toward the Cific Ocean, in the not-so-far west. It seemed to set the tips of the pines on fire with a blazing radiance. Pale tendrils of white mist gathered around the peaks of the Sierras, drifting down into the valleys.

Jak had gone inside, followed by Dean and Doc, his arm around the boy's shoulders. J.B. had led

Mildred in by the hand, leaving Krysty and Ryan standing together in the cool of the evening.

The setting sun dazzled off her fiery hair, making it seem as though her skull were ablaze. She turned and smiled at Ryan, the bright emerald light from her eyes filling him with a wave of fondest love.

"We made it again, lover," she said, squeezing his fingers in her hand.

Ryan nodded. "Yeah. Been plenty of blood spilled in the last couple days."

"Not ours."

"No."

She looked up at him, scuffing the silver toes of her boots in the dust. "How much longer, lover?"

"Who knows. Just keep on to the end. When we get to the end, then I guess we'll know it."

Krysty tightened her grip. "You still think about settling down, lover?"

"Course. Not a day passes without thinking about it. One day it'll happen."

"One day."

THE FRIENDS TROOPED through the control room with its rows of desks with the cheeping consoles and flashing banks of lights, into the little room and on to stand together in front of the actual gateway chamber.

"Sec doors all locked behind us, Dean?" Ryan asked. "Best be safe."

"Sure are, Dad. All locked."

The armaglass walls were glistening with a deep,

deep maroon color, the door slightly ajar, showing the hexagonal interior of the unit.

"Everyone ready for the jump?" Ryan looked around the circle of friends, getting nods from all, though Doc was his usual unenthusiastic self.

"I confess that I shall be more than delighted when the jump is over and done," he said.

Despite his reluctance, he led the way into the chamber, crossing the floor and sitting down slowly, his knee joints cracking like pistol shots, and leaned his back against the vivid-colored translucent wall.

Jak and Dean were next, sitting on either side of the old man, Jak's white hair a startling contrast to the maroon armaglass.

Mildred made herself comfortable next to the albino youth, patting the floor next to herself for J.B. to sit down. "Here we go again," she said.

The Armorer carefully removed his spectacles and folded them into a pocket of his jacket, laid the scattergun and the Uzi alongside himself and finally took off his fedora and settled it into his lap.

Krysty took a last quick glance around before taking her place between Doc and Dean, leaving a gap for Ryan to join at her side.

He took a long, slow breath before moving, feeling suddenly tired, in need of a long vacation.

Maybe the next jump down the line could take them someplace like that.

"Yeah, mebbe," he muttered.

He stepped inside the gateway chamber, aware that the maroon walls were giving everyone, even Jak, a healthy, ruddy glow to the skin.

Before sitting down between Krysty and Dean, Ryan unslung the Steyr from his shoulder and laid it on the metal disks in the center of the floor.

As he stood by the door, he looked around at the group of old friends, his mind flashing back for a moment over some of their adventures together, knowing that a man couldn't ever have better companions.

"Ready, Jak? Dean?"

"Ready," the youths chorused.

"Mildred?"

"Let's get on with it. Sooner we start, the quicker we get to finish."

Her beaded plaits rattled softly against the maroon armaglass wall behind her.

"J.B.? Ready to jump?"

The Armorer, true to form, simply nodded.

"Doc?"

There was no answer, just a faint snoring sound from the old man's open mouth.

"Guess he's ready as ever," Mildred said, smiling.

"Lover?"

Krysty looked up at him, lines of strain etched around her mouth. "Let's move on, lover. Like Mildred says, sooner we start the jump, the sooner we'll be someplace else."

"Here we go."

He tugged the heavy door firmly shut, feeling the solid click as the lock engaged, triggering the mattrans mechanism and feeling the system engage.

He sat down quickly, giving Krysty's hand a firm

squeeze, settling himself comfortably, and adjusted the holstered SIG-Sauer and the long blade of the panga.

The opaque white mist began to gather between the metal disks set in the ceiling of the gateway, coiling around and becoming thicker, and the humming sound started, so faintly insistent that you couldn't tell whether it came from outside or inside the maroon chamber.

Or from inside your own skull.

Ryan took a last look at the others as the mattrans process began to suck at his mind.

Doc was either asleep or already unconscious, head to one side, a thread of yellow bile trickling between his cracked lips, staining his ancient jacket. Jak and Dean had also passed out, slumping sideways, a worm of blood on Jak's chin where the teenager had bitten the end of his tongue.

Mildred had her eyes closed, holding J.B. by the hand. The Armorer seemed to have gone, but he sensed Ryan looking at him and opened one eye in a reassuring wink.

"See you soon, lover," Krysty whispered, her voice muffled and echoing into Ryan's mind from a vast distance.

"Yeah, see you..." he tried to reply, but the effort of speech was enormous.

The maroon walls of the chamber were receding from him at an alarming rate.

The darkness came, and Ryan Cawdor closed his eye.

COMING NEXT MONTH

Meet the Trader

in

ENCOUNTER,

a full-length Deathlands story
in the Collector's Edition.

Here is an excerpt....

Trader exited the galley and headed up the narrow, windowless companionway toward the portside door. He intended to track down each of his drivers and let them know that he wanted one member of each wag crew to do some hunting for the pot come sundown.

Despite the wind outside, it was hotter than rad blazes inside the MCP. The hilltop was a treeless knob of dirt and rock, so there was no shade to park beneath. Using War Wag One's battery-powered fans was a luxury, under any conditions. And in the present situation, Trader knew he didn't want to draw down the level of stored current. If things went sour during the exchange with Cooper, he figured he'd need all his available battery power for flood-lights and the like. A prolonged firefight could run well into the night.

Always nice to see who you're chilling, he thought.

He was halfway down the corridor when he heard muffled explosions outside. A cluster of them, like a short string of firecrackers popping off under a wet blanket. He didn't know what they were, he only knew what they weren't. They weren't frag grens, blaster shots or incoming HE rounds. He spit out the stub of his cheroot and ran for the closest exit. As he did so, he was thinking two things. If it was an attack from Cooper's sec men, he had to contain and repel it. If it wasn't an attack, he had to keep his crackerjack gun crews from raining all of hell's fury down on Cooperville. The second cluster of explosions, which burst virtually on top of the MCP, convinced him that the convoy was, in fact, under assault.

"Dix! Dix!" he shouted.

The armorer appeared ahead of him, at the far end of the corridor. Right off, Trader could see something was very wrong. Dix was moving strangely. Staggering off balance, like the wag was rocking from side to side. Before Trader could reach him, J.B. slumped to his knees on the deck, his face going purple, greenish foam ringing his lips.

At the same instant something tickled deep in Trader's lungs. He tasted battery acid and his heart began to flutter wildly. Suddenly everything became clear to him. Horribly, horribly clear. Trader turned and rushed back the way he had come, the strength draining from his legs with every step. Gasping, he reached up to the interior wall and slapped the power switch to the wag-to-wag intercom system. "Hit the fans!" he shouted into the microphone. "It's nerve gas! Hit your fucking fans!"

Whatever the poison was, it wasn't quick.

And it wasn't painless.

As he slipped helplessly down the wall to the floor, his skin was on fire and his heart felt squashed in his chest, crushed into a space so terribly small that it could barely beat against the surrounding pressure. Likewise, each agonized breath took all of his effort; he couldn't even manage to whimper. He labored against the pain and the terror for what seemed like an eternity, then both seemed to miraculously diminish.

Trader realized he was looking down on his own body from a vantage point along the ceiling of the corridor. He watched his own legs kick and jerk, and his head banged against the floor, leaving a broad smear of blood.

It didn't matter.

The pain was no longer part of him.

It belonged to the body, the dying physical form to which he felt not the slightest kinship.

When Trader looked up, instead of seeing the MCP's ceiling, he was confronted by a widening, brightly lit aperture, like the canal of birth. Or resurrection.

RYAN, HUN, AND POET ARRIVED at the viewing point as the second volley of gas grenades burst amid Trader's circled wags. Each of them knew instantly what was going on, that the smoke released wasn't CS or CN. Announcing an attack on a superior force with a barrage of non-lethal gas would have been nothing short of suicidal. Each of them knew that the wild rumors about Shabazz's stockpile were true. They were too far away from the hilltop to do anything but watch in horror as the nerve agent settled down over the convoy.

"The fuckers!" Hun sputtered in frustration and outrage. "The dirty fuckers!"

Ryan and Poet stared in silence at the swirling gray mass that now hid the circled wags from view.

After a minute or two, the steady breeze had whipped the clouds of gas away from the convoy and dispersed them. Ryan raised his spotting scope to his eye. He could see the bodies on the ground, sprawled, in the center of the circle. So could Poet, who looked through his own binocs.

"Is anybody alive?" Hun demanded. "Could anybody still be alive?"

Before either of the men could answer, there came a series of three tightly spaced gunshots.

"Signal," Ryan said, at once.

"Yeah," Poet agreed, turning his gaze back down the road to the ville. "The all-clear."

Out from the barricade came a line of sec wags. They roared up the road toward the hilltop, and as they did, they honked their horns.

Ryan caught movement around the convoy, four figures quickly advancing from the far side of the knoll.

"It's Shabazz," Ryan said, lowering the scope.

"Lemme see," Hun insisted, taking it from him. "Son of a bitch!" she said. "The bastards are turning over the bodies on the ground, making sure they're chilled."

Actually, it was worse than that.

Shabazz and his crew were dragging the fresh corpses to the very center of the ring, then lining them up side by side, like trophies of the hunt.

"They're smiling and laughing," Poet said.

Ryan grabbed his scope back from Hun in time to see the bearded road pirate Shabazz wave his men over to Wag One. They cracked the portside door, climbed in, and started pulling the bodies out. They threw them out the doorway in a heap.

Ryan saw them throw Trader out. His body was limp when it hit the ground. It did not move.

Under the circumstances, this was something Ryan expected. But surprise or not, the sight of his dead leader treated like so much garbage was more than he could handle. His anger exploded. And it exploded close to hand.

"You got him chilled!" Ryan snarled at Poet, hurling down the spotting scope. "You gutless sack of shit!"

Poet growled a curse under his breath.

What happened next occurred in the space of a heartbeat. It occurred because the two men involved were both in their prime, both skilled in the deadly arts, and hardfocused on chilling. Their handblasters cleared holsters and came up simultaneously. Ryan's thumb locked back the Blackhawk's hammer as Poet dropped the safety of his own sidearm.

They were standing close, virtually toe to toe. There was no room for either of them to maneuver, no time for one to try to block the other's draw or deflect the aim.

The muzzle of Poet's longslide Government Colt came up hard against Ryan's mouth. And as it did so, Ryan jammed the barrel of the Blackhawk under the older man's chin. Cawdor smiled, letting the muzzle of the Colt push between his lips and grate against his front teeth.

Point.

Counterpoint.

Two coldhearts locked together; three eyes, unblinking.

Both warriors had drawn their triggers hard up to the break. All that separated either one from oblivion was an ounce or two of pressure on the other man's index finger.

Ryan smelled the familiar sweetness of gun solvent and he tasted its poison bitterness. Somewhere, miles away it seemed, Hun was yelling something at him. Ryan couldn't make it out. He thought she might have been slugging him in the back, too. Hard to tell. He was that tightly focused and caught up in the moment. What he had in his right fist was what he had wanted all along. An ending. No fear.

Just fury.

And fulfillment.

In Poet's eyes Cawdor saw a landscape of resignation, as flat and smooth as his forehead. The old man was ready to die. Maybe he even wanted it a little bit. Then Poet opened his mouth a crack and words came out of his throat in a harsh rush. "As sure as this blaster's in my hand, I will send you to hell, Cawdor, but I am not your Demon."

Ryan gave the Ruger a savage twist, making the front blade sight cut into the skin of the older man's throat. "What the fuck do you know about my Demon!" he demanded.

"Only what I said, that it isn't me. It's somebody else."

"Never said it was you," Ryan hissed.

"No, but you let yourself think it. And you acted like it was me from the moment we crossed paths. A man calls things by their true name. Always by their true name."

Despite himself, Cawdor blinked.

The true name of his demon was Harvey. His own brother Harvey. Who, out of greed and envy, had murdered their oldest brother, Morgan. Who had cunningly turned their father against Ryan. Harvey, who had slashed out Ryan's left eye and had driven him from family, friends and ancestral home.

Hun moved in closer beside them. She had a deft touch. Her quick, light fingers slipped between hammers and firing pins and locked down, preventing them from firing, for an instant at least. "Enough of this!" she exclaimed. "Stand down, the both of you. We got enough trouble without your blowing each other's brains out for no good reason."

Neither man moved. They stood on a tightrope, face-to-face over the abyss.

The dawn of the Fourth Reich...

THE Destroyer™

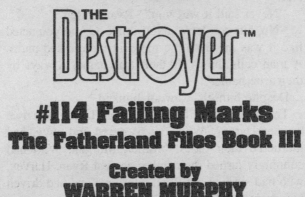

#114 Failing Marks
The Fatherland Files Book III

Created by
WARREN MURPHY
and RICHARD SAPIR

From the mountains of Argentina the losers of World War II are making plans for the Fourth Reich. But when the Destroyer's brain is downloaded, he almost puts an end to the idea. Adolf Kluge plans to save the dream with a centuries-old treasure. But then, the Master of Sinanju may have different plans....

The third in The Fatherland Files, a miniseries based on a secret fascist organization's attempts to regain the glory of the Third Reich.

Available in February 1999 at your favorite retail outlet.

Or order your copy now by sending your name, address, zip or postal code, along with a check or money order (please do not send cash) for $5.99 for each book ordered ($6.99 in Canada), plus 75¢ postage and handling ($1.00 in Canada), payable to Gold Eagle Books, to:

In the U.S.
Gold Eagle Books
3010 Walden Ave.
P.O. Box 9077
Buffalo, NY 14269-9077

In Canada
Gold Eagle Books
P.O. Box 636
Fort Erie, Ontario
L2A 5X3

Please specify book title with your order.
Canadian residents add applicable federal and provincial taxes.

GDEST114

TAKE 'EM FREE
2 action-packed novels plus a mystery bonus

NO RISK
NO OBLIGATION TO BUY

SPECIAL LIMITED-TIME OFFER

Mail to: Gold Eagle Reader Service
3010 Walden Ave.
P.O. Box 1394
Buffalo, NY 14240-1394

YEAH! Rush me 2 FREE Gold Eagle novels and my FREE mystery bonus. Then send me 4 brand-new novels every other month as they come off the presses. Bill me at the low price of just $16.80* for each shipment. There is NO extra charge for postage and handling! There is no minimum number of books I must buy. I can always cancel at any time simply by returning a shipment at your cost or by returning any shipping statement marked "cancel." Even if I never buy another book from Gold Eagle, the 2 free books and mystery bonus are mine to keep forever.

164 AEN CH7Q

Namo	(PLEASE PRINT)
Address	Apt. No.
City	State	Zip

Signature (if under 18, parent or guardian must sign)

* Terms and prices subject to change without notice. Sales tax applicable in N.Y. This offer is limited to one order per household and not valid to present subscribers. Offer not available in Canada.

GE-98

James Axler

OUTLANDERS™

HELLBOUND FURY

Kane and his companions find themselves catapulted into an alternate reality, a parallel universe where the course of events in history is dramatically different. What hasn't changed, however, is the tyranny wrought by the Archons on mankind…this time, with human "allies."

Book #1 in the new Lost Earth saga, a trilogy that chronicles our heroes' paths through three very different alternate realities…where the struggle against the evil Archons goes on….

THE LOST EARTH SAGA
BOOK 1

Available March 1999 at your favorite retail outlet. Or order your copy now by sending your name, address, zip or postal code, along with a check or money order (please do not send cash) for $5.99 for each book ordered ($6.99 in Canada), plus 75¢ postage and handling ($1.00 in Canada), payable to Gold Eagle Books, to:

In the U.S.

Gold Eagle Books
3010 Walden Ave.
P.O. Box 9077
Buffalo, NY 14269-9077

In Canada

Gold Eagle Books
P.O. Box 636
Fort Erie, Ontario
L2A 5X3

GOLD EAGLE®

Please specify book title with order.
Canadian residents add applicable federal and provincial taxes.

GOUT8

Journey back to the future
with these classic

DEATH LANDS ®

titles!

#62535	BITTER FRUIT	$5.50 U.S.	☐
		$6.50 CAN.	☐
#62536	SKYDARK	$5.50 U.S.	☐
		$6.50 CAN.	☐
#62537	DEMONS OF EDEN	$5.50 U.S.	☐
		$6.50 CAN.	☐
#62538	THE MARS ARENA	$5.50 U.S.	☐
		$6.60 CAN.	☐
#62539	WATERSLEEP	$5.50 U.S.	☐
		$6.50 CAN.	☐

(limited quantities available on certain titles)

TOTAL AMOUNT	$ _____
POSTAGE & HANDLING	$ _____
($1.00 for one book, 50¢ for each additional)	
APPLICABLE TAXES*	$ _____
TOTAL PAYABLE	$ _____

(check or money order—please do not send cash)

To order, complete this form and send it, along with a check or money order for the total above, payable to Gold Eagle Books, to: **In the U.S.:** 3010 Walden Avenue, P.O. Box 9077, Buffalo, NY 14269-9077; **In Canada:** P.O. Box 636, Fort Erie, Ontario, L2A 5X3.

Name: _____

Address: _____ City: _____

State/Prov.: _____ Zip/Postal Code: _____

*New York residents remit applicable sales taxes.
Canadian residents remit applicable GST and provincial taxes.

GDLBACK1

GOLD EAGLE ®

Stony Man moves to snuff out the kill fire of a demented terrorist....

STONY MAN™ 38

Enemy Within

It's up to the Stony Man warriors to stop the deadly plan of a high-tech pyromaniac, which includes the bombing of federal buildings in a dozen large U.S. cities. For this demented soul, the federal buildings are just for practice, since he has a bigger target in mind: the White House.

Available in January 1999 at your favorite retail outlet.

Or order your copy now by sending your name, address, zip or postal code, along with a check or money order (please do not send cash) for $5.50 for each book ordered ($6.50 in Canada), plus 75¢ postage and handling ($1.00 in Canada), payable to Gold Eagle Books, to:

In the U.S.

Gold Eagle Books
3010 Walden Avenue
P.O. Box 9077
Buffalo, NY 14269-9077

In Canada

Gold Eagle Books
P.O. Box 636
Fort Erie, Ontario
L2A 5X3

Please specify book title with your order.
Canadian residents add applicable federal and provincial taxes.

GSM38